PRAISE FOR REBECCA BEHRENS

"Disaster-related action keeps pages flipping… A believable heroine finds her strength during a disaster."

—*Kirkus Reviews* on *The Disaster Days*

PRAISE FOR *WHEN AUDREY MET ALICE*

"Should please teachers and librarians…shouldn't dissuade those who are looking for nothing more than an entertaining middle-grade romp—albeit one set at America's most famous address."

—*New York Times*

"This charming debut… An appealing journey and a fascinating life."

—*Kirkus Reviews*

"[An] entertaining debut… Details of life in the White House, combined with Audrey's more ordinary struggles (including the potential for a first boyfriend), will keep readers hooked."

—*Publishers Weekly*

"A terrific work of blended realistic and historical fiction… The combination of humor, history, light romance, and social consciousness make Rebecca Behrens' debut novel a winner."

—*BookPage*

"The juxtaposition of Audrey and Alice's stories creates an interesting counterpoint of past and present…the first-person narrative is consistently engaging. An enjoyable first novel."

—*Booklist*

ALSO BY REBECCA BEHRENS

When Audrey Met Alice

Summer of Lost and Found

The Last Grand Adventure

THE DISASTER DAYS

REBECCA BEHRENS

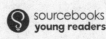

sourcebooks
young readers

Published by Sourcebooks Young Readers, an imprint of Sourcebooks Kids
P.O. Box 4410, Naperville, Illinois 60567-4410
(630) 961-3900
sourcebooks.com

Library of Congress Cataloging-in-Publication Data

Names: Behrens, Rebecca, author.
Title: The disaster days / Rebecca Behrens.
Description: Naperville, IL : Sourcebooks Young Readers, [2019] | Summary:
    Thirteen-year-old Hannah's first real babysitting job turns into a
    nightmare when a major earthquake knocks out power and phones,
    cuts off the island, and leaves her stranded with two children.
Identifiers: LCCN 2019008891 | (hardcover : alk. paper)
Subjects: | CYAC: Earthquakes--Fiction. | Survival--Fiction. | Self-reliance--Fiction. |
    Babysitters--Fiction. | Islands--Washington (State)--Fiction. | Washington (State)--Fiction.
Classification: LCC PZ7.B38823405 Dis 2019 | DDC [Fic]--dc23
LC record available at https://lccn.loc.gov/2019008891

Source of Production: Maple Press Company, York, Pennsylvania, United States
Date of Production: August 2019
Run Number: 5015800

Printed and bound in the United States of America.
MA 10 9 8 7 6 5 4 3 2 1

For the helpers

NOTHING WAS REMARKABLE THAT morning, except the postcard-perfect view of Mount Rainier. Most of the time, clouds and fog hid it, but the volcano was always there, watching us, even when we couldn't see it. We forgot that we were living right on top of a fault zone.

And we never could feel the power struggle happening deep beneath our feet, the fight our North American tectonic plate put up as the ocean's Juan de Fuca plate slowly, determinedly slipped beneath it. For years and years—longer than any of us have lived, longer than most of the evergreens had stood tall in our forests—our plate had held tight. Straining against the pressure. Refusing to give way. Protecting us.

Then, it budged.

None of us on sleepy, safe Pelling Island knew what was about to happen. If I had, I would have done everything differently that day.

Starting with my last words to my dad. They definitely wouldn't have been *yum* and *thanks*.

I would've shrugged off missing the bus. I wouldn't have pouted the rest of the morning, which probably made my mom feel bad. I would've let her ruffle my hair and pull me in for an awkward car hug.

I would have hugged her back. Hard.

And I never would've sent that text.

But like I said, I hadn't known.

1

MORNINGS IN MY HOUSE were a natural disaster. My mom raced back into the kitchen, still shrugging into her sweater. Seconds later, she yelped as the toaster spat out a piece of singed bread. Meanwhile, she kept trying to talk to me, but I was focused on untangling my headphones and thinking about Neha. How yesterday she hadn't waited at her locker for me after last period like she always does. How I had worried that she'd gotten sick and had to go home or something. Eventually, I'd walked outside without her. Right before the bus pulled away, she came running through the double doors—arm in arm with Marley.

"Why the frown?" Mom peered at me from across the table, where she was shoving a mess of papers into her bag with one hand while shoving peanut butter toast into her mouth with the other.

"Nothing," I said, looking down at the still-knotted earbuds. I didn't want to get into the Neha stuff. Mom would stop getting ready and come sit next to me to talk it out, because she was a good mom like that. Even at the busiest times she would stop, sit down, and listen. But we were already running very late, and I felt like just ignoring it instead.

The phone rang, and Mom pirouetted to answer it. "Hello?" Her face brightened as she pulled away from the handset to tell me, "It's Dad."

"Let me talk!" I scooted over, making grabby hands for the phone.

"Here, Hannah wants to say hi." She zipped her bulging bag shut, signaling me to pull on my backpack.

I pressed the phone to my ear while I worked my arms through the straps of my backpack. "Hi, Dad. How's the trip?" He was in Seabrook, this cute town nestled on the Pacific Ocean, where he'd been working on a new project.

"It's gorgeous here today. When the hotel is finally finished, we're taking a family beach vacation. Well, if they'll give the architect a special room rate." Dad laughed. "Listen, I was telling your mom that I'm going to be stuck here an extra night because we're having a problem with the irrigation system. But I'll be home tomorrow, okay?"

"That's cool," I said. Then I heard the double-honk of the bus—the warning sign that it was leaving. I glanced at the microwave clock. So late. "Dad, I gotta go. I hear the bus."

"Oh, the honk tolls for thee. Have a great day, kiddo! I'll try to bring back some saltwater taffy for you."

"Yum, thanks," I said, passing the phone back to my mom.

I grabbed my cell phone and notebook from the table before I bolted down the hallway. I flung the front door open just in time to see the yellow back of the bus driving away. Mr. Fisk was ruthless about keeping to the morning pickup schedule.

My heart sank. I had really wanted a chance to talk to Neha. Marley got a ride to school from her parents, so the bus had become one of my only chances to be alone with my best friend. Now I wouldn't see Neha until lunch, when she'd probably already be sitting next to Marley and laughing about something from yesterday's soccer practice or the team group text, a joke that would be hilarious to them but unintelligible to me.

I stomped back into the kitchen. Mornings were generally less disastrous when my dad was home. I only ever missed the bus when it was just Mom and me.

She saw me glowering in the kitchen doorway. "Missed it?" I nodded. "I'm sorry, Hannah. Time management: you know it's not my forte. Let's hope that's not genetic. Don't worry—I'll give you a ride." I slumped into a chair to wait for her to finish gathering the rest of her stuff, turn off the coffee maker, shrug on her purple coat, grab her library work badge, and then find her always-misplaced keys.

We finally got in the car and started down the road toward the bridge. Technically I live in a suburb of Seattle, but it doesn't feel like a suburb. At least not the kind you see on television or that my California cousins live in. Pelling Island has wild berry bushes growing along the main highway and a hint of salt water in the air. It has a real downtown, too, with shops and yoga studios and cafés, but the rest of the island is covered in a patchwork of dense woods. It feels like the country, but it only takes thirty minutes on the ferry to get to downtown Seattle (or you can go the long way via car, circling the island and then driving across the two-lane Elliott Bay Bridge—but the traffic is often a nightmare). We've got everything on Pelling: the water, the forests, even a view of the Cascade Range off in the distance.

"Whoa, the mountain is out!" Mom said, pointing.

There are a few special spots on Pelling where you can see Mount Rainier, although its snowy peaks are usually hidden by drizzly clouds. Catching a glimpse of the mountain is kind of a special thing—a good omen, like seeing a rainbow. Sometimes when that happens, my mom will pull over so she can stare at it, and I can take a photo. Not when we're running late, though. My mom glanced away from our street, Forestview Drive, to catch it again. "So imposing," she murmured. I shifted in my seat. Something that big and powerful makes me feel like a little ant. I went back to staring at my phone.

We were crossing the bridge over the inlet that separates our mini neighborhood—a smattering of houses before the forest preserve—from the rest of Pelling Island. Between us and the bridge lives Mr. Aranita. He's retired and usually is either visiting his grandkids in Portland or on another bucket-list trip, though, so most of the time our only neighbors are the Matlocks. They're "next door," but I once measured the walking distance between our front doors with the fitness tracker on my phone, and it's nearly three-quarters of a mile. I guess if you cut through our yards instead of going along our driveways and the road, it would be less, but the bramble bushes don't really allow for a shortcut unless you're wearing pants, a long sleeve, and some protective eyewear.

"Don't forget, I'm watching Zoe and Oscar after school," I reminded my mom. I'd only babysat for the Matlocks—for anyone, actually—once before. It's kind of funny that parents let a kid watch younger kids. I mean, my parents still barely let me stay home alone and won't allow me to bake cookies if they're not around, to make sure I don't explode the oven or something. But the Matlock kids are pretty fun. Zoe is a fifth grader and Oscar is in third—babysitting them must not be nearly as hard as taking care of preschoolers or babies.

"What time do you think you'll be home?" Mom slowed down for a stop sign and let the doppelgänger Subaru opposite us make its turn.

"Ms. Matlock wasn't sure. She's going to a gallery opening in the city, but she said she'd try to be home by nine."

"Oh wow, so you're *really* sitting this time." The first time, I babysat while Ms. Matlock ran errands on island, and she was only gone for an hour and a half. "I'll be right next door if you need anything. Don't hesitate to call."

I hugged my arms across my chest. I was a teensy bit nervous, and she wasn't helping. My mom doesn't exactly have a ton of confidence in me. When Ms. Matlock had first asked me to sit, Mom kept saying, "I just don't think you're ready to be alone and in charge. I didn't babysit until I was fourteen."

"It's not a big deal, Mom." I could totally handle two kids for a few hours without needing my mom as backup. Right? After all, Neha and I had taken the official childcare course over winter break at the community center. She was too busy now with soccer to take on any babysitting gigs, though.

"Text me whenever you're done. I'll pick you up—that way she doesn't have to load the kids in the car."

"I can walk home." I mean, it's kind of ridiculous for your mom to pick you up, by car, from your next-door neighbors' house.

"I don't like you walking alone in the dark, okay?"

"Fine," I said. But it seemed like overkill. Nothing bad ever happened in our neighborhood, and if a person was old enough to take care of younger kids, wasn't she also old enough to walk home by herself? "You're being kind of overprotective, Mom."

"Hey, it's in my job description!" She laughed. I fought back a smile.

We inched along the driveway leading to my school, slowly because the bus ahead had its stop sign out while kids streamed off. I watched for Neha to step onto the curb. Maybe I could still catch her going inside.

"Do you have gym today?" Mom asked.

I saw a flash of turquoise: Neha's puffy coat, as she hurried down the bus steps. Neha was always in constant motion—probably why she was such a good athlete. "Yup, it's a gym day." I started to unbuckle my seat belt.

"So you have your inhaler, right?"

I stopped putting my backpack back on, mid–arm slide. I pictured my inhaler, sitting on top of my nightstand. *Shoot.* "Um…"

"Hannah Kate." Using my middle name always means disappointment. My mom sighed, glancing at the clock. She drummed her fingers on the wheel. "I think we should go back and get it."

Then I would miss homeroom altogether. "No way, Mom. I haven't even used it since I got over that cold."

"You're not supposed to use it all the time. It's a *rescue* inhaler. You never know when you might need it."

"We're not even going to be running around in gym. Ms. Whalen is starting a yoga unit. We'll be stretching and relaxing, listening to her wind-chimes music."

My mom sighed again. "But you forgot it last week too. I need you to be more responsible about this. You're thirteen years old now, and—"

"I know how old I am!" And I was plenty responsible. I was on the honor roll, I always recycled, and I had that babysitting certificate. The only thing wrong with me was my lungs. I reached for the door handle. Neha was getting farther and farther away, and I saw a grinning girl standing by the double doors, waving at *my* best friend. Marley. She was wearing a matching puffy coat. I glanced down at my old windbreaker. "Maybe, if we weren't always running late in the morning, I would remember…"

"Fair enough. Just promise me you'll take it easy today. Why don't you text me while you're at the Matlocks' so I know how the babysitting is going, okay?"

"Sure, whatever." I pushed the door open. My mom unbuckled her seat belt and reached over to give me a hug. I could smell her lavender body lotion, mixed with the cinnamon she always sprinkles into her thermos. Whether at home or in the car, she always hugged me goodbye; it was as essential a part of her morning routine as pouring the coffee. I knew it would bug her if she didn't get one in.

But I had to catch up with the puffy coats.

I swung my feet onto the pavement and hopped out of the car. I turned back to my mom, who leaned over the seat with her arms outstretched. "*Loveyoubye*," I said, giving her nothing more than a brisk wave before I shut the door and—even though she'd just asked me to take it easy—ran down the walkway. I don't like thinking about how my mom's face probably looked, crestfallen and worried, before she settled back in her seat and drove to the ferry terminal, on her way off the island and far from me.

2

CAUGHT NEHA ALONE AT her locker after last period. "Hey!"
I scooted through a huddle of sixth graders. She was busily
shoving notebooks and papers into her backpack. Another bag
was at her feet—her soccer duffel. Her last name, Jain, was
stitched on the front in big proud letters, and all her Pelling
Pirates teammates had signed it in puffy paint.

I wanted to talk to her about the Earth Day expo—I had
finally come up with a good idea for a project. My dad's building
designs always feature green roofs—not, like, painted green but
"green" because they have plants growing on top of them. They
save energy, help with air pollution, and can even be a home for
wildlife. Plus, they look really cool. Green roofs are kind of his
signature thing; there's even one on our house. Anyway, my idea
was to design one for school. Dad could help me create the plans.
Neha is super talented at art—she's super talented at everything,
honestly—so I thought she'd like to work on the renderings.

We hadn't talked about the project since the assembly when it
was first announced, but of course we'd partner up for it. Neha

and I were always partners. If there were an official code of best friendship, "always be partnering" would be in it.

"What's up?" Neha mumbled from deep in the locker. She popped up and smiled, like she was really happy to see me, but only for a second. "I gotta hurry—Marley's mom is driving us."

"Oh yeah?" I leaned into the locker next to hers, feeling my shoulders slump. "Where's the game?" I used to be on the team. After I started struggling to breathe when playing and turned a really embarrassing shade of red, the doctor diagnosed me with asthma. Then my parents didn't think it was a good idea for me to keep going. "Maybe next fall," they'd said. "Let's see how the inhaler works." To be honest, I didn't really miss soccer. I'd seen how my teammates would look at me as I struggled to run the field: like I was holding them all back. Even Neha hadn't seemed particularly sad when I left. Being with her was the only part I actually missed.

She popped out from behind the locker door again. "Bremerton. They're *really* good."

"*You're* really good." It was true. Neha was the star forward. When I played, even before the asthma attacks, I was the kind of midfielder who got distracted by dandelions and realized three seconds too late that the ball was headed my way.

She swung the door shut. "Aw, thanks, Hannah." She already had her backpack on and was spinning her lock. She hoisted her duffel. "I don't want to make them wait. Text me, okay?"

I hurried down the hall and followed her through the double doors. "Yeah, I will. I'm babysitting tonight."

"Good luck!" She blew me an air kiss and dashed off to Marley's car. I sighed and trudged toward the bus. I'd have to text Neha my idea.

While waiting for the bus to fill up, I watched their car leave, Marley's and Neha's silhouettes visible in the back seat. I could imagine them giggling and sharing red licorice and probably gossiping and doing all the stuff I loved to share with Neha. Or maybe just talking endlessly about soccer. Somehow this season, the Pelling Pirates had become the most important thing in Neha's life. Her teammates, the most important people. And I wasn't one of them.

The bus ride home always feels thousands of times longer than the ride to school. I watch everyone else get dropped off at their stops and start their after-school lives, while I'm on board till the bitter end. Seriously—my house is the last stop. And Mr. Fisk's ruthless punctuality only applies to the morning ride; afternoons are for "the scenic route," according to him. By the time we hit the inlet bridge, and I'm the only kid left on the bus, he announces that he's become my private chauffeur. Literally, he gets on the PA and tells me that—every single day. On days when I get out at Neha's stop, about halfway through the ride, he jokes that I've fired him.

I forgot to tell him that I wasn't getting out at my house, though. "Mr. Fisk?" I called from my seat toward the back.

"Yes, Miss Hannah?" That's another part of the joke—calling me "Miss." Or, when he was really into some British TV show about rich people, "Lady Hannah."

"I'm babysitting today—can you drop me off at my neighbors'? They live just past our house."

"Not a problem, m'lady."

Crossing the inlet bridge, I couldn't see Mount Rainier anymore. The sky had clouded over. Speeding down the hill on the other side always gives me this peaceful, happy feeling— I'm tucked back in our private little corner of the island, where everything is green and calm and familiar. We passed my house and I smiled, even though I hadn't been able to shake off the feeling of being left out. Forestview Drive never feels isolated, even though it is. It feels safe—like home should.

The bus lurched to a stop at the Matlocks' drive. "This it?" Mr. Fisk called back to me. "I hope so, because I don't see any other houses. I think I've found where the sidewalk ends."

I laughed. Actually, we don't even have sidewalks, because other than people driving into the forest preserve, there's no traffic on our road. "Yup, this is perfect." I grabbed my backpack and walked down the aisle. "Thanks, Mr. Fisk." He saluted me goodbye.

I stopped to grab the Matlocks' mail, watching Mr. Fisk navigate the bus into a three-point turn so he could head home. He tooted the horn and I waved.

The driveway leading up to their house is so long, the cross-country club could use it for trail-running practice. I walked slowly so I could soak up the quiet before the chaos. The serene look of the Matlocks' house and yard is one big fake-out, because it's kind of bananas once you get inside. By the time I was halfway to the front door, I could hear the sharp, dissonant strains of someone learning to play a recorder. The butterflies in my stomach fluttered harder in response.

I rang the bell, waited a few seconds, then opened the door anyway.

"Hannah? Did anyone let Hannah in?" a voice called from upstairs.

"I let myself in, Ms. Matlock!"

"Oh, good. Welcome! I'll be down in a minute." A pause. "And seriously, please call me Andrea!" She always said that, but I couldn't *not* start out by calling her "Ms." My mom had drilled that into me since I was a preschooler. It felt too weird to call a grown-up by her first name.

I put my backpack down next to the mess of shoes and umbrellas and galoshes in the entryway, and I slipped my phone into my pocket. Then I pulled it back out to text my mom. She's a stickler about making sure I check in.

I'm at the Matlocks'

Thanks, honey.

Have fun with the kiddos!

Keep me posted on your adventures in babysitting.

Ok

The recorder was still going strong somewhere upstairs, and earsplitting crashing and booming noises bellowed from the TV. I wandered into the living room through the open kitchen. Oscar was curled up on the couch, intensely focused on a video game.

"Hi, Oscar."

"Hi, Hannah—watch me get this guy!" Something neon burst on the TV screen, and Oscar jumped up from the cushion, piercing the air with his fist. "Yeah!"

"Nice," I said, flopping onto an armchair.

"Okay, Hannah, I need your opinion." Andrea had breezed downstairs during the explosion. "These earrings?" She held out a dangly silver pair. "Or these?" The ones in her other hand were jade.

I hopped up to join her in the kitchen. "I like the dangly ones."

She held both palms out and studied her options. "Yup, you're right. Good taste." She started fastening them into her ears. "And my dress is okay? Do I need a scarf or anything?" Andrea did a twirl. She looked great—the dress was a deep teal color and made of a very flowy fabric that swirled like waves as she moved.

"You look amazing," I said, standing up a little straighter. Andrea grinned at me. I liked how she asked my opinion about her outfits, almost like I was her friend, not just the kid next door. That, plus the fact that I was there to watch Oscar and Zoe, not play with them—it all made me feel pretty mature. The opposite of how it felt when my mom insisted I text her to check in or freaked out about me not always remembering my inhaler.

"Except there is a teensy bit of lipstick on your teeth," I pointed out.

"Lifesaver," she said, running her index finger over her front teeth to erase it. She smiled wide again. "Better?"

"Perfect."

"I'm going to a gallery opening—a friend's show. There'll be lots of people who write reviews or represent artists. Honestly, I'm nervous," Andrea admitted, stuffing her wallet and keys into a purse. "I'd love to get them interested in my work."

Her drawings were all over the house: framed ones lining the walls and in-progress ones covering most flat surfaces. They were awesome-looking, even if I didn't always quite get what they were supposed to be showing. Sometimes, I thought the people in them were dancing, and sometimes it looked like fighting. Maybe that was on purpose. Her pottery—big tubular vases lining the mantel and the tops of bookshelves—was easier to understand.

"Anyway," Andrea continued, glancing around the kitchen. "I'm going to drive all the way there, even though it'll take forever. I don't want to be at the mercy of the ferry schedule. Nor do I want to navigate the sidewalks in heels." She bent to refasten one of the buckles on her fancy shoes. "I'll have my phone with me the whole time. If anything comes up, I can head back right away." She paused, chewing on her lip. "Don't hesitate to call."

I nodded and said, very confidently, "I'm sure everything will be fine." Famous last words.

The recorder by then was making loud screechy noises that couldn't be part of a song. It sounded more like a warning siren. Andrea winced. "Well, whenever the racket's finished, could you help Zoe with her math homework? That would be excellent." She motioned to Oscar in the living room. "For that one, don't let him play video games the whole night. They both already used up their screen time for the day." She glanced at a calendar taped to the fridge. "It's Oscar's turn to clean Jupiter's cage." Jupiter was the Matlocks' pet guinea pig.

In between booms from the living room couch: "Noooooo!"

"Sorry, O. The schedule doesn't lie." Andrea pulled open the fridge door and scanned inside. "There's veggie pasta to heat up for dinner. And basically nothing else to eat—my cupboards are worse than Mother Hubbard's. Tomorrow's grocery day. But if you guys get desperate, I think there's a can of refried beans somewhere." We both laughed.

"That's it for instructions. You know the drill. Emergency numbers are by the phone." She pointed.

"Zoe! Come downstairs and say goodbye!" The bleating of

the recorder stopped, and I heard her feet thudding down the stairs. Andrea swooped Zoe into a hug, spun her in a circle, and called for Oscar to come over.

"But I'm almost through this level!"

Andrea rolled her eyes and walked over to kiss him on the top of his curly head. "After this one, the TV's off. No more games, okay?" She looked out the window. Blue sky was attempting to pierce through the clouds. "Unless they're outside. It's not raining." To me, she added, "Maybe get them some fresh air?"

I nodded as my phone buzzed inside my pocket. I didn't want to pull it out right in front of Andrea, which would make me look distracted, but I was also dying to see if the buzz was from Neha. I sneaked a look. The text was from my dad—a picture of the Seaspray Resort's roof, covered in cool-looking succulent plants. The ocean glistened in the background.

Good job! I texted back.

"Okay, you're on your own now. Behave, you two!" Andrea slung her purse over her shoulder and grabbed her coat off the back of a kitchen chair. The bracelets on her arms tinkled. "I know they're in good hands with you, Hannah," she said, which made me blush. *I wish she'd tell my mom that.* Andrea paused in the doorway, taking one last look at Zoe and Oscar. She seemed slightly nervous about leaving, so I gave her a big smile.

Immediately after she walked out of the house, Oscar went back to his video game and Zoe picked up her recorder again. I paused for a moment, next to the door, listening to the car roll down the driveway. I couldn't tell whether the prickle I felt was nerves or excitement about being in charge. *It's just babysitting*, I reminded myself. *You got this.*

3

I DECIDED TO TACKLE THE hard stuff first: getting Zoe and Oscar to do the two things their mom had requested. "Zoe, go get your math homework." She wandered out of the kitchen, recorder still bleating, and came back with her polka-dotted backpack.

"Math is easier when you're not playing an instrument," I suggested, and she put the recorder down. *Thank goodness.* There's only so much "Hot Cross Buns" a person can take. At least, I think that's what she was practicing.

"I need a calculator. Can I use your phone?"

"Sure." I wasn't sure if she was supposed to use a calculator for the worksheet, but I didn't think it could hurt. I sent a quick text to Neha.

What's up? How's the game?

Then I handed over my phone, and Zoe got to work.

On to Oscar. "It's time to clean Jupiter's cage, buddy."

"Noooooooooo!" Oscar jumped from the arm of the sofa to the cushions, grabbing at his chest like he'd been wounded. "It's so stinky."

He wasn't lying. When I walked over to the corner of the living room where Jupiter lived, my nose was hit by the unmistakable combination of musty wood shavings and guinea pig pee. Good thing Jupiter was ridiculously cute. Most guinea pigs I'd seen had short fur, but Jupiter's was more like thick, glossy locks of hair that fell to his tiny paws. It was so long you could braid it. Zoe and Oscar had done that before. There were pictures of it on the fridge.

When I stood next to the cage, Jupiter started jumping around and making little *squeak-whoop* noises. "You're excited to get a clean cage, aren't you?" Except I didn't know how they cleaned it. With soap and water? A vacuum?

"Zoe, how does your mom clean Jupiter's cage?" From the kitchen table, she shrugged. "Oscar, do you know?"

He had hopped off the couch and joined me. "She uses one of the sprays under the kitchen sink." He reached in and gently pulled out Jupiter, cuddling him in his arms and cooing at him. Jupiter made a contented noise, almost like purring.

While Oscar held him, I went into the kitchen and checked under the sink. All I saw was blue glass cleaner, and that didn't seem like what you'd clean a cage with. *Maybe they're out. Better not use the wrong stuff.* So I put on some rubber gloves and carried the trash can over to the cage. I grabbed as much of the gross used shavings as I could and dumped them into the trash, then covered the cage floor with fresh stuff. It looked, and smelled, cleaner at least.

"Good enough," I pronounced.

"Yay! I get a checkmark on the calendar," Oscar said nuzzling Jupiter with his cheek.

"No, all you did was hold Jups!" Zoe cried from the k table.

"Actually, I think you're going to have to clean the cage real later on. When your mom's home." After I put the trash back, peeled off the gloves, and washed my hands, I checked Zoe. "How's the math?"

"All done," she said, but she was still hunched over my phone It was making the camera-snap noise.

"Zoe, what are you doing with my phone?"

"Nothing!" She sat upright, and I snatched it back. My photo album was now full of pictures of Zoe's nose. Along with video slow motion of her sticking out her tongue and wiggling it.

"Please tell me you didn't post any of these?" The last thing I needed was everybody at school seeing close-ups of nostrils and assuming they were mine.

"I didn't?" The question in her voice suggested the opposite. I sighed, opening all my apps to check my latest posts. So far, babysitting felt like one long, continuous sigh.

But everything looked okay—no bizarre posts from Zoe-Me. Also, no texts from Neha. The game was probably running long. I sent another.

I have an amazing idea for our Earth Day project

Text me when ur done so I can tell you!

I thought back to Andrea's instructions. Zoe's homework: check, thanks to my phone's help. Oscar's cage cleaning: check-ish, thanks to me. No more screen time and maybe play a game: up next. "Hey, how do you guys feel about going outside?" I glanced through the big picture window in the living room, above Jupiter's less-stinky cage. While most of their property was dense with evergreens and bushes, they did have a large backyard. Spread throughout the open grass was Andrea's veggie garden; a small fish pond that the previous owner had put in; a firepit; and a redwood swing set with two swings, a platform, slide, and rusted monkey bars. It looked almost exactly like the one Neha used to have in her backyard before the Jains landscaped it and Neha begged for a soccer goal. I smiled, thinking of the hours we'd spent on hers, swinging and climbing and laughing. Before she became the star of the Pelling Pirates, that was our pirate ship. I missed playing like that, sometimes. There was nothing like the feeling of lying back on the grass, letting the blue—or cloud-covered (after all, we live in the Pacific Northwest)—sky overhead help you to catch your breath. Now when we hang out, Neha and I spend almost all our time on laptops or phones. It makes you tired in a different way.

"Nah," said Zoe. She'd joined Oscar on the couch. He was back to scrolling through his video game options, and she'd picked up a tablet and was questing for candy on an app. I

sank down in the love seat across from them. Suddenly, I was exhausted. Kids wear you out.

"Guys, your mom said you were out of screen time." I tried to sound firm. But my phone had finally buzzed with a text.

"If Oscar puts on his headphones, Mom doesn't care if he keeps playing," Zoe said. Oscar obediently grabbed the pair from the coffee table and put them over his ears.

"Okay, but only for a minute—then we're going outside," I murmured, as I swiped to check my messages. Now I had a bunch from Neha.

Hey! We WON!!!!!

I got a goal :) And Marley made an awesome save

Anyway she had this idea to do water-quality testing at the pebble beach by the ferry

Maybe you could work with us?

I slumped deeper into the love seat.

Maybe I could work with them? So she was definitely working with Marley and had ignored me in all this planning. I felt my heartbeat hasten, and my stomach knotted.

I thought we were doing the project together

And why wouldn't I? We did everything together. Or, at least, we had. We were a perfect pair. Even our names were coordinated: *Hannah*, *Neha*.

Dude we can still work together!

with Marley

It's NBD

Actually it kind of is

My fingers had started typing without the consent of my brain.

For the longest time, Neha's side of our conversation showed /
three "still typing" dots. I glanced up to check on Zoe and Oscar. Both were totally absorbed in their games. Once, the Pelling community center had hosted a "silent dance party" where everybody danced while listening to music with their own headphones on. So it was a party, but totally quiet. The three of us, sitting in the living room but not playing together at all, glued to our respective devices, reminded me of that. Then, finally, Neha's reply buzzed through.

What is ur problem lately?!

I broke the silence with a huff. Zoe and Oscar didn't stir.

My problem?!

I dunno

Maybe the fact that all you're interested in now is Marley

And soccer

Soccer and Marley

Ur being ridiculous

It's not my fault you can't play

And it wasn't mine either. The blame belonged to my lungs. My phone buzzed angrily.

You need to check your jealousy

LOL I'm not jealous!

I'm

I sent that accidentally, before I could think of what exactly I was feeling. Left out? How could I explain that to Neha without sounding needy or clingy?

Marley is super nice

You'd know if you would actually like talk to her

That stung. It isn't easy to jump into conversations full of inside jokes and game recaps.

Whatever

She's not my friend

I knew I sounded sulky. And I'd always been friendly with Marley, even if I didn't know her well. I just had all these feelings, bubbling up inside, and I was too overloaded to control what I was typing.

Three dots again from Neha. And then:

Srsly Hannah?

Right now I don't even want to be ur friend anymore.

She even used a period. As soon as I read it, Jupiter started to squeak. The timing was uncanny, like he was paying attention to our text drama and wanted to weigh in. I glanced over at his cage. He was whooping while he ran in circles, making small hops.

Neha's last text was slowly sinking in. I blinked to prevent tears. Somewhere deep inside I knew I wasn't being very fair.

But she wasn't being fair to me either. I couldn't think straight with all the squeaking. I turned to Zoe. "Is Jupiter okay?"

I waved a hand until she came out of her tablet trance. "He's never done that before, at least not when we aren't by his cage with treats."

Out of the corner of my eye, I saw a commotion outside. Birds scattered out of the trees in the Matlocks' backyard, cawing and soaring up high into the sky. The scene kept me distracted from the words on my screen for a few seconds longer. My phone buzzed again, reminding me I had gotten a message. An awful one.

I replied in kind.

I don't want to be ur friend either.

The jolt was so strange, and sudden, that at first, I thought only I had experienced it. Like it was some kind of physical symptom of how I felt about Neha's texts—and my replies. People always describe bad news as a "punch to the gut" or being "shaken to their core." It was like that. A jerk, a thud, a jolt—something had just shifted, or broken, in our best friendship, and I felt it inside and out. Neha and I had never said words like that to each other before. I didn't even know we could. It was a tectonic moment in our friendship.

"What was that?" Zoe's eyes lifted again from her tablet, and they were wide with alarm. On the other side of the couch, Oscar sat up straight and pulled off his headphones.

"I woke up a huge dragon, and I actually *felt* its roar!"

The jolt wasn't only mine. Even though my phone was practically burning in my palm, I focused on the room around me. I held my breath, looking and listening. Everything seemed fine...

Then the shaking started.

4

ONE SECOND, WE WERE sitting down, quiet and still, wondering what we'd felt. The next, it was like the whole house had turned into a washing machine and we were inside. Sudden, violent, and loud, the noise of everything shaking and—within seconds—crashing around us. Along with our shrieks, once our disorientation shifted to fear.

"What's going on?" *Is this an...earthquake?* I didn't know what else it could be. But I'd never, ever felt one before.

The first crashes I could identify were from the pottery and vases that lined the mantel toppling off, one by one, like synchronized swimmers diving into a pool. As each piece hit the stonework at the edge of the fireplace, it shattered. The coffee table, which Zoe and Oscar had both rested their feet on seconds before, began to lurch across the floor. My love seat was starting to move too. I crouched on all fours on top of the cushions. I was afraid to stay on a moving piece of furniture but equally afraid to jump off. It's like the house was suddenly on top of a cresting wave.

Zoe pointed at something in the kitchen, yelling. It took me a second to realize she was shouting about the fridge. I turned and watched the huge stainless steel appliance shuffle out of its spot between the countertop and the cupboards. It advanced toward us in the living room, "walking" like Frankenstein's monster.

I heard creaking above me and brought my eyes up to see a metal pendant light fixture swinging. It looked heavy. And it could fall on us. I scrambled off the love seat. "Zoe! Oscar! Get under there!" I pointed to the heavy wooden dining table in between the living room and the kitchen. The table would be sturdy enough to protect us. It was at least better than staying on the couches while the house crashed down around us and giant pieces of metal swung sickeningly overhead.

Zoe, shielding her head, darted to the table. Oscar and I followed. It felt like running on top of a surfboard. Underneath the table, we huddled together, too shocked to cry or yell or do anything but watch the living room fall apart. The shaking was making me feel sick, so I braced my hands on the floor. But that only made me feel the wavelike movement stronger.

Zoe curled herself into a ball, hugging her knees. "Make it stop," she begged. The rumbling was so loud, I could barely hear her, even though Zoe was right next to me.

Oscar gasped and started to stand, almost knocking his head into the underside of the table. "Jupiter!" He pointed at the cage, below the windows way on the other side of the living room. It was sliding across the floor, and Jupiter cowered inside near his food dish.

"I have to save him!" Zoe wailed, crawling out from under the table.

"No, stop!" I shouted, sticking my arm in front of Zoe to block her from darting into the open room. "You have to stay here, where it's safe." Zoe howled as I held her back. I didn't even know if underneath a table was where you were supposed to hide during an earthquake. *If* that was what was happening.

For a moment, I covered my eyes because I couldn't bear to watch poor, sweet Jupiter. But I could still hear his squeaks. That cage was a death trap, with everything falling around it. I took a deep breath. "Don't move!" I shouted at Zoe and Oscar, before I army-crawled out from the safety of the table.

Ducking my head, I hunched and ran in the direction of the cage, but the shaking and all the furniture moving around me forced me on a zigzag path. *This is not smart*, I thought. *Really not smart.* Mrs. Pinales, the babysitting course instructor, had said during the first aid part of the class that rule number one is to always make sure a situation is safe before you try to rescue someone else. *Well, I'd rather be whacked by books flying off a shelf than leave a guinea pig to die.*

The floor shifted up and down, side to side. I struggled to move forward. Finally, I stumbled to my knees in front of Jupiter. There was no way I could drag the whole cage back to the table—it was too heavy and moving was already difficult enough. I unlatched the top and reached inside, scooping Jupiter into my arms. He was trembling so hard. His tiny paw-nails dug into my skin as I held him tight. My own fear didn't even register. All I could focus on was getting us back to safety.

Curling myself over his furry little body to protect him, I dodged and ran across the floor. Zoe and Oscar peeked out from under the table, tears streaming down Oscar's face.

"It's okay. We're both here," I said as I reached them. I held Jupiter out for Oscar to grab, then dropped to my knees to scoot underneath. As soon as heavy wood was overhead, all the fear I'd put on pause during the rescue flooded me. *What is happening? What should we do? Why isn't someone here to tell us? I can't handle this on my own.* I felt my pocket for my phone, only to realize I didn't have it. I'd left it somewhere out there, in the danger zone.

"Good job," Zoe said, wiping at her nose. I panted and closed my eyes, trying to slow down my racing heart. My breaths felt shallow. How long had the shaking and buckling been going on? Was it ever going to stop? I wanted it to, more than I'd ever wanted anything.

We all startled at the loudest crash yet, followed by the sound of glass cracking and shattering. Something—maybe a vase, or one of Andrea's paintings?—had flown through the big window behind Jupiter's now-empty cage. Thick shards of glass rained down on it and the floor. Oscar whimpered and pulled Jupiter in for a hug, burying his face in the guinea pig's fur. I wanted to cry, and I could feel tears welling in my eyes. But I had to keep cool, for Zoe and Oscar. I tried some of the yoga breathing Ms. Whalen had taught us in gym class. In for four counts, out for eight counts. *Stay calm. Just stay calm.*

"What if you hadn't..." Zoe started to say, but I shushed her. I didn't want to think about what would've happened to Jupiter. And I didn't want to think about what would've happened to me if I'd dashed to the window only a few seconds later, or lingered at Jupiter's cage during the rescue.

"What's going on?" Oscar whispered.

"I'm not sure. I think...it's an earthquake?" As far as I knew, Pelling Island had never experienced one. *But that's the only thing this could be, right?* My dad sometimes talked about the local building codes, how the new buildings he worked on had to have an earthquake-resistant design—which had always seemed silly to me, considering we lived in a place where quakes never happened. *Where they hadn't happened yet.* We lived on top of the North American tectonic plate. The Juan de Fuca plate was sneakily slipping below it. I had learned all that in the geology unit. But I hadn't understood that it meant *this*.

Thoughts of my dad and my mom lingered in my head. I shut my eyes tight. *I wish they were here.* Or Andrea. Anyone old enough for a driver's license, really. They would know what to do, how to stay safe. I wanted a grown-up to say to us, "Hey, it's going to be okay."

I wasn't sure how long we'd been hiding under the table. It felt like forever, but it must have been only minutes. Earthquakes didn't last for hours, right? I mean, maybe the aftermath did, but not the actual quaking. Pretty much everything I knew about them I'd learned from movies and TV. I didn't want to think about those shows, tense and shocking stories in which people died and everything was reduced to rubble. Something like that couldn't be happening here. Not in Seattle. Not on sleepy, safe Pelling Island.

"I don't feel good," Oscar said.

I scanned him to make sure he wasn't bleeding or bruised anywhere. I didn't think he'd been hit by anything while we ran under the table, but I could have missed that during the chaos. Everything had happened so fast. It was like we were trapped in a bad dream.

"You look fine. What hurts?"

"My tummy." He grimaced.

I patted his shoulder. "It's okay. You know, mine doesn't feel good either." It felt like I'd been riding the ferry on a really rough day. With the stomach flu.

"Mine too," Zoe said, leaning over to wrap Oscar and Jupiter in a hug.

The shaking seemed to soften. I closed my eyes and held my

breath, feeling and listening closely, hoping to detect a slackening. *Yes, it's slowing down.* A few more seconds and the quake stopped, as suddenly as it had started. The noise continued, though—stuff falling over or off of surfaces. Pops and hisses and creaks and drips. Stray crashes and thuds. Then the toppling sounds faded, and it was quiet again. Eerily quiet, the only sounds our shallow breaths and galloping heartbeats in our ears.

I didn't trust the calm. Not one bit.

"Can we get out of here?" Zoe's eyes were shiny and wide. She crouched at the edge of the safe circle of shadow below the tabletop, like a scared rabbit ready to bolt. She pointed at the door that connected the living room to the screened porch.

"No, we should stay put." I was watching a bookshelf that teetered, having been wrenched away from the wall. Gravity needed a few more minutes to do its work, so we didn't crawl out only to get crushed by a cabinet or something. Also, I wasn't convinced the quake was truly over. People always talked about aftershocks. Did they happen right away? Or did they sneakily wait a few minutes until, dazed and relieved, you climbed out of your hiding spot and regained trust in the floor, stock-still beneath your feet?

Maybe we would be better off waiting under the table until Andrea came home. I closed my eyes to ward off dizziness.

Where was Andrea during this? The thought slid into my mind like a spear, sharp and sudden. *And where were my parents?* My dad might not have even felt it, hours away on the coast. But my mom was probably late leaving work, like always. Had she felt the earthquake in the library? I looked again at the slumping bookshelf across the living room. There were hundreds of shelves and cases loaded with heavy books in the big Central Library downtown. I wondered if they were secure, or if they could've toppled or started to walk like the Matlocks' fridge.

What if my mom had been shelving and was sitting right in the middle of an aisle full of books when the shaking started? I shuddered as I pictured hardcovers raining down.

Or what if she'd been in the elevator, taking a book cart up- or downstairs? I doubted elevators were safe places during an earthquake. I imagined the car slamming into the sides of the shaft, the cables fraying like the scene in that action movie...

I felt a rising in my throat, like I was going to be sick.

No. None of that happened. I willed myself to stop thinking about my parents and Andrea. They were all fine. They had to be. As soon as I got my phone, I'd call them.

"I have to pee," Oscar announced, sniffling.

"Me too," Zoe added.

"Can't you hold it?" I longed to stay under the table. I didn't trust anywhere else.

"No!" Oscar said, shifting on his knees and wincing. Zoe nodded.

"I'll crawl out first, then hand me Jupiter." I took another deep, calming yoga breath, then scooted into the open room. I looked up—the big pendant light was hanging at a weird angle, but we could avoid that part of the room because the love seat was no longer underneath it. I scanned the edges of the space, looking for anything big or heavy that might fall over. We'd need to stay clear of the bookcases. The walls still stood—most of the art had come crashing down, but the pieces left up looked light and stable. About half the windows were shattered. The door to the porch had come ajar. Dust swirled in the breeze that flowed in from outside.

"Okay, you guys can come out now," I said, bending down to take Jupiter from Oscar's outstretched hands. The guinea pig was shuddering, so I hugged him close and gently petted his fur to soothe him. "*Shh*, it's all over, Jups." I really hoped I wasn't lying.

Zoe and Oscar slid from under the table and stood up next to me. They looked as dazed as I felt. Somehow, we'd all gotten a dusting of plaster or dirt or something on our heads. With my free hand, I brushed it off theirs and then wiped at my own. Nobody appeared injured, thank goodness.

"Let's head to the bathroom together. Zoe, take Jupiter?" I carefully passed him to her. "I'll lead the way." They followed me, single file, as I slowly crept into the kitchen. The fridge was smack in the middle of the tile floor. It had "walked" so far that it yanked its own plug out of the socket, which trailed behind the fridge like a tail. Zoe pointed to it and laughed.

"That's hilarious! I gotta take a picture."

"Later, once we're back from the bathroom." I needed to find my phone. But I also needed to pee, badly. Must be from all the adrenaline.

The cupboard doors had flung open and spewed their contents all over the countertops and the floor, so we had to step through spilled boxes of cereal, around piles of lentils, and carefully over some shattered glass jars that once held what looked like pasta sauce and pitted olives. The floor was slick with sauce and oil and dusted with flour. Plus the trash can with Jupiter's used shavings had toppled over, so that was part of the mix too. Yuck.

"Be really careful, guys." What a colossal mess. I felt glad that I'd get to go home and avoid the cleanup. *Except my house might look the same inside.* I swallowed hard. No, my house would be okay. My dad had renovated it, after all. I bet it could withstand anything.

In the hallway right off the kitchen, evening light shined through the window in the bathroom. The door was wide open, and Oscar darted inside, slamming it.

"Don't slam anything!" I called after him. Like it was punctuating me, a framed photo fell off the mail table across from the door. While Oscar did his business, I glanced around the hallway. A lamp had also toppled off the table, and two chairs had been knocked over, legs sticking up in the air. Otherwise, the hallway area looked relatively unscathed. I walked to the bottom of the stairs and gasped.

"What is it?" Zoe ran to my side and looked up. "Oh no."

Blocking the stairs was another big light fixture, like a chandelier but not fancy-looking with crystals or anything. Normally it hung dramatically from above the second floor landing. It had come crashing down from upstairs and landed smack in the middle of the staircase, covering the steps with glass and sharp bits of light bulb and twisted spikes of metal. Cords and frayed wires splayed out in all directions from the broken iron chain. The pieces of wood below the staircase's handrail—they're called balusters, I know that thanks to my dad, who let me use old design plans as coloring books when I was little—had been knocked out like teeth.

"Well, that's not safe." I turned to Zoe. "No going upstairs." She nodded in agreement.

When Oscar came out of the bathroom, Zoe passed Jupiter to him before dashing in. Oscar mournfully assessed the hallway. "Our blue lamp," he said, his bottom lip trembling. "I helped my mom glaze that one."

"It's okay; lamps can be fixed," I offered. But honestly, it looked beyond repair. I swallowed hard, thinking of the things I loved in my home, like the big colorful bowl we bought on a trip to Mexico and the shelves my dad had carved out of the old tree that fell down in our backyard. A painting of whales that my grandma had made when she decided to become an artist at seventy-one. I bet I could think of a memory attached to every single item in my house. It hurt to imagine them broken all over the floors.

Oscar slumped to sit against the wall, Jupiter in his lap. "I want my mom." His chin quivered dangerously.

I crouched next to him. "I know. I do too." I really meant it. Babysitting in the best of circumstances was nerve-racking. These were definitely not the best circumstances. Mrs. Pinales hadn't covered how to deal with a natural disaster, unless you consider feeding a toddler one. I shouldn't be alone in a damaged house with two younger kids. This was only the second time I'd ever been left alone with anyone! What if I did something wrong and made things even worse? *Andrea is probably already on her way back,* I told myself. *I have to keep things under control for an hour, tops, before one of our moms gets home.* But my chest was still tight, and I felt dread like it was right before a big test.

As if to show me I was right to be afraid, we felt a subtle side-to-side shake again, like a shudder. Oscar cried out and grabbed my hand. "An aftershock," I said, squeezing his. The tremor passed quickly.

A minute later, Zoe came out of the bathroom. "The sink in there is cracked."

"Good catch. Did you try to use it?" She shook her head. "That's probably smart."

"Wait—Oscar, did *you* use the sink?" she asked. He shook his head, sheepishly. Zoe rolled her eyes. "Oh my God, how many times has Mom told you? Wash your hands after you go to the bathroom. Ew!"

"Maybe right now is the exception to that rule," I said. "But, yeah, otherwise—wash your hands." I wrinkled my nose, thinking about how I'd just held his post-bathroom-break hand. I wiped my palm on my leggings. Oscar shrugged.

I hurried inside to pee. At least the toilet flushed normally.

When I came out, the three of us stood in the hallway for a moment. I didn't know what to do next. *Find my phone, then a safe spot; huddle there until Andrea gets back?* I didn't want to hang out in the kitchen, with the floor covered in food and stinky cage shavings, not to mention glass. "I guess let's go back to the living room," I said. "Turn on the news, see if there's any info about what happened."

Zoe and Oscar trailed me like ducklings through the kitchen again, both giggling at the fridge's tail. That *was* funny. I allowed myself to giggle too. And right then, it seemed like maybe everything was going to be okay. It was awful, the damage in the house. It had been scary to experience the shaking. But that was over, we were all unharmed, and soon our parents would start taking care of everything. Including us. "We really do need a picture of the fridge." I laughed harder, thinking of what Neha would say when I texted it to her. Only then did I remember how we'd left things before the jolt. My smile faded.

Once we made it back to the living room, Zoe ran to the

area by the coffee table to grab her tablet, which had ended up halfway under the love seat. She tiptoed back over to the edge of the kitchen to take some pictures.

"Stay off the kitchen floor for now—there's broken glass." I started hunting for the TV remote. "Oscar, do you remember where the remote was?"

He shook his head. "Somewhere by the couch. What about Jupiter? He doesn't have a house anymore." He pointed at the mangled cage, sitting below the shattered window on the opposite side of the room.

"Hmm. We'll take turns holding him until your mom gets back." *Their mom*—I still hadn't texted her. I shook my head at my own mistake. Contacting Andrea should've happened first after we crawled out from the table, even though it had been a bathroom emergency. She must be super worried, assuming she knew what had happened on Pelling. "Can you keep holding Jupiter while you look for the remote? I'm going to find my phone."

Oscar nodded, tucking Jupiter into the crook of one arm while he slowly walked around the safe zone of the living room, turning over pillows, papers, and magazines that were now covering the floor, the surfaces of the couches, and the coffee table. "There's dirt on the carpet," he said, pointing with his free hand at a spot where a planter had toppled over.

"Okay, maybe stay off that part of the carpet. We should

probably all wear shoes…" There was too much to manage at once. I focused on the most important thing, my missing phone, scanning the area around the love seat—that's where I'd been using it. I felt a pinch in my stomach, remembering my last text. Had Neha written something back and now I'd ignored it for all this time? What if she'd apologized? Maybe she'd understand when I explained what had happened to us.

Had the shaking happened to Neha, too, all the way in Bremerton?

"Are you guys looking for the remote?" Zoe asked, from the edge of the living room. She held up the black cylinder. "It got all the way over here."

"That's wild," I said. "Turn on the TV—let's check the news."

Zoe carefully made her way to stand next to where I was searching, on hands and knees, for my phone. We were all moving around like we were in a game of The Floor Is Lava. *Come on, where is it?* When I didn't hear the television make its turning-on blip, I paused in a squat.

"It's not working," Zoe said, pressing random buttons.

"Could the batteries have run out?"

She shook her head. "Mom put in new ones last week."

"Hmm. Let me see?" She handed me the remote, and I pressed the red power button hard, then again. Nothing. "Wait a minute." I stood all the way up and walked to the edge of the kitchen, studying the overhead light. Wasn't that on before the shaking started? Now it was off. I scanned the walls for a switch, then started flipping them all. Nothing turned on, nothing turned off. A chill ran down my spine.

The power was out.

Andrea needs to know what's going on here. Now. I could look for my phone later—I'd first call her on the landline. I carefully crossed the kitchen floor, avoiding a big puddle of debris that had formed, with shards of glass and chunks of plaster mixed in along with syrups and cereal and spices. The base part of the phone wasn't turned on, because of the power outage, but hopefully the handset had been fully charged when it went off. The list of emergency numbers was posted right next to the phone, with Andrea's cell and the kids' dad's number as well as the pediatrician, dentist, vet, poison control, and even the number for my house, I guess since we're the closest neighbors and Mr. Aranita is gone a lot. I clicked the handset on and punched in Andrea's number, but when I put the phone to my ear, it was dead silent. Not even a dial tone. I clicked it off, then back on. Nope. Nothing. My breathing felt shallow again.

Calm down. This isn't a huge deal, I told myself. *The phone line is probably connected to the power or something. It'll be back on soon.* Anyway, I could still call Andrea on my cell; I just had to find it. Clutching the list of emergency numbers in one hand, I returned to searching for my phone. Outside, evening was slipping into night, and the light was fading fast. Soon it would be totally dark in the house.

"Okay, we're going to race—the person who finds my phone gets to eat a bowl of ice cream. Before dinner, even!" I figured that wasn't a bad idea, if the power was out and everything in the Franken-fridge's freezer compartment was going to melt anyway.

"I'm going to find it!" they shouted, almost in unison. So that was an even-better idea, because I'd found a way to distract the kids from the disaster—literally—around us.

"Ready, set, go!" Oscar, still cradling Jupiter, used his free arm to start tossing everything on the floor up into the air. Normally that would create a huge mess, but it really made no difference now. *Everything about this is so weird.* I had another impulse to text Neha and tell her. The other time I babysat, I sent her regular updates on what the Matlock kids were doing and how the snack situation was panning out. But now I couldn't text Neha any updates—not just because my phone was MIA, but because our friendship had been shaken up almost as strongly as the house. At least it was still standing. I hoped Neha and I would be too.

Then two things happened at once.

"I think I found it!" Oscar squealed from beyond the love seat. He bounced up in the air, clutching my phone in its glittery case. "*Yes!*"

And Zoe screamed. At first, I thought she must be really upset about not getting ice cream, which was silly, because obviously it was bound to melt and we'd been through a real trauma, so we would all eat as much as we wanted. I was only going to let Oscar have first pick of the flavors. Maybe I should've made that clear.

But then I saw her near the windows, where she'd been crawling in the hunt for my phone. She was sitting on her heels, eyes squeezed shut, clutching her right forearm with her left hand. When she opened her eyes and turned to me, she lifted her hands and I saw. The light caught the glass sticking out of her arm, making it sparkle. A line of red was trickling down, pooling near her elbow.

"Freeze! Everybody stop right where you are!" I shouted. I didn't like blood. I didn't even like looking at grainy pictures of it in the first aid workbook. During that part of the class, I had shielded my eyes while Neha shook her head. *It's just blood; it's not a big deal.* But it made my stomach turn to see it.

I could not turn my head from this. "Zoe," I said, faking calm as best as I could. "Carefully come to the kitchen." She nodded and whimpered, and then she slowly walked over to where the carpet ended and the tiles started. A few droplets of blood left a trail behind her. I swallowed hard. *This is my fault. I made them crawl around in a room full of hazards. What was I thinking?*

"Wait right here," I said, my voice trembling, once she was in the kitchen. I hurried over to Oscar, still frozen by the love seat, watching us. I scooped him up. His legs and bare feet dangled almost to the floor as I held him up by his armpits and walked us both back to the kitchen tiles.

"Don't move from this spot." He nodded, nuzzling Jupiter. Then I led Zoe over to the sink. I forced myself to look again at her arm. The cut was bad. It was on the inside of her forearm, closer to her elbow than to her wrist, with glass still poking out of it. There was a lot of blood. *She might need stitches.*

I cleared my throat, trying to make my voice sound as soothing as Ms. Whalen's had during the yoga lesson. "I'm going to rinse off the…blood. Then I'm going to make sure the glass is out, and we'll put on a bandage, and it'll all be fine." I paused. "Do you know where the Band-Aids are?"

Zoe, unlike me, couldn't stop staring at her arm. Her voice trembled as she said, "In the drawer next to the sink."

"Okay. That's great." I turned the tap on. Cold water or hot? I think you're supposed to rinse wounds with cold. Hot might hurt. I guided her arm under the water, adjusting the stream so it was gentle but still strong enough to rinse out any bad stuff. The drawer was already open, and once I flung away a bag of marshmallows that had fallen into it from a cupboard, I found a box of bandages of assorted sizes. Luckily, all the little ones were used up and only the extra-larges were left, the size people hope they'll never have to use. One would be big enough to cover the cut, deeper than it was long. I dug around in the drawer, but there wasn't any antibiotic ointment, as far as I could tell.

I turned off the water. The blood didn't stop flowing, so it was hard to see if it was clean of dirt. *What if she cut an artery? Aren't there arteries in your arm?* That chunk of glass still stuck out. "Close your eyes," I said, because she was staring at it. Zoe squeezed them shut, and before I could think too much and lose my nerve, I pulled the glass out. Zoe winced and gasped. The piece was almost an inch long, sharp like a knife. *I shouldn't have let them crawl around like that. I'm the worst babysitter.*

After rinsing the wound again, I grabbed a paper towel from the roll mounted over the sink and blotted her arm dry. The towel darkened with red, and I thought I might throw up. But I kept going, reaching for the bandage. This was no time to be squeamish.

The first bandage started reddening right away, so I stuck on another one. That seemed to hold it back. "Done," I said, even though I wasn't convinced the bandages would last. "Why don't you sit down and keep your arm up?" You're supposed to elevate a wound to stop bleeding. And something else...*apply direct pressure!* "Press on it." I took her hand and touched it to the area around the bandage. "Not so much it hurts. Just enough to help it stop." Tears rolled down Zoe's face.

Looking at the blood-soaked paper towels made me dizzy. I wanted to cry too. Actually, I wanted to go to sleep, to slip away into a happy—or at least boring—dream, which seemed like the only way I could escape what was happening around me. But I couldn't. I was there, I was in charge, and I'd already made one really awful mistake. Mrs. Pinales's words sounded in my head, like a reprimand: *"The first thing to do in an emergency is get an adult."* I blinked and glanced up. Oscar was still watching us, warily, from the edge of the kitchen, holding my phone. There was a clear-ish path from his spot to where we sat, next to the sink. I motioned him over. He handed me my phone.

I didn't realize how dim it had gotten until I pressed the home button and the screen lit up. Outside, the sun must've dropped beyond the tree line. It was already past seven, and the house would get very dark, very fast. "As soon as I call your mom, let's find a flashlight."

I swiped to unlock my phone, realizing that the blank lock screen meant no texts had come through the entire time it had been missing. *Nobody messaged me? Neha never wrote back? And my mom didn't call?* A nervous chill made me shudder, but I ignored it. My phone was working fine. It looked like I had bars. Was it really possible that nobody else knew yet what had happened on Pelling?

Except, if it was nearing dark, shouldn't my mom have gotten home from work already? And why hadn't she texted when she saw I hadn't updated her on my babysitting "adventures"?

I pressed Andrea's number in the list of recent calls. I held the phone to my ear, waiting for her to pick up. But the call didn't go through. I put it on speaker and listened to a few unfamiliar blip noises, but it wouldn't connect. I pressed end and checked my bars. Now they'd disappeared.

"No service," I muttered. The network was probably overloaded. Maybe the earthquake had rattled a cell tower or something. Zoe was eyeing me with concern. But the Wi-Fi symbol was still at the top of my screen. "I'll text."

I typed it out quickly, all in one superlong message so there would be fewer to send:

Hi Andrea, I don't know if you already heard but I think we had an earthquake or something on Pelling. There was all this shaking, now the power's out and the phone too. I'm sorry there's a lot of damage inside from things that fell and Zoe got a cut. It looks bad. Can you come home right now? Also where are the flashlights and stuff? It's getting dark.

The zippy green line showed that the text was sending, and my shoulders relaxed with relief. My mom sometimes gets on my case for texting too much: *"Every time I look at you, I only see the top of your head, because your face is looking down. You're transfixed by that phone! At least swap it out for a book once in a while."* I would take great pleasure in pointing out how, in this case, texting saved the day when every other form of communication failed us. Although I suppose I didn't try any passenger pigeons.

The green line stalled at about 80 percent sent, but that didn't worry me. It did that a lot when using Wi-Fi instead of the cell network. I held the phone over my head, waving my arm back and forth, to try to wake up the signal. I checked the screen again. No movement. Now the Wi-Fi icon had disappeared too. If the router used electricity… My pulse started speeding up again. I walked closer to one of the windows.

"Is your phone broken?" Zoe asked. Tears coursed down her cheeks. Oscar, eyes big and fearful, was biting his thumbnail. Even Jupiter, on Oscar's lap, still looked wary.

"No, it's just slow," I reassured. The signals were probably cutting in and out. There was nothing I could do but wait—and keep the kids calm. "Hey, let's get you that ice cream." I sent a shorter message to my mom:

Mom help emergency please come over if you get this

I placed my phone on the countertop nearest the window, after turning the ringer on and the volume up as loud as possible. I nudged the fridge with my toe to make sure it was stable in its new, middle-of-the-floor home. It seemed fine. I opened the freezer door and, waving away the cloud of cold air, quickly scanned the cartons. "Mint Moose Tracks and Salted Caramel."

"Mint Moose!"

"Caramel." Zoe's voice wavered.

Thank goodness they didn't want the same flavor. I pulled out the cartons and quickly shut the door. Luckily there wasn't a ton of food in the freezer. Just the ice cream, some vacuum-sealed packages of fish and garden veggies, a box of freezer-burned

Popsicles, one packaged burrito, and frozen berries. "Spoons?"
I asked.

Zoe nodded toward a drawer behind me. It was already open,
the spoons jostled with the forks and knives inside. I didn't want to
go hunting for bowls. "You guys can eat straight out of the cartons."

"Aren't you having some?" Zoe asked, when I took out
only two.

I shook my head. "I'm going to let my stomach settle." I was
too nervous even for ice cream. And, looking at her bandages,
I didn't feel like I deserved it. I handed a spoon to Oscar, then
realized Zoe couldn't apply pressure to her arm and eat at the
same time. "Just a second, then I'll help you eat." I went back to
the counter to check on my phone.

Message delivery failed. Try again? I sucked in my breath.

"What's wrong?" Zoe quickly asked.

"I guess my phone isn't working after all." Oscar dropped
his spoon with a clatter. I hurried back to them, to head off a
meltdown. I slid down next to Zoe, replacing her left hand with
mine over the bandage. I could feel that it was moist. *What if it
never stops bleeding?* With my other hand, I opened the carton
for her and held it out so she could eat. "But I'm trying to send
the text again. We probably need to give it a minute. I'm sure
everybody is texting right now."

"It's getting kind of hard to see in here," Zoe pointed out, in
between spoonfuls.

The flashlight. I'd forgotten we needed to find one before it got totally dark in the house. *Stay focused*, I reminded myself. *And calm.* Moods were contagious, like yawns and laughs. If I panicked, so would Zoe and Oscar.

"How are you doing on the ice cream?"

"I'm already done with mine," Oscar said. When I gave him a look, he replied, "What? There was barely any Mint Moose left."

"It's hard to eat with my left hand." Zoe sped up her pace. "But mine's almost gone too."

"Finish quick, so we can find a flashlight."

"Can we not race this time?" Oscar asked quietly. It made my heart cramp.

"I promise we're not going to race anymore. We're going to stick together."

While we waited for Zoe to scrape out the last caramel bits, I listened to the quiet. A house without power seems silent, but it's not. There are all kinds of strange, unfamiliar sounds. Creaks and knocks and whirs. Although some of the sounds might have been the aftereffects of the shaking-up. Who knows what kinds of damage it did to the house, in places we couldn't see… We had no idea what things were like upstairs or outside in the yard or in the basement, with all the pipes and the boiler and flammable art supplies and whatnot. Important things that might be on the verge of toppling over or caving in. I swallowed hard. I wished my dad could take a walk-through and tell me that everything was safe and structurally sound.

Scenes from news reports and movies of people wandering through earthquake rubble flashed in my head. Those were always in far-off places—or California. After a quake, wasn't the power sometimes off for a long time, hours or maybe even days? Weren't people stranded on highways, trapped in building collapses, stuck without food and water… I wanted, more than anything, for Andrea or one of my parents to burst in through the door. Hug us and tell us that it wasn't like that here. That we were all going to be fine.

But I couldn't dwell on that. The only reason we could see anything in the kitchen was because our eyes had been slowly adjusting as the light dimmed. It was dangerous to be in the kitchen—to be anywhere in the house, in its present state—in darkness. I squinted to see if Zoe's bandages were holding up. The wound pad was red beneath the plastic coating, but blood wasn't leaking out of the adhesive sides, at least.

"Done, Zoe?" I worked hard to keep my voice calm and even. Enthusiastic. The opposite of how I felt: scared and ragged. Wanting to curl into a ball. My breathing was starting to feel funny. Like I was trying to suck in soda through a straw with a hole; like I wasn't getting what I was owed with each inhale. When this happens, I know I'm supposed to use my inhaler. But I didn't have it. I pictured it sitting on top of my nightstand, next to a framed family portrait and a photo of me and Neha on the stage at fifth-grade graduation. I inhaled for four counts and exhaled for eight. I'm not sure if that helped.

Zoe swallowed her last spoonful and nodded. I guided her hand to take mine's place on her arm. Then I rose up to check my phone one last time. The text had failed again. No Wi-Fi icon, no bars. I didn't tell the kids. I just pressed to try again, even if that was pointless without service, and then switched on the flashlight app, to help us see what lay ahead. "Oscar, let's find a real flashlight. Zoe, I think you should stay here and keep your arm elevated."

She shook her head. "I can hold it up while I walk. I don't want to be alone in the dark." She paused. "You promised we'd stick together."

"That's right, I did." Slowly I led Zoe and Oscar out of the kitchen, our tentative footsteps, and Jupiter's chirps, drowned out by the pounding in my ears of my own panicked heart.

5

WHERE DO WE KEEP *the flashlights in my house?* I closed my eyes, trying to picture their hiding spot. *There.* Tucked away in the closet next to the kitchen, a small plastic tub of emergency stuff—some water, food like granola bars, and a big flashlight with extra batteries. I know this because during spring cleaning every year, my mom changes out the water bottles and checks to make sure the food isn't expired. She tests the batteries too. I asked her once what kind of emergency the tub was meant for, and she gave me a vague "just in case" answer. I think she didn't want to scare me by mentioning what could actually go so wrong to make us have to subsist on granola bars and water, eaten by flashlight. But honestly, it's scarier not to know what exactly has freaked out your parents enough to make them designate a special tub in an overcrowded closet.

We were back in the Matlocks' front hallway, but it looked different than during our bathroom trip. Through the window, the trees outside cast creepy twilight shadows that slid around our feet as we stepped carefully across the runner.

"Shouldn't I go first? It's my house—I know which doors are which," Zoe said.

That was true, but I didn't think her leading the way was such a great idea. It was as though the whole house had been booby-trapped. "You can direct us, but let me go first—in case something is in the way." Like a pile of glass or sparking wires or who-knows-what. Another appliance that had toddled like the fridge. I gripped my phone tighter. I didn't particularly like wandering around dark houses in normal times, and especially not when I had no idea if actual danger lurked around a corner.

"Stop!" Zoe commanded. When I shined the phone's light on her, she nodded toward the door in front of me. "That's the coat closet. There might be a flashlight somewhere inside."

I opened the door, an inch wider at a time, in case something was about to tumble out. I waved my light into the dark space—a mess of parkas, galoshes, umbrellas, and shoeboxes. It looked like the entire lost-and-found bin at school had been dumped onto the closet floor.

"I guess the shaking messed this closet up pretty bad," I said, kneeling down to sort through it one-handed. I was holding Jupiter.

"No, it always looks like this," Oscar said, managing to make me laugh.

"I can hold the light while you look," Zoe said. "Since you've got Jupiter, and I have to keep my arm raised anyway."

"Great idea." I stood and passed my phone to Zoe, who held

it overhead, shining it down on us like she was a human street-light. Oscar and I sifted through the stuff until he found his missing tennis racket and started plucking at its strings. "Let's stay focused, guys." He put it back down and crawled deeper into the closet.

"What does it say on this box?" he called up to me. I leaned in, and Zoe swept the beam of light toward him.

"It says 'emergency'! Bring it over here." Oscar crawled back to me and tugged open the lid. Zoe shined my phone over the inside of the box. A metal cylinder reflected back at us.

"Yes! A flashlight." Oscar pumped his fist in the air.

"What else?" I asked. Jupiter was getting tired of being in the crook of my arm, and I had to keep readjusting so he wouldn't wiggle out to freedom. It wasn't safe for him to run free.

Oscar pulled out a small, clear plastic box with something red inside. "A…radio?"

"Oh, sweet. An emergency radio. Can you hand it to me?" I reached down to take it. Having a radio packed away for times like this was really smart of Andrea.

"That's pretty much it, just a big water bottle and…wrappers." Oscar wrinkled his nose and held up several shiny granola-bar wrappers. "I guess someone ate them?"

Zoe looked sheepish. "Sorry. I got hungry playing hide-and-seek with Liliana."

"It's fine," I assured her. "It's not like we need them. We'll eat everything in the fridge first, since the power's out. Oscar, can you turn on that flashlight, so I can look at this?" He shined it at me. The box the radio was in said: **Emergency Radio with USB Phone Charger—Crank-Powered and Solar-Powered**.

"Perfect, this thing has a phone charger too." Which was excellent news, because my battery had only been at 70 percent before the shaking, and using the flashlight app and trying to send desperate SOS texts had surely drained it even more.

Oscar had moved the flashlight underneath his chin and was flicking it on and off, making spooky faces. "Great faces, Oscar, but now let's keep it on so we can find our way back to the living room, okay?"

Feeling flush with the ability to charge, I kept my phone's flashlight app on, for extra light while we crept back through the hallway to the kitchen. Last thing we needed was another incident with broken glass. "How's your cut, Zoe? Are the bandages holding up?"

"I think so," she said. "Can I put my arm down now?"

I wasn't sure. I hadn't paid great attention during the first aid part of my babysitting course because, really, what would I have expected to do other than slap on a bandage? For anything serious, you'd call the parents or a doctor. We were passing the kitchen phone as I thought about calling doctors, and I shivered. That wasn't even an option. *Andrea will be home really soon*, I reassured myself. It was close to eight, which made me wonder why my mom hadn't already come over to check on us. Even if she somehow missed the shaking, she must've tried to text me by then and I hadn't replied. *If there's ever a time to be overprotective, I think this is it.*

In the kitchen I had the brilliant idea—although it probably came rather late—to get the kids to put on their shoes. They were lined up by the door to the carport and had only moved a foot or two during the quake, like they'd all shuffled in a line to the right. With shoes on, we could walk in the living room without risking more wounds. I helped Zoe get hers on one-handed and checked her arm again. "We should change your bandages." When I peeled them off at the sink, the pads were heavy with blood. It seeped onto my fingers as I dropped them to the countertop. I shuddered and gagged. But her bleeding had slowed to a trickle, to my relief. To conserve the supply, I only put one bandage back on.

We had almost reached the safe zone of the couch when it happened again. A vibration surged through my feet up along my spine, followed by shaking so hard my teeth rattled. It was harder to tell what was happening around us now that it was dark. But we knew right away to be scared. Zoe and Oscar screamed. I turned and enveloped them in a hug. Jupiter, now in Oscar's arms, squealed. The noise was louder this time, or maybe it only seemed that way because we couldn't see. The beams from my phone and the flashlight Oscar held wavered like a light show at a concert. There was a huge crash—the biggest yet. So loud we all cringed. I held my breath, wondering if the falling thing was about to squash us.

A few seconds later, the shaking stopped.

We huddled there, my arms still around the kids, afraid to stand tall. Zoe and Oscar were crying. Where were *my* tears? I'd been numbed by fear.

"What's going on?" Oscar's voice was barely above a whisper.

It took me a few seconds to catch my breath. "Another aftershock. But it's over." *I think. I hope.*

The really big crash had come from behind us. I lifted my hand to shine the beam of light into the kitchen. The fridge had loomed in the center of the room before. Now, it was gone.

"What… Where…" I took the real flashlight from Oscar and focused it on the middle of the kitchen. The beam landed on a huge rectangular shape, covering the floor. The fridge.

We'd been sitting in front of it, eating ice cream. Only seconds before the shaking, we'd walked directly in its path, after I'd changed Zoe's bandage. What if we had paused right there when the aftershock started? It could have crushed us. I'd thought that, aside from avoiding the debris, we were safe in those moments. But we hadn't been.

We weren't safe anywhere in the house.

One time, Mom and I were driving home at night and a deer wandered across the road in front of us. It froze as the car approached, and then Mom slammed the brakes. We were honking and yelling for it to move. The deer stared at us, unblinking. After a few seconds, it seemed to wake up, then bolted away. That's when I realized what "deer in the headlights" really means—when you're so scared you can't even move. And that's what happened after I saw the fridge flopped on the kitchen floor and imagined us flattened by it. I froze.

"Hannah?" Zoe sounded tentative. "Um, what should we do now?"

Her voice woke me up. But unlike the deer, I didn't even have a safe place to run to. *I don't know—Mrs. Pinales never covered deadly refrigerators.* Nothing I'd learned had prepared me for this. *I can't handle this all on my own.* But I had to at least determine somewhere safe-ish for us to hide out until help arrived. *What's the farthest spot from anything that could hurt us?* I shined my flashlight across the living room. The couch seemed the best place, not near any shelves and far enough away from that precarious pendant light. "Follow me to the couch." I didn't feel calm or sure, but I tried my best to sound it.

After I checked for pottery shards and glass, we curled up on the cushions together. I turned off the flashlight app on my phone, checking for bars again. None. I reopened my messages, crossing my fingers that my text to Andrea had somehow gone through. I turned away from Zoe and Oscar, so they couldn't see the screen. They were busy comforting Jupiter anyway.

Message failed. I swallowed a groan. *Come on, phone.* I pressed to resend it again, crossing my fingers. *Please go through. Please, please go through this time.* My chest began to ache.

It was unnerving to sit in the silent dark. "Hey, let's try out the radio." Oscar tossed it to me, and while Zoe shined the flashlight on the box, I opened it and pulled the little red radio out. "When's the last time you guys listened to a radio? And I don't mean a podcast." Maybe if I acted like everything was totally normal, it would be.

"Um…" Zoe tapped her fingers on the flashlight, thinking. "Never?"

I tried to remember. "Yeah, I don't think I've ever used one. Maybe at my grandma's house." In the car, I mostly talked to my parents or we played music off one of our phones. "This is like time travel, back to the olden days," I said with artificial cheer, flicking the buttons. I turned it on, but no sound came out. I pulled the antenna out as long as it would stretch. I spun the volume all the way up, but still, nothing. "Maybe I need to crank it first." The solar-powered feature was unlikely to help us.

I began turning the crank on the back, which took a surprising amount of arm effort. For some reason, Oscar found this hilarious to watch, and he dissolved into a fit of giggles on the sofa. I was grateful for anything to distract him. We were all on the verge of total freak-outs, and I didn't know how—or whether I had the strength—to stop tears once they started. Including my own.

When my arm grew tired, I quit cranking. "I seriously hope that was enough," I muttered, flicking the on button again. Static filled the room.

"It's working!" Zoe bent to kiss Jupiter's head—the noise had startled him into chattering.

I slowly tuned the dial, searching for words instead of sandpaper sounds. Finally, I heard a series of beeps, followed by an official-sounding voice. "*Shh*, everybody quiet." I made a silent wish to hear good news, like that the power would be back on momentarily.

"*This is Beth Kajawa with the latest on the Cascadia earthquake event.*"

Even though the woman speaking sounded professional and calm, how fast and forcefully she spoke worried me. *This is urgent,* her voice communicated. *This is a big deal. You must pay attention to this.* It also occurred to me that she wasn't calling it the "Pelling earthquake." *Cascadia* meant she was referring to the whole Cascade mountain range. So the earthquake must have been felt beyond our island. I sucked in a breath. And then another, because the first one wasn't sufficient.

"*In brief: At 6:17 p.m. Pacific Standard Time, an earthquake occurred along the Cascadia Subduction Zone, which runs approximately seven hundred miles from Cape Mendocino, California, to Vancouver Island, Canada. Preliminary reports suggest a magnitude in excess of 8.6. There are widespread reports of serious damage to*" *homes, roads, and other infrastructures throughout the Seattle metropolitan area. All communities west of the Cascades are presumed to be affected by the event. The power grid is currently down as well as most cellular phone networks. Parts of I-5 are closed due to damage. Ferry service to and from Seattle is not operating. There are several reports of bridge and highway collapses in the region. It is difficult to estimate the number of casualties with the current disruption to mass communication, but anecdotal reports suggest area hospitals already are becoming overwhelmed with patients. Residents are advised to shelter in place."*

I had stood up while cranking the radio. Hearing that news, I slid back down to the carpet next to the couch. Highways shut down, no ferries, hospitals overwhelmed with patients... That was bad. Really, seriously bad. Tears pricked at the corners of my eyes. I fought them. I couldn't fight the urge to cough, to get enough air. *I wish I had my inhaler.* Why hadn't I remembered it that morning? Now it was another kind of rescue I needed.

If the damage was everywhere in and around the city, the shaking had happened where Andrea was, where Neha was. Wherever my mom was. What about my dad? Seabrook was hours away from Seattle and the Cascades. At least he would be safe.

"We will continue to keep you updated as information becomes available. Now we have a message from Seattle's Director of Emergency Management..."

I heard a whimper from Oscar. He had curled into a ball on the far cushion. Zoe sat next to him, hugging Jupiter close. Fresh tears rolled down the tracks on her cheeks. I turned the radio dial off. The silence in the living room felt thick with dread. I looked away from the kids.

Andrea wasn't going to be home anytime soon. Neither was my mom.

We were all alone, in a shaken and shattered house, in the dark.

One of us was bleeding. All of us were terrified.

And I was in charge.

6

I WAS A BABYSITTING NEWBIE, but Neha actually had a lot of experience with little kids—she loved to help watch her younger cousins at family parties. So when Mrs. Pinales had asked at the end of her class if anyone had questions, I'd been surprised that Neha's hand shot up in the air.

"What do you do if the kids you're watching start crying? Or if they're super grumpy and refuse to play *any* of the games you suggest? Like, their answer to every single suggestion is screaming 'No!'" Huh. I hadn't thought of moodiness as being a potential babysitting problem.

"Great question, Neha. It's tough when your charges aren't in the best spirits—but we all have blue days, even as babies." Mrs. Pinales had smiled reassuringly. "My advice is that when you're in charge, you set the tone. Stay positive, and give the kids a little space. Usually, they'll come around—especially if *you* seem to be having a good time."

As Zoe and Oscar sniffled in the dark, I focused on that advice. I couldn't follow Mrs. Pinales's instruction to wait for an adult's help; I was going to be in charge for however long we had to wait for our parents to come home and take control of things. Hopefully, that would be soon, but it was going to be pretty awful for the three of us to sit and wait in tears. Or squeaks, in Jupiter's case. For now, it was my job to turn things around, or at least try. I needed to distract the kids with something fun, even if pretending like any part of this awful situation was fun seemed ridiculous. At the least, I could pretend like I wasn't terrified. I focused on my breathing, so when I broke the silence my voice would sound normal and calm.

When I'm freaking out, what do I distract myself with? I squeezed my phone in my palm, then glanced up at the TV. Well, those weren't options. I needed to think of ways to have fun in the dark, without electricity…like camping? But indoors.

It hit me: the best part of camping is always s'mores, and when I'd been cleaning up Zoe's cut, I'd noticed that bag of big marshmallows that had landed safely in the open drawer when everything went torpedoing out of the cupboards. *That's perfect.* What kid wouldn't perk up with a little chocolate and marsh-mallow? Even in a situation like this.

"So." I paused to clear my throat, because my voice had gotten thick and gravelly. "That broadcast was kind of intense." Oscar's head bobbed in vigorous agreement.

"Kind of?" Zoe snorted.

"But the good news, from an otherwise scary report, is that

everybody in Seattle knows what happened. The emergency people are on it. Help is probably already on the way." *How will help even get to Pelling if the ferries aren't running and the highways are closed… What if the Elliott Bay Bridge is one of the ones that collapsed?* We lived on a secluded peninsula on an island. The only way we could be more difficult to get to would be if our neighborhood were bordered by quicksand instead of a forest preserve. *Stop it, you're spiraling.* "Everything's going to be fine." I smiled, in an attempt to convince both them and myself.

"But it's dark, and we're home alone." Oscar whimpered.

"Don't worry about the power. This'll be fun, guys—like camping, but inside! Sit tight and give me a minute." I stood up, turning my phone's flashlight app back on.

"Where are you going?" Zoe's voice was panicked. "Don't leave us!" She grabbed for my wrist. Her nails dug into my skin as she tried to pull me back.

"I'm not leaving you!" I shined my phone's light toward the kitchen. "I'm getting something in there, and I'll be right back. You can watch me the whole time." After a few seconds, Zoe reluctantly let go.

I had to squeeze past the fridge to get into the kitchen, and my stomach twisted as I saw how much space it took up on the floor. I nudged its stainless steel side with the toe of my sneaker. Of course it didn't budge. A fridge when it's set back against a wall and surrounded by cupboards doesn't seem so huge and heavy, but lying on the floor I realized how massive it was. A scene flashed into my mind: one of us trapped below, the others struggling to lift the fridge away. *Another death trap.* I shook my head to clear the picture. It hadn't hurt us. We'd been lucky. Now that the fridge was prone on the floor, it couldn't fall again. Right then, we were safer than we'd been all night; we just hadn't known the dangers before. Still, I decided it was probably wise to spend as little time as possible in a room full of appliances and cutlery.

The marshmallows, miraculously, hadn't landed anywhere gross when I'd tossed them. I hugged them to my chest. Now for the graham crackers and some chocolate. Everybody had those squirreled away in their cupboard, right? I called back to the living room, "You guys holding up okay?"

"Yeah." Oscar's voice was so forlorn. It made my heart squeeze.

"I promise you'll be excited about what I have planned!" *Graham crackers, graham crackers, wherefore art thou, graham crackers?* I shined my phone's light into a cupboard containing a big cereal spill. *Aha!* Far in the back, still standing upright, was the familiar blue box. I snatched it. Now I only needed chocolate. There were lots of baking ingredients jumbled in that cupboard—it seemed like the right place to keep hunting. I swept my hand left to right, using the phone like a searchlight. A metallic wrapper glinted.

Jackpot.

The bar was hard as a brick, and the partially peeled label said Baking Chocolate, but it would have to do. With my arms full of ingredients, I carefully walked through the kitchen, squeezing past the sharp edge of the fridge again, and back into the living room. I plopped onto the couch, in between Zoe and Oscar. They scooted right next to me, and Jupiter made a whoop like he was happy I was back too.

"You know what you have to do when you're camping, even indoors?" Oscar shook his head no. "Make s'mores!" I grinned like a maniac.

Oscar's face brightened—and not from the flashlight he was shining on and off again. Zoe looked skeptical. Maybe that was because of my unintentional rhyming. Now I understood how my mom felt whenever she tried way too hard to get me excited about something, like doing yard work or helping her reorganize our bookshelves in accordance with the Dewey decimal system.

It turns out that s'mores without a source of heat—be it a crackling campfire or a lowly microwave—are not quite as good. It's a dessert that hinges on gooeyness; without melting, it doesn't quite gel. Also, baking chocolate is totally not the same thing as regular chocolate. Oscar took the first bite of a dusty square and promptly spat it somewhere on the floor.

"Ugh! That chocolate tastes awful. Can it go bad?"

I picked up a square and failed to break off a piece—it was

really hard. I nibbled on the edge, and my nose scrunched up. "Yuck. It's like there's no sugar in it."

Zoe nodded. "Mom only uses that stuff for making fudge. And then she dumps in loads of sugar." I wished she'd told me that before I ate it. I looked down at the sad imitation of s'mores in my hand. The marshmallow was barely squished. The graham cracker had crumbled all over the couch when I'd bitten into it. Crumbs were the least of my worries, though.

My throat had that tight feeling, like there was a lump in it that I couldn't swallow past. The feeling you get when your voice rises and your eyes sting, right before you start to cry. I gulped in air to make it loosen.

Zoe was watching me. She could tell I was struggling. "I love marshmallows," she said quietly, offering a tiny, tentative smile. She took a big bite of hers. "Yum." Watching her try to act happy for me made my heart squeeze tighter.

"How many do you think I can fit in my mouth?" Oscar asked, grabbing for the bag. He crammed a few in, forced his lips closed, and then shined the flashlight again from under his chin while grinning and waggling his eyebrows. Despite everything, Zoe and I laughed. My tears stopped welling, and my throat relaxed. Mrs. Pinales had been right—they were coming around. I just had to keep them distracted and all three of us calm. Four, if you count Jupiter. Periodically he would make this weird angry purring sound, which Zoe insisted meant he was stressed out.

Continuing to pretend like we were in the dark on purpose—camping indoors—seemed like the best strategy I had. I'd only gone camping once, with my Girl Scout troop. We'd stayed in tents at a campsite in the mountains and went on a nature walk during which we identified plants in order to get a special badge. At night, we stargazed and told stories by a campfire. I definitely didn't want to herd the kids outside to try to see stars—who knew what conditions were like out there, and even if it weren't drizzling, then the sky had probably clouded over anyway. We didn't have a campfire, but we could still tell stories. By flashlight.

"While we eat the marshmallows, let's tell some scary stories. Pretend we're around a roaring campfire," I said.

"Or at a sleepover!" Zoe added, her face brightening. "I went to one last week for Liliana's birthday. She told us a *really* scary story."

"Super!" I said. "Do you want to go first?"

She nodded. "Oscar, give me the flashlight." He stretched it out and, with her good hand, Zoe took it.

She cleared her throat, then spoke in a low whisper, while the flashlight below her chin illuminated her face. "This is the story of the scritch-scratch." Oscar's eyes widened. "At night, when children are sleeping in their beds, sometimes a shadow creeps up to their windows. If they were smart, they closed the curtains before they went to sleep, or rolled down the shades. If they had shades instead of curtains. Or blinds, I guess. Anyway, foolish children don't remember to cover their windows."

"I never close my curtains," Oscar piped up. "I like to watch the moon."

"Well, I guess we know that you're one of the foolish ones, then. As I was *saying*—some children sleep with their windows uncovered, and that's how the shadow finds them."

"Their own shadow? Isn't it already there?" Oscar sounded confused. So was I.

"No—it's a different shadow, like a monster. Just listen, okay? So first the shadow lurks below the windowpane, listening. Once the kid is snoring, it knows the time has come…for the scritch-scratch test. It takes its long, bony shadow finger, and with its even longer, grimy shadow fingernail, it goes *scritch-scratch* against the glass."

Zoe raised her other arm, the one she'd cut, to mime the scratching. To my relief, her bandage appeared to be holding up—it looked clean and white; no more blood had soaked through.

"If the noise wakes them, the shadow slips away. They're not in deep-enough sleep. But if they don't stir, it…attacks!" Zoe switched off the flashlight and we were plunged into darkness. Oscar screamed, and then Jupiter began chirping frantically.

"I don't want a shadow to attack us!" He started to sob.

"Zoe, turn on the flashlight!" I yelled.

The light snapped back on, showing her apologetic face. "Jeez, Oscar. It's just a story that Liliana made up."

I crawled across the back of the couch cushions so I was

sitting next to Oscar, and I put my arms around him in a hug. He felt so much tinier than I expected. Maybe because we were in the dark, or because he was curled over Jupiter in his lap. His little shoulders shook. I rubbed his back and tried to soothe him. "It's only make-believe, Oscar. There are no shadows out hunting kids. I promise."

He kept on crying. "I want my mom."

My heart panged. *I do too.* "I know. She'll be home as soon as she possibly can."

"I can tell another story," Zoe offered. "Without any shadows or scritch-scratching."

"Thanks, Zoe—but maybe we should leave the stories for later." That idea had been a mistake, clearly. I pressed the home button on my phone to check the time. It was closing in on nine. No wonder I felt so exhausted.

"Guys, I think we should start getting ready for bed." Before they could protest about Andrea not being back yet, I added, "Your mom will really appreciate it if you're all ready for sleep once she gets home." If *she makes it here tonight.* I paused, sinking back into the couch. Till that point, I'd still believed that eventually I'd be going home, changing into my favorite fleece pajama pants, and curling up in my bed. I only knew of the chaos the earthquake had caused at the Matlocks' house. In my mind, mine still stood strong, waiting to welcome me.

But until Andrea made it back—I would be staying right where

I was. In their upturned living room. If my mom came back first, though, maybe she could take the four of us to my house.

Mom must be frantic, I thought, if she knew I was there alone, with two kids and a guinea pig. She would stop at nothing to get to Pelling, if she hadn't already been on the island when the earthquake happened. So the fact that she wasn't here…

A bit of the news broadcast popped back into my head: *Area hospitals already are becoming overwhelmed with patients.* What if my mom was one of them?

My stomach twisted. The reporter had said there were lots of casualties already. Did that mean people had…died?

A rushing noise filled my ears, and I felt my pulse start to race. My chest started to tighten, like my lungs were a balloon with a hole, one that couldn't quite expand.

"Hannah? How are we even going to go to bed?" Zoe asked. "We can't go upstairs, remember… Are you okay?"

I gripped the arm of the couch, forcing myself to calm down. *Focus, Hannah. You have to stay in control.* "Uh, good point." We couldn't go up to the kids' bedrooms, but that was probably for the best. We needed to stick together, and it would be easier to get out of the house from the first floor if anything else happened. "We're camping, remember? Here in the living room. Yeah—we're going to make a tent." I held up a soft throw.

"I love making blanket forts." Oscar sniffed.

"Now it'll also be like a sleepover," I added, for Zoe's benefit. "Let's find some more blankets."

A tall wicker basket full of them had overturned in front of the fireplace, which was now blocked by a heaping pile of broken pottery and everything else from a shelf that had collapsed. Facing away from the couch, I shook out all the blankets, hoping that if any shards had fallen, they'd be flung away before we snuggled up in them. Then we draped the biggest blanket over the space in between the couch and the coffee table a few feet away, tucking the corners into the couch seams so they'd stay tight. We laid out the couch and love seat cushions on the carpet below the blanket covering, for a softer place to sleep. It would be pretty tight for us three to fit in that space, but I didn't mind being curled up together.

"What about Jupiter?" Oscar asked. "I can't hold a guinea pig all night long."

"We can't put him back in his cage… Is there a box anywhere? Like a shoebox or something."

"We have the emergency box." Zoe had carried it back from the closet.

"Perfect. Jupiter, congratulations on your new home." Zoe handed me the box, and then Oscar gently settled Jupiter inside. The walls were tall enough that a guinea pig shouldn't be able to climb out, but it was open so he'd have enough air.

We made another group expedition to the bathroom, grabbing

sweatshirts from the mess inside the closet, and on the way back we stopped in the kitchen to brush our teeth—but with our fingers, since their toothbrushes were upstairs and mine was at my house. "It feels so weird to not use toothpaste. Weird and wrong," Zoe said.

"I know," I agreed. I ran my tongue over my teeth, wishing I at least had a piece of gum or something. Slimy marshmallow residue still coated them. I couldn't remember the last time I'd gone to sleep without brushing. Although, that was probably the least weird part of the night, considering I was going to bed inside a blanket fort with two elementary-schoolers and a guinea pig.

The whole time we were "getting ready for bed," I kept my fingers crossed. Hoping that a knock would come at the door, followed by my mom calling for me. Hoping that we'd hear Andrea's key in the lock, or that we'd see flashing lights, even, from a police car coming to check on the house. If our parents couldn't get back, wouldn't they tell someone to come wait with us? I couldn't believe that we'd been left alone this long. I mean, my mom knew I couldn't remember my inhaler half the time. She didn't think I was very capable—she'd made that clear this morning. There's no way she would let me handle this situation alone. Unless there was nothing she could do about it. That was the scariest possibility.

I didn't want to go to bed, not without an adult in the Matlocks' dark, demolished house. What if the shaking started again, and I was wrong in thinking that our blanket fort was in the safest possible spot? Watching *The Wizard of Oz* taught me that during a tornado, people go into basements and cellars. Are you supposed to go to a certain place during an earthquake? I had no clue. I looked longingly at my phone's dark screen. If only I could Google it.

"I don't want to go to bed before our mom gets home," Zoe announced, echoing my thoughts.

Oscar spat the water he'd been swishing around his mouth into the kitchen sink and nodded. "Yeah, I'm waiting up for her." He'd barely finished the sentence before he punctuated it with a yawn. I bit at my lip, thinking. The later we stayed up, the more worried they were going to get, and we were all exhausted. In the bathroom, I'd caught a glimpse of myself in the cracked mirror, thanks to a sliver of moonlight coming in through the window. I hardly recognized my weary face. It was strange to think that only hours ago, it had been a perfectly ordinary day. Now, it was like we were stranded in some alternate universe, without power or parents or a phone. Where refrigerators were deadly. I missed the regular buzz from Neha's texts. I wanted so badly to shut my eyes and travel home. To click my heels, like Dorothy.

Maybe when we woke up, everything would be back to normal. Power, phone, parents. For that to happen, though, I had to convince the kids that it was safe to let ourselves sleep. Even if that meant lying.

I took one step back from them and pressed the home button on my phone so the screen lit up. Both Zoe and Oscar whipped their heads toward me and the light.

I faked a gasp. "Guys, a text must've come through while we were making the fort! Your mom is finally on her way. We can stop worrying."

"I want to send her a text!" Zoe cried.

I shook my head, although I'm not sure she could see me in the dark. She lunged for my phone, which I pulled back to my chest. "No, I should conserve the battery—and the connection is spotty."

"Then I'm going to stay up." Zoe crossed her arms over her chest, flinching when she pressed on the bandage. She released her hands to her sides. "If she's on her way."

"It's going to be really late when she gets back," I said. "She wants you to go to bed. How about I wake you up when she's home?" It felt wrong to lie, especially about their mom. I wouldn't want someone to do that to me. But I needed a break. My chest was hurting again, and my heart kept racing. No matter how deeply I tried to breathe, I couldn't get enough air. I felt like I'd been trying to keep up with Neha on the soccer field. Lying down on the couch cushions might help.

Zoe sighed. "Fine, I guess."

Holding hands, we tiptoed out of the kitchen and back into the living room. We bent down and crawled into the blanket fort, first Oscar, then Zoe, last me. Oscar curled himself around the emergency box holding Jupiter, who was quietly huddled in a corner. Zoe lay down next to Oscar. I grabbed the softer of the two remaining blankets and wrapped it around them, tucking it tightly. Burrito-style, as my dad used to say. "Okay, sleep tight. It's going to be better in the morning."

"It'll be better once Mom gets home tonight," Zoe said, yawning.

I winced. "Right." I lowered myself onto the cushion and pulled the last blanket over me. It was small, barely long enough to cover my legs—and I'm pretty short. It was also scratchy, made of that knitted fabric with lots of holes. Afghans, I think they're called. I didn't know how warm it was going to keep me. I scooted closer to Zoe and Oscar, greedy for their body heat.

They seemed to fall asleep in minutes. I don't know how that was possible. My mind—and my heart—wouldn't stop racing. I lay awake, listening. The house sounded strange. There wasn't the hum of a single device, but it wasn't exactly quiet. Many of the windows had shattered, and in through them wafted noises from outside. Rustling trees. The hoot of an owl. Something that howled—I hoped that was a faraway neighbor's dog, although it would have to be *really* far away, because my family doesn't have one, the Matlocks only had Jupiter, and Mr. Aranita is a cat person. Otherwise the howl came from the forest preserve. There are coyotes—and cougars and even black bears—that live in it. They've never bothered us before, other than sometimes leaving scat in the backyard, but that's when we had lights and, more importantly, unbroken windows. I started thinking about the story that Zoe had been telling about the scritch-scratch shadow hunting children. Did I hear any...scratching outside? I switched from lying on my back to my side, trying to roll away from the thought.

But my ears would not stop listening. They were vigilant. Every sound made my breath catch, before I identified it as something harmless. *Wait, is that a car?* I sat up, straining to hear the crunching sound, like car tires. It was so faint. *Please, let someone be coming to help us.* I held my breath and listened, but I couldn't hear the noise anymore. Maybe it had only been the damage settling, or my imagination. I tried not to think of any sharp-toothed creatures that could make crunching sounds outside.

I sank back onto the cushion. Earlier moments from the day kept replaying in my head. What had I said to my dad before I hung up the phone—*"Yum, thanks"*? Why didn't I say, "Love you" or listen for a minute longer? After all, once I heard Mr. Fisk's honk while still in the kitchen, I knew missing the bus was inevitable. Why hadn't I given my mom that hug in the car, when I knew how she craved it?

And why had I told Neha that I didn't want to be her friend because of a stupid Earth Day project? She was as close to me as a sister. Even if I was a little mad or hurt right now, I still wanted to be her friend. But now those horrible words were my last message to her before…this. I swallowed hard, because I didn't know if Neha was okay.

Or if Zoe, Oscar, and I were going to be.

The wind rustled something on the living room floor. I curled into a ball, hiding my head under the afghan. A tear slid out from the corner of my eye, and I was surprised by how warm it felt as it rolled down my cheek, all the way to my chin. If I had been able to see anything in the dark, I'm sure I would've been able to see my breath. I scooted another inch closer to the blanket cocoon encircling Zoe and Oscar.

Everyone I loved was somewhere out there, in a dangerous new world. I hoped they were somewhere at least as safe as our blanket fort. I hoped they weren't alone. I hoped they knew that I was thinking of them, wishing as hard as I possibly could that they were okay. That they were…alive.

That was all I could do. Hope.

7

OPENED MY EYES AND saw a beak, frighteningly close to my face. A bird's opaque but curious eyes stared into mine. I must've sensed it watching me, and that stirred me awake. *Or am I dreaming this?* I looked to my left, then to my right. Somehow, in the night, my top half had wound up outside the blanket fort, although my legs were still tangled in the afghan and stretched across the top of the cushion nest. The bird was also outside the fort, although perhaps it wanted to come inside. It hopped toward my face, slightly too close for comfort, and I shrieked and scooted back underneath the fort. That made the bird flap its wings and attempt to fly away, but because it was in a *living room* and not the great outdoors, it just made panicked racetrack loops around the ceiling.

"What's going on?" Zoe startled to an upright position, rubbing at her eyes. On her other side, Oscar rose onto his elbows, yawning sleepily.

"A bird just woke me up. Literally!"

"Are you serious?" Zoe began to scoot on her hands and knees to get out of the fort, till her bandage made contact with the carpet and she winced. She switched to crab-walking out from the blanket. Oscar followed her, and so did I.

We stood there, blinking in the bright morning light, watching the bird continue to circle the ceiling. It felt really good to see our surroundings again, but that meant we could clearly see what bad shape the living room was in. We were in a scene from a disaster movie, which I suppose made sense. Everything was overturned. Lights dangled from the ceiling. Half of the floor-to-ceiling windows facing the backyard were broken. That must be how the bird got inside. Now, it was too scared to fly back out, even though it was circling no more than a foot above a wide-open window frame. I wanted to help it.

"Come on, bird!" I waved my arms, hoping the bird would prove the "bird brain" stereotype wrong and understand that all it had to do was fly a teensy bit lower to get to freedom. It didn't do it.

A fireplace broom was lying on the floor not far from where we stood. I grabbed it and walked to the edge of the room, stopping in front of another shattered window. When the bird flew my way, I tried to shoo it out with the broom. "Come on, silly bird! I'm showing you exactly where to go!" It kept circling, and then it pooped. The glob was inches from landing smack on my fleece vest.

Zoe and Oscar dissolved into a fit of giggles. I had to admit, this was hilariously weird. I wished I could take video of the avian intruder and send it to Neha, who loved to watch funny animal videos online. *Neha.* All the worries came flooding back. I swung the broom down for a second, leaning over with my hands on my thighs so I could catch my breath. It had gotten even chillier in the house overnight, and cold always seems to make the breathing stuff worse for me.

The bird buzzed past me—so close I could've almost touched its wings—before it passed through the window frame and finally found its way outside. I watched it cross the backyard, flapping madly, heading for the evergreens of the forest preserve. On its way home, wherever that was. I wondered if its nest would have been damaged during the earthquake, or if it had left any baby birds behind and was desperate to return to them.

I dropped the broom and carefully walked back to the blanket fort, hugging my arms to my chest. I wore a long sleeve under my vest and thick leggings, but I was still shivering.

"The heat was on in your house yesterday, right? Before *this* happened?" I motioned at the debris filling the living room.

Oscar shrugged. Zoe looked thoughtful. "It must have been… I remember Mom turning it up when we got home after school." Now she shivered, hugging her chest. Then her arms dropped to her sides. "Wait. Where is Mom? You said you'd wake us up when she got home!" Her tone was more panicked than accusing.

Oh. "So, the bad news is, she's not back quite yet—"

Zoe interrupted before I had to come up with good news, which was a relief, because that was definitely going to have to be a big white lie. "Why not? She, she…" Zoe's eyes welled with tears.

"She texted after you fell asleep." Another lie, but I had no other choice. If Zoe and Oscar thought our parents had checked in, it would be much easier to keep them calm. "She had to spend the night in Seattle…with friends," I said. "Um, my mom is there too, but it's okay. They'll definitely be back before dark."

Zoe narrowed her eyes. "My mom said that?"

I took a breath, then nodded. "Yup."

Zoe and Oscar let the news that we were still on our own sink in. I waited, hoping that they wouldn't pout or cry. My head ached, and I hadn't slept enough. When it seemed safe to change the subject, I said, "Well, I don't think the heat's on anymore." This time of year, it's usually in the fifties during the day. At night, the temperature drops into the forties. Without the heat on, it gets cold—and damp—really fast.

"I know where the thermostat is," Zoe said with a sigh, starting to pick her way through the mess to the far side of the living room.

"Wait—I'm not sure that's the best idea," I said. Our house uses electric heat, and the Matlocks' likely did the same. As long as the power was out, the heat would be too. Even if it wasn't off because of the outage, I wasn't sure it would be smart to try to crank it up. Fires were in the background of every earthquake movie I'd ever seen. "Why don't you guys get back in the blanket fort, put on those sweatshirts, and I'll grab a few coats from the closet?"

As they dutifully crawled back inside, I swiped the emergency radio from the top of the coffee table, where I'd left it the night before. While I was away, I could sneak an update on what was happening. Hopefully, today's broadcast would be better news, but if it wasn't, I didn't want Zoe or Oscar to hear. I patted the pocket of my vest, making sure my phone was still inside, in case service came back. I kept feeling phantom buzzes, and then I would optimistically press my hand to its outline through the fabric, only to feel nothing but the phone's still, silent weight. I'd checked the volume dozens of times.

The rest of the house was in worse shape than I remembered. Maybe yesterday when we'd walked to the bathroom, we'd been so shell-shocked that the damage hadn't registered. Or maybe things had simply gotten worse after dark. It had been night by the time the fridge-toppling aftershock had happened. Now, in the harsh morning light, I could see that dust, possibly from plaster, covered every surface. It made me cough, and I pulled up the neck of my shirt to cover my mouth and nose as I slowly made my way down the hall. All the furniture was broken or overturned, or both. The beautiful amber-colored paint was streaked bone white in all the places where bits of wall had cracked or crumbled down. The door to the closet had flung open during the shaking, and the junk that had been inside was now strewn across the hallway floor. The staircase leading up to the second floor had lost even more "teeth." Balusters lined the floor like I'd stumbled on the tooth fairy's stash.

Before trying to sort through the closet debris for coats, I needed to pee. I headed into the bathroom. Its door refused to actually shut. *So much for privacy*—although right then, I was alone.

I quickly did my business. Flushing made kind of a weird sucking noise, but the bowl refilled with water, like it was supposed to. I closed the lid and sat down on top of the seat. The floor had been really crunchy when I walked in—I glanced over at the sink and saw that the mirror above the faucet had broken, shards now covering the tile floor. *I should probably try to sweep that out or something, before the kids come in again.*

The lid was freezing cold against the backs of my thighs, even with my leggings on. I pulled my knees up to my chest and huddled in that position. The emergency radio was on the floor next to me. I should turn it on. I *needed* to turn it on, but I was afraid of what I might hear.

It's like ripping off a bandage. Just flip the switch, quickly. Get it over with. I yanked the antenna thingy out and turned the dial, making sure the volume was high enough so I could hear, but low enough so the sound wouldn't carry from the bathroom back to the blanket fort.

I held my breath as I listened to the crackle. Then a voice came in. The same one from last night. *What was her name? Beth Kajawa.* Only this time she sounded a lot more freaked out than she had before.

"*…is unable to estimate at this time when an update on restoration will be available. For those just tuning in, we have the latest developments in the Cascadia earthquake. The U.S. Geological Survey now estimates the initial quake as a 9.0, the first major quake in the Pacific Northwest in three hundred years, and perhaps the second strongest to hit North America. Ever. The power grid is down for the whole region, from Seattle all the way to Portland. Many cell towers have been damaged, so, as I'm sure our listeners are aware, there is little if any service. All local airports, including Sea-Tac, are closed. Ferry service is not operating. Many roads, including much of I-5, are impassable. We're currently compiling a list of all highway and bridge closures and will get that to you as soon as possible, but as a reminder to our listeners: the Seattle Office of Emergency Management still asks that you shelter in place. There are reports of landslides, fires, and flooding, and we're working to get you more details. Until then, if you are in a safe place—please stay there.*"

Maybe that's why our mothers weren't home yet; they were somewhere safe and were obeying the emergency people by staying put. But even as I tried to convince myself, deep in my heart, I knew that couldn't be true. My mother would never "shelter in place" elsewhere if she hadn't at least spoken to me. Andrea, I'm sure, would be the same.

Beth Kajawa paused, letting out a barely audible sigh before she continued, *"Authorities tell us they predict thousands of fatalities and tens of thousands of people injured along the Cascadia Subduction Zone. Seattle Medical Center is working to evacuate critical patients due to hospital damage. Northwest Hospital is accepting patients, we're told."*

I squeezed my eyes shut, resisting the urge to cover my ears. *"Thousands of fatalities."* I slid off the toilet seat and crouched next to it, in case I might throw up. *What if our moms…* I couldn't let myself continue that thought.

Another pause in the broadcast, during which the static crackled. I started to worry that I'd lost the signal. When Beth Kajawa spoke again, her voice was throaty and pained. *"We also have an update on the tsunami."* I notched up the volume. She hadn't mentioned that in the broadcast last night. *"First, to clear up any confusion, we're only hearing of a small amount of tsunami damage on the interior of Puget Sound, mostly to low-lying structures."* She sounded distraught, but wasn't that good news? Seattle was on Puget Sound. *"On the coast, that is not the case. The wave hit eighteen minutes after the earthquake. The areas affected are from the ocean to approximately one mile inland, and everything—"* Her voice cracked on the word. *"Everything is...destroyed. All structures wiped away. The people there... I'm sorry. There's no easy way to put this. It's just...unimaginable."*

My pulse thudded in my ears. I gripped the sides of the radio so hard, my knuckles turned white. The broadcast kept going, Beth Kajawa trying her hardest to sound calm and reassuring, but I couldn't hear her words anymore, not over the buzzing in my head. *The coast.* Slowly, I moved one hand off the radio. I reached into my vest pocket, pulling out my phone. I opened my messages and scrolled to the conversation with Dad. I saw that picture he'd sent me, the one from the Seaspray Resort. The glistening ocean, its waves gently lapping at the sand right in front of the brand-new building. There was even a bit of Dad's thumb at the edge of the frame, undeniable proof that he had been right there. Right where it had hit. Right where everything was destroyed. *The people there* what?

I started to cry, silently even as it changed to sobs. My shoulders shook like I was in another kind of quake. Even though I was gulping in air, it wasn't enough. My chest tightened, and it had that funny straw-like feeling again. It was making me dizzy.

I moved the radio to the floor and clutched my phone with both hands. My fingers flew across the surface as I texted. Messages to my dad, my mom, Neha. I prayed that somehow, they'd get through.

Dad, you have to be okay! Tell me you are!

I really need you, Mom, please come home we're here all alone

I didn't mean what I texted, Neha, I'm so sorry

"Hannah?" Zoe's voice, followed by a tentative knock on the not-quite-closed bathroom door. I choked back another sob, wiping at my eyes and my runny nose. Clutching the radio, I stood up, slowly because I could feel the impending head rush. The doctor who prescribed the inhaler had told me that it wasn't just running that could trigger asthma symptoms. Having a cold, certain types of weather, and strong emotions could too. *In terms of strong emotions, I've never felt this scared and overwhelmed.* She'd explained it in a gentle, caring way, which almost made me feel worse. I remember thinking, *How can I possibly be so fragile that my lungs can't even handle feelings?* It's funny how you think you know yourself and your body, and then all of a sudden it betrays you. I used to feel like a strong person. After the asthma, I wasn't sure anymore. I didn't trust my own lungs.

It wasn't the time to worry about whether a chronic illness changed who I was. If I needed more air, I needed to calm down. I forced myself to take a few slow, deep Ms. Whalen–approved breaths. *You can't show Zoe and Oscar how bad it really is.* I was so grateful that I'd listened to the radio alone. I flicked off the dial.

"Hannah?" Her second knock was firm.

"Just a sec," I finally said, my voice wavering. I hoped she wouldn't notice I'd been crying. I peered down at one of the biggest shards of mirror on the floor to check my reflection. *Nope.* The tearstains were obvious.

I took another good breath. The tightness relaxed a smidge. I walked to the door and tugged it the rest of the way open. "I wanted you guys to stay in the blanket fort," I said.

Zoe darted past me into the bathroom. "I know, but I really had to go!"

Oh. I guess I should've had us all take a bathroom break first thing. "My apologies to your bladder." I sniffled again, then called down the hallway, "Oscar, if you have shoes on, you can come to the bathroom!" Seconds later, I heard him thudding down the hall. "Slowly and carefully!"

Zoe had barely emerged from the door before he burst past her into the bathroom. One look at Zoe's face, and I knew she had been crying too. Her eyes were puffy, and her nose was red and raw. "Are you doing okay?" It was kind of a stupid question. None of us were anything near okay.

Zoe tried to nod, then shook her head. "Why isn't my mom home yet?"

Beth Kajawa's words echoed in my head. *"Tens of thousands of people injured."* I made a silent plea that Andrea wasn't one of them, even though the sinking feeling in my stomach told me she absolutely could be. Same with my mom. Same with Neha, and even Marley. "Um, your mom texted and said not to worry, but it's taking a long time to get back because of…damage on the bridge." Zoe's eyes widened. "*Minor* damage," I added. "Something they can definitely repair." Lying still felt wrong, but like a necessary kind of wrong.

"Did you tell her about my cut?" Zoe asked.

I bit at my lip. What would make me feel better? Knowing my mom had promised I would be *fine*. Knowing that she was actually proud of how I was handling things. I nodded slowly. "She said it'll be just fine, and she's super proud of how tough you're being." I heard the toilet flush from inside the bathroom. "You too, Oscar."

I hadn't checked on her injury yet that morning. "Let me see your cut," I said, motioning her over. I gently took her forearm in my hand. The skin around the bandage looked perfectly normal. "Does it hurt badly?"

She shrugged. "It stings. And the Band-Aid itches."

"My mom always says itching is a sign of healing." I hoped that was true. "I'm taking a peek under the bandage, okay?" She nodded. As carefully as I could, I pulled the adhesive edge from her skin, Zoe wincing as it tugged on her downy hair. With a corner up, I could see the cut. I gritted my teeth, willing myself to not feel faint or barfy from looking at it. The wound had crusted on the edges, and it didn't look like it had scabbed yet at all. But there wasn't any bright red, fresh blood. "The bleeding has stopped—that's great! Can you move your hand and arm

normally?" Zoe flexed her hand into a fist, then opened it. She circled her wrist for me.

"I also think you're going to be fine." I hoped I hadn't just jinxed it.

I T TURNS OUT MARSHMALLOWS don't do a great job of keeping you full. I'd thought that my stomach ached only from anxiety, but while Zoe and I were grabbing the coats from the closet mess and Oscar used the bathroom, it made a plaintive growl. Loud enough that I startled, clutching at the coat's arm like it might protect me.

"My tummy's been talking to me too," Zoe said, patting her midsection.

I relaxed my grip on the coat sleeve. "Yeah, as soon as Oscar's done in there, we need to scavenge for breakfast."

I hadn't meant *scavenge* literally, but that's what we ended up doing. At least 50 percent of the food from the Matlocks' cupboards was now pooled on the sticky, slimy, powdery kitchen floor and therefore inedible. Everything in the fridge was inaccessible, because it had landed door-side down when it fell. Now it was a giant tomb of perishable food. I once read that the ancient Egyptians buried people along with jars full of delicacies. Tutankhamun's tomb had eight baskets of fruit inside it. I thought longingly of the yogurts and veggie pasta and cheese and berries I'd seen inside that fridge. The pitcher of water and dregs of a gallon of milk too. At least I knew that no ice cream had been lost, because we'd eaten it all.

But then again, with the electricity out, all the food inside the fridge was bound to spoil whether we could access it or not. Probably faster than we could possibly have eaten it, even though the house had become as chilly as the freezer section at Safeway.

The cupboard doors were all open and some cabinets had even pulled away from the wall. The one closest to where the fridge had formerly stood was hanging by a couple of screws. I didn't want to poke around in it, because I feared it would fall on me if I touched something wrong. Luckily the big pantry cabinet had held up okay, aside from everything inside of it having been shaken up. I gathered a dented can of mandarin oranges, a half-empty plastic jar of peanut butter (the full, glass all-natural one had rolled out, shattered, and splattered on the floor), and a slightly crushed bag of potato chips. I thought about scooping the spilled bran cereal into bowls, but then I got worried that the bits of plaster dust covering the countertops could have settled on the cereal, and I didn't think we should eat that kind of "frosted" flakes. A box of unopened almond milk had landed on the floor unharmed, so I picked that up too, along with a hardy box of mac and cheese. I grabbed a slightly wet shopping bag from the floor, loaded it with all the salvageable food, and handed it to

Zoe and Oscar, who I'd made wait at the edge of the kitchen, away from the broken glass. "Take this stuff back to the blanket fort—we'll have a picnic on the couch."

I crouched to scan the floor for anything else salvageable. While standing up, I bumped my shoulder on a drawer stuck partially open. Whatever was inside rolled and bounced off the sides of the drawer like pool balls. Grumbling, I tugged the drawer open the rest of the way. *Oh, sweet.* An egg carton full of chocolate crème eggs, left over from Easter. *Perfect for breakfast.* In spite of everything, I smiled. If only the bunny had gifted candy bacon in their baskets. I scooped up the loose eggs and put them back in the carton.

I made my way to the couch, holding it behind my back. "Do you guys want eggs?"

Oscar frowned. "Don't you have to cook them?"

"Not this kind!" With a grin, I whipped out the carton and tossed him a foil-wrapped egg. He caught it and squealed with delight.

"I'm going to eat *eggs* for breakfast!" He unwrapped it and bit the chocolate open to see the fake yolk inside, giggling. "I love this kind."

Zoe smiled. "I'll have an egg too." I tossed her one, then unwrapped another for myself.

Oscar and I ate greedily, taking turns sipping straight from the almond milk carton—not the best idea in terms of sharing germs, but none of us felt sick, and none of the dishes that had survived the earthquake were clean. Oscar ate about half the carton of chocolate eggs by himself, which I realized too late was going to set him up nicely for a major sugar rush and, later on, a crash.

Zoe picked at her oranges, staring at the picnic spread in front of us. Then she lowered her hand to her lap, frowning. "Can we listen to the radio again? Maybe it will tell us when my mom might be back…if there's an update on the bridge repairs."

I wondered if she'd overheard any of the broadcast when she'd come to find me in the bathroom. If so, she would've heard the fear in Beth Kajawa's voice. For Zoe's sake, I hoped she hadn't. I didn't want her to feel the panic and dread that simmered inside me, no matter which distraction I struggled to focus on. It was excruciating to know how bad things were out there—and inside this house—yet have no clue if our families were okay.

I swallowed, forcing the glob of peanut butter I'd eaten—scooping it out of the jar with a sturdy potato chip, because the only other option was my dirty fingers—to slide down my throat. "How about later on, after we've finished eating? I need to crank the radio more first, anyway."

"Did you listen to it this morning? You took it with you when you went to the bathroom." Zoe was eyeing me in a way that suggested she knew the answer to her question already, and this was a test.

I swallowed harder. The glob of peanut butter did not want to move down my throat. I stalled with a sip of the room-temperature almond milk. "There wasn't really any new information." *Other than that lots of people are hurt. Some have died. Nobody seems to know what to do. A tsunami destroyed the coast. My dad was there.*

"Is there anything we can feed Jupiter?" Oscar piped up. He motioned to the emergency box. "He's squeaking like he's hungry." I beamed at him, grateful for ending the other conversation.

Zoe scooted over to peek in the box and give Jupiter a loving pet. "He needs water too," she said.

I stood up, rubbing potato chip grease on my already filthy leggings. Most of our problems, I couldn't fix. This one, I could. "I can get his water bottle out of the old cage. Fingers crossed it wasn't crushed." I shuddered, thinking of how narrowly I'd managed to rescue Jupiter from the glass shards that had rained down on his home during the shaking.

I made my way through the obstacle course of the living room toward the shattered window. The large wire cage now rested up against the wall, flipped over on its side. Shavings and glass and pellets blanketed the floor around it. Even though I'd halfway cleaned the cage, it reeked. The bottle had leaked out some water, but it was still clipped to the side. I worked the bottle free, careful not to cut myself on the glass bits lying next to it. The wire edges of the cage were mangled and poked menacingly in multiple directions. Jupiter would definitely be staying in the emergency box until Andrea could buy a new cage.

Which made me wonder: When would people even be able to go shopping again? Cute shops clustered along the main street of downtown Pelling, their shelves lined with scented candles and quirky letterpress cards and locally made granola and, of course, fancy coffees roasted right here in Seattle. I pictured those shelves toppled and collapsed, all the wares wrecked on the floor. The glass storefronts shattered onto the sidewalk, cracked and uneven. And that was a best-case scenario, if the buildings themselves were still standing. I had no idea what condition the rest of the island was in. Maybe we'd experienced the worst of it, here in our mini neighborhood. Maybe something about being on a peninsula, on the other side of the inlet, had made us more vulnerable to the quake, but based on the broadcasts I'd heard, I doubted it. If anything, we'd been lucky.

"I got the water bottle," I called. As I started to walk toward the kitchen for water, my nose wrinkled. At first, I thought the smell must be from the stew of debris on the floor. Last night, when I dumped the shavings from Jupiter's cage, I'd noticed that the trash can was filled to the brim with coffee grounds and old melon. Now, that plus the majority of the contents of the kitchen were all mixed together, baking in the soft rays of morning sun coming in through the skylight.

But the smell wasn't like the guinea pig shavings or melon or coffee. It was kind of like eggs—not the Easter candy kind. Real ones. I recognized that scent from my kitchen. When you light a burner, especially if it takes a moment or two to spark, you can smell it. It's gas. Or rather, a chemical they put in the gas so people know when it's swirling into the air around them. The gas itself is odorless. My mom taught me that. *"A flatulent scent can save lives."*

I stepped onto the tiles of the kitchen floor, sniffing. The scent was barely noticeable when you were in the living room. In the kitchen, it was faint but definitely present. I moved closer to the oven. Unlike the fridge, it hadn't lurched from its spot during the shaking. But it did stick out farther into the room than it had before. It should have hugged the back wall, and now there was almost a foot of space between them. I peeked over to see if anything was visibly wrong with the tangle of cords and tubing connecting the stove to the pipes within the wall. I inspected the burners, making sure that one hadn't accidentally been turned on. All were definitely off.

Was there a soft hissing noise, too, like when you're letting the air out of an inflatable pool floatie?

Did that mean the stove had a gas leak?

This is really, extra, super not good. I sniffed again, as deeply as I could, at least, with my chest never having gone back to its normal level of tightness since the earthquake happened. What if the gas had been leaking the whole night? What if it was slowly poisoning us? Sometimes there were news stories about people falling ill in their homes because they had filled with carbon monoxide. I didn't think that came from stoves, but I wasn't sure. I glanced at the kitchen window, which, surprisingly, was still intact. Even though it was going to make the house even chillier, I flipped the latch and pushed it wide open. Maybe once I aired out the kitchen, the smell would go away. Maybe it was a temporary thing.

I leaned my upper body through the window, taking in the fresh scents of evergreens from the yard. The clouds were breaking up, revealing a bright blue sky. Frankly, it looked safer out there than inside.

"Guys, put on those coats," I called to the living room. We were going to venture outside.

***

It *felt* a lot safer outside too. The backyard looked mostly like it always did—the veggie garden, fish pond, firepit, and swing set had stayed in their usual spots. There weren't any big gaping chasms in the ground, as far as I could tell. The bramble bushes seemed to have been unharmed by the earthquake. One or two trees had fallen, but the rest surrounding the property were standing tall. Big branches and sticks with leaves littered the yard, but not more than you would see after a particularly windy day. Although the news had said that fires, flooding, and landslides were happening all over the place, which made it seem like Seattle had turned into a dystopian novel's setting, none of that was happening in the Matlocks' backyard. The grass smelled sweet. The birds chirped. It even felt a couple of degrees warmer than it had inside the living room. For the first time since 6:17 p.m. Pacific Standard Time the day before, I felt my shoulders and chest relax a bit. I could breathe more easily.

We stood next to the small screened porch that connected the Matlocks' living room to the backyard, unsure of what to do. Play? It seemed wrong to run around merrily, but it was a rare sunshiny spring day. The weather, perhaps, was trying to make up for what we'd been through the night before. It seemed no less wrong for Zoe and Oscar to sit on the damp ground and worry with me.

"What's that?" Oscar pointed to a section of open grass at the side of the backyard. I did a double take. Mounds of sandy dirt that looked like gigantic anthills had cropped up, and they were spitting out sprays of wet mud like geysers.

"I have no idea," I said. We watched the silt spew out and plop onto the grass next to the volcano-like mound. They didn't seem particularly dangerous—just weird. I guess the backyard wasn't as untouched as I'd thought. "Stay away from that area."

"Can I go on the monkey bars?" Oscar asked. He was hopping on one foot in a small circle, clapping his hands over his head whenever he switched feet. It made me dizzy just to watch him.

The sugar high from his "eggs" was really kicking in. Eventually, we'd have to go back in the house, and I wanted him to burn off that energy before we had to hunker down for the night.

I'm already expecting we'll be alone in the house overnight. For me to be in charge. Again. I shivered, hugging Andrea's coat tighter around me. I was wearing it over my windbreaker, which was over my long sleeve and vest. Four layers, both inside the house and out. Still I couldn't escape the damp chill. My house had a generator. If it was running, we would be a lot warmer over there.

"You guys can do whatever you want out here," I said. "In the backyard, I mean. This is maybe not the best time to go traipsing into the forest." Zoe was still clutching the emergency box with Jupiter inside. "I can watch Jupiter, if you want."

Oscar took off galloping across the backyard, toward the swing set, dodging sticks on his way. Zoe handed me Jupiter's box and then followed him at a shuffling pace. I think she felt as conflicted as I did about enjoying the nice weather, pretending like a crisis didn't surround us. All I had to do was look down at Jupiter in the box, clearly marked **Emergency**, to be reminded.

I stared at the swing set, which Oscar had already reached. It reminded me so much of the one in Neha's yard. I wondered if she'd even made it home before the earthquake hit. If she hadn't— where was she? Still stranded on a soccer field, maybe. At least there, no furniture could've fallen on or near her. Although if she was in a place where the landslides were happening…

No. My chest was tightening again, my throat narrowing. The more I worried, the harder I had to work to breathe normally. I was torn between trying to calm myself and surrendering to the fear, because it almost felt like worrying about my parents, Neha, and Andrea was important. Protective, even. Like if I kept them in my mind, I might keep them safe. If I let go and stopped worrying, even for a few moments—*Boom!* That's when something awful would happen to them. If it hadn't already.

Whenever I let go of fear and let in the hope I was trying to preserve in the kids, even for just a moment, guilt immediately followed.

Oscar started climbing around on the swing set. Zoe sat in one of the swings. Her injured arm rested in her lap; her other hand grasped the chain. She barely pumped her legs, instead letting the breeze twirl her in gentle half-circles.

I sat down on a large smooth rock at the edge of the fish pond, about halfway to the swing set. I tilted my head back and closed my eyes, letting the sun shine on my face. It felt nice and warm. In the house, I had seen my breath when I spoke. Maybe, when we eventually went back inside, I should use dish towels as blankets to make sure Jupiter stayed cozy inside his box. Assuming I could find some usable towels in the kitchen mess. Shavings would be good to add too, if they weren't already covering the floor. The box already had gained several pee stains.

With my eyes closed, I listened carefully to our surroundings, hoping for some nearby sound of civilization. I hadn't heard a car on the road since Andrea had driven away the afternoon before and not even a distant horn or siren. Although only my family, the Matlocks, and Mr. Aranita live on this side of the inlet, plenty of cars pass through our neighborhood. People like to hike in the forest, and at night they even go in to stargaze if the sky is clear. The rangers patrol the preserve road too. But as far as I could tell, not a single vehicle had driven by since the shaking had begun. That was alarming. Maybe later we should walk down the driveway to the road, see if it looked like anyone had been by.

Or maybe we should just head all the way to my house, where there was plenty of food, probably less damage, that generator (although I had no clue how to turn it on), and—best of all—my inhaler. But we had no way of telling our parents we were leaving. Although, we could always write a note…

Oscar was laughing, so I peeked an eye open to see what he was up to: he'd climbed down and was giving Zoe a push on the swing. I smiled. They were actually doing great, considering. A tiny bud of hope bloomed in my chest. Maybe I wasn't a failure of a babysitter. Sure, Zoe had gotten cut pretty badly, and it was partly because I encouraged them to crawl around on a glass-shard-covered carpet. We'd also eaten mostly from the "use sparingly" parts of the food pyramid since I'd gotten there: ice cream, marshmallows, chocolate eggs, chips. Even the mandarin oranges had been syrupy sweet.

But Zoe and Oscar had still slept through the night. They were in decent spirits. I'd smartly moved them away from the kitchen when I smelled the funky gas scent. If Mrs. Pinales were going to grade me on the job I'd done so far, I would pass. She'd give me an A for effort, definitely.

I daydreamed about my mom and Andrea racing up to the house. Panicked and breathless. They'd fling open the door to find the kids and me, safe inside, playing cards by flashlight— even though I didn't know any card games, much less know where playing cards might be kept. It just seemed like the kind of thing a great, responsible babysitter would do while watching kids in a house with no electricity. Or—better yet—we'd be loading big black trash bags with debris from the kitchen floor—with rubber gloves protecting our hands, of course. Starting the cleanup effort before our parents had even returned. Even though it was only a fantasy, I felt the rosy flush of pride in my cheeks. My mom would probably never again chide me for a little mistake like forgetting my inhaler…not if I'd shown so much responsibility in such a tough situation. Maybe she'd even start letting me use the oven on my own.

I lifted Jupiter out of the box and onto my lap, stroking his soft, silky fur. He didn't feel too cold but instead like a furry hot-water bottle. He cooed as I petted him, and he nestled next to my stomach. I stretched my legs out onto the damp grass and went back to watching the strange sand geysers. My dad would probably know what they were. My heart panged, as I wished he were with me. I did not allow myself to think of where he could be.

I heard the crack first, loud and sharp like a baseball hitting a bat. Instinctively, I looked up. But, of course, in the Matlocks' yard there was no ball spinning through the air above me.

Next, I heard a shout, more surprised than scared. It came from the swing set. *The swing set.* I thought of all the things far more solid than wood inside the house, and how they were now toppled, shattered, cracked, peeled, pummeled. The swing set had looked fine...from a distance. *I should've inspected it first. I should've checked to make sure nothing was split or bowing or sunken.* Instead, I'd let Oscar tear across the yard and climb up the ladder, let Zoe dangle by a chain on her swing.

I hugged Jupiter to my chest as I hopped to my feet. I was running toward the swing set before I even looked to it, before I saw the piece of the monkey bars bent and drooping in the air. Before I saw the heap of sky-blue parka crumpled on the ground; Zoe, frantically screaming, on her knees next to him.

9

W E DIDN'T COVER MUCH first aid in the babysitting class. Mrs. Pinales taught us the basics, of course—make sure to wash a cut before you bandage it, elevate whatever's bleeding, cool water instead of ice for a minor burn, flush out someone's eyes if chemicals get in them. But mostly she reminded us of whom to contact, aside from the parents, for various medical emergencies. The answer was always 911, although she did say if you had the number for poison control, you could also call that if a kid swallowed something from underneath the sink. "I can't emphasize enough how important it is," she'd said, "to *not* try to handle a medical issue on your own. Even if you think it's not a big deal. Sometimes the most responsible thing a babysitter can do is actually nothing—because you need help from an adult. Preferably one with first aid training." I wrote that down in my notebook, underlined it, and even drew an exclamation point next to it. It had seemed like a really serious point. Neha had whispered to me, "Doing nothing—sounds doable." I'd stifled a giggle. It was funny partly because Neha was too much of a doer to ever follow that advice. Case in point, Neha had then given me her cousin-sitting pro tip that "boo-boos" almost always need a kiss in order to heal, even if the boo-boo is somewhere gross, like a toddler's bare foot. "So be prepared for that." She'd wrinkled her nose but still looked proud.

I wished she were with me—or better yet, Mrs. Pinales—as I hunched next to a howling Oscar on the grass. When I first reached the kids, huddling below the swing set, and I dropped to my knees—still carrying Jupiter in the crook of my elbow—I was relieved that there wasn't any gushing blood. Visible to me, at least.

"Did he hit his head?" I asked Zoe. Head injuries could be really serious. My dad once got bonked on his hard hat at a construction site and wound up in the emergency room for a CT scan.

"No. He fell straight down, like he was jumping, but he landed hard on his leg." She pointed, and my eyes followed the tip of her finger. My stomach lurched, and I had to glance away for a second before turning back.

Oscar's right leg, near his ankle, was bent at a sickening angle, like he was an action figure and someone had turned its foot the wrong way. I used to pull mine out of their storage tubs and their limbs would all be bent—"akimbo," my mom called it—and I would laugh, never thinking about what it would be like for an actual human body to twist like that. How painful and scary. *His leg looks broken.* My body flushed with panic. Now *this* was an emergency, and like Mrs. Pinales said, I definitely needed an adult. Not just an adult, but a doctor—right away.

The yard seemed to grow very quiet around us. I didn't even hear the breeze or the birds. We were entirely alone. We had no way to call 911 or run to the nearest grown-up for help. Unless Mr. Aranita was home for once, the closest adult was somewhere across the bridge that spans the inlet. Only trees loomed around us, watching this crisis unfold. I felt incredibly small. Powerless.

Figuring out what to do was entirely up to me. I had all the responsibility and few of the skills, but doing "nothing" wasn't an option.

"Oscar, it's going to be okay," I said, working hard to keep the tremor out of my voice. My words sounded hollow, and they didn't soothe him. Oscar kept crying and moaning. He stared up at the sky, tears running so fast down his cheeks I worried he'd choke on them. His face was red as his shoes.

His cries upset Jupiter, who started chittering and clawing his way out of my elbow nook. "Zoe, can you take him?" That broke her out of the position in which she'd been frozen. She tucked Jupiter to her chest with her good arm, the bandaged one hanging limp. *They're both hurt. How did I let this happen?* Guilt and shame washed over me. My throat squeezed.

I don't know what to do. I'm just a kid. I need help.

I fumbled to unzip Andrea's coat so I could reach inside my windbreaker to get to the vest pocket where I'd zipped my phone. It was a reflex, whenever I had any kind of question—from *What's the capital of Bolivia?* to *Best chocolate-chip cookie recipe* to *How do you cure asthma?*—to pull out my phone and Google it. Or I'd ask one of my parents, but then they'd more often than not grab *their* phones or a laptop and type my question into a search box. And ta-da, there was our answer. *Bolivia actually has two capitals, Sucre and La Paz. The best recipe is from the back of the Toll House package. Asthma can't be cured, but it can be managed and here are some ways...* With shaking fingers I swiped to unlock my home screen so I could search *How to tell if a bone is broken?* and then *First aid for broken bone.*

The browser wouldn't even load. No bars, no Wi-Fi. My phone was no longer my oracle. It was simply a hunk of aluminum and glass, useless aside from the flashlight app. I was stranded without it or the internet.

I sat back on my heels, my head spinning. More than anything, I wished I'd thought to ask Mrs. Pinales about a situation like this. *What if you can't get ahold of the parents in case of emergency? What if there are no adults around, so you can't just wait for help? What if you can't even search for a wiki how-to article to show you how to deal with a problem in fifteen not-so-easy steps, with unintentionally funny illustrations? What do you do then?*

Zoe pointed at my phone. "Why aren't you calling my mom? Or texting her?" Upon hearing the word *mom*, Oscar wailed even louder. "Is your phone even *working*?" She lunged for it, reaching with the hand that wasn't cradling Jupiter, but I swiped my phone out of her reach at the last second.

She knew right then that I'd been lying all along.

"Let me see the messages from my mom!" she bellowed, startling the birds in the nearby trees. The louder her voice got, the louder Oscar's cries. "Right now!" The veins on her face and neck had suddenly become very visible.

"Zoe, I'm sorry. I didn't want you to worry. I wanted you to be able to sleep. I honestly thought she'd be here when we woke up," I pleaded. "When she wasn't, I didn't know what to do…" I stopped to catch my breath. "I didn't want to lie. I really, really didn't." Zoe looked stung.

"I don't care, just get my mom!" Oscar's scream snapped at me like a rubber band. The problems piling up around me needed triage. Zoe finding out I'd lied didn't matter *right now*. Taking care of Oscar did, even if I didn't know how to properly do that.

"Zoe," I leaned in so I was inches from her furious face. "I know you're upset with me, and I totally get why. But we can't focus on that. Oscar needs our help. Badly. We have to focus on him. You can yell at me later."

She nodded.

"We should move him inside," I said. Clouds had formed overhead, boxing out the blue sky. Eventually, it would rain, and the air felt cooler than it had when we first ventured out. "Oscar,

I know it hurts. I know you're scared. We're going to help you get back to the couch, where you'll be more comfortable. Then I'm going to figure out what else to do. To make it better." *Make it better.* It reminded me of Neha's advice, kissing boo-boos. Neha always knew how to take charge of a situation, whether it was guiding the ball down the field or organizing a fund-raiser for a charity she cared about or studying for an intimidating test. Once Neha Jain got an idea in her head, nothing could stop her. I loved that about her.

I hoped, wherever she was, that glint of determination was still in her eyes. To survive this moment, I was going to have to borrow it.

"Does anywhere else hurt?" I asked Oscar. "Other than your leg?" With some injuries—like ones to the spinal column—I know you aren't supposed to move a person, but so far he was moving the rest of his body okay.

He shook his head no. I sucked in another breath. We could pick him up, then, so long as we kept his leg safe. I turned to Zoe. "We'll carry him chair-style—you take one side, I'll take the other. His right side, so I can protect his leg."

"I still have Jupiter," she said, motioning to the guinea pig in her arms.

"I want to hold him!" Oscar wailed.

I didn't want to deny him any comfort, but I shook my head. "You'll need to hang on to us tightly so we don't jostle you. Here,

Zoe—give me Jupiter and I'll run him back inside." She handed the guinea pig to me and I took off across the yard for his box, still sitting next to the fish pond.

I hate to admit this, but running away, I wished I didn't have to go back to them. I wanted to keep running, all the way to my house. I wanted to burst through my front door and race up the stairs to my bed, then dive inside my covers. It would be easy to breathe there. My inhaler would be waiting on my nightstand. Underneath my lavender comforter, it would be quiet and warm and cozy. I wanted to be somewhere safe like that. Where I wasn't in charge, but I was simply a kid again. As soon as I wished all that, I hated myself a little. *And what—strand two injured children?* Sure, I hadn't asked for this kind of responsibility, but nevertheless it was mine.

By the time I reached the porch with Jupiter, I was winded. I placed his box, partially closed, on a rocking chair and then propped open the door for when we came back with Oscar. I gave myself two seconds to rest, leaning over with my hands on my thighs. Then I gulped more air and raced back across the yard, dodging fallen tree limbs and those sand volcanoes like I was on an obstacle course.

The night before I'd been surprised how small and fragile Oscar had felt when I hugged him. His bones had seemed as delicate as a bird's, and maybe that wasn't untrue, considering what had happened to his leg. But when Zoe and I hoisted him off the ground, he sure felt heavy. We pressed our hands to his back as his arms wrapped around our shoulders, and we clasped hands below his thighs so he could rest on us like he was in a swing. His hurt leg dangled next to me, and I kept my eyes on it the whole time, careful not to bump it into anything, including myself. "Zoe, you lead. I need to keep track of Oscar's leg."

We inched our way across the Matlocks' yard toward the house. I worried about the ground starting to shake. I worried about potential holes or cracks or stumbling points that the grass hid. I worried more sand volcanoes would crop up underfoot. "We're almost there," I said to Oscar. He'd stopped wailing, but the tears still streamed down his face, and every other step he'd let out an agonized moan. His fingertips dug into my upper arm.

Finally, we reached the screened porch. "Keep going to the living room. I think he'll be most comfortable on the couch."

Zoe grimaced. "He's getting heavy."

"I know." *Channel Neha. Remember how she used to psych everyone up during Pirates games? Even when we were exhausted and losing, and it was starting to drizzle.* "A little farther—you got this, Zoe, I *know* you do." Zoe nodded, clenching her jaw and tightening her grip.

We had to scoot around a few boxes that blocked our path into the living room from the porch. They were too heavy to quick kick out of the way. "What's in all these?" I asked, my voice strained and wheezy.

"Books," Zoe said, in between pants. "Grandpa's encyclopedia set...some other old ones. Mom's gonna donate them." I almost bumped Oscar's foot into the door frame, missing it by no more than half an inch. Sweat beaded around my hairline, even though it was cold. Four layers were too many for that level of exertion. We still had the obstacle course of the living room to navigate. *More Neha-speak.* "You're doing great, Zoe. You're killing it." Bad choice of words. "I'm so proud of you."

The couch cushions were all still tucked inside the blanket fort, so we had to lay Oscar down on the flimsy fabric that separates plush cushion from the sharp couch innards. "Give us a sec, and we'll get you some padding." I dove underneath the blankets to pull out the big sectional cushion that had made such a nice mattress the night before. My arms burned from carrying his weight. Inside the fort, where the ambient noise was dampened, I heard my own breathing clearly. There was still a hint of a wheeze. I ignored it.

We lifted Oscar up one more time to get the cushion in place, then carefully lowered him to rest on top of it. With his legs stretched out, the right one didn't look as obviously twisted as before—but his pants were now covering it. "Can I check on your leg?" He nodded.

Gingerly, I lifted the hem of his sweatpants and began to roll it upward, careful not to put any pressure on his body. At least the hem was loose and not an elastic fit, so I didn't have to tug. Already the skin around his ankle was discolored. It was puffy from the top of his foot to his shin. There was a lump-like deformity on the outside of his ankle above the knobby part. I winced—it hurt to look at.

"Um, I have a problem," Zoe said.

"Right now?" I turned to her.

"My cut is bleeding again." She raised her arm to show me the splotch of red seeping through her bandage.

"Okay. Okay," I repeated, as though if I kept saying that word, things would actually become *okay*. Like it was a magic spell. Maybe if I clicked my heels three times it would work. "Raise your arm again, above your head. I'll get you a new bandage." I'd also check if there were any stray pain relievers in the drawer the bandages had come from.

The kitchen was freezing. Not surprisingly, because the window was still wide open. I sniffed deeply, hoping the rotten-eggs scent was gone. I sniffed again. If I did smell it, it had become faint. That was a relief, at least.

I got a fresh bandage, but I didn't see pills anywhere in the drawer or spilled on the counters or among the debris piles on the floor. Maybe Zoe would know where their mom kept children's Tylenol.

I ran back into the living room, waving the bandage with one hand and rubbing at my chest with the other. It ached. Before I saw the doctor and got diagnosed with the asthma, I used to feel like this during soccer practices. My face would turn beet red and everything from my rib cage to my shoulders would feel so tight after I'd been running up and down the field. "Do you have a side stitch? Try raising up your arms while you run," Neha had suggested. That never helped. I hated feeling so much weaker than everyone else on the team. Even after I got diagnosed, I didn't want to go back to playing. Having asthma made me feel kind of ashamed. I didn't want to have to stop in the middle of games for puffs of my inhaler with everyone watching. Maybe sometimes that's why I forgot to bring it to school.

Although I really wished I had my inhaler as I hustled through the Matlocks' house.

While changing Zoe's bandage, I could see that the bleeding was only seeping a little—Oscar's legs must have been pressing directly on the cut when we were carrying him, and that had opened the wound again. "If you rest that arm, it should be fine," I said. "But keep it raised for now."

We stood shivering next to Oscar, who lay motionless on the couch. I had absolutely no idea what to do next. I pressed my hand to my phone, willing the internet to come back to it. For text messages from my mom and dad, Andrea, and Neha to flood the screen. But without power, that wasn't going to happen. *How am I supposed to figure out what to do?*

I blinked, remembering the boxes that had blocked us on the screened porch. *"Encyclopedias...some other old books."*

"Wait here—I'll be right back." When Zoe opened her mouth

to protest, I added, "I'm going to be moving around those book boxes, and you can't help me—not with that." I pointed at her injured arm. "Stay with Oscar."

"Why are you going through the book boxes?" she asked. "How is that going to help us?"

"You'll see!"

"Are you going to bring Jupiter back inside too?" she hollered after me.

"Good call," I yelled back at her. Poor Jupiter. I'd forgotten his box was on the cold porch. Although it was equally cold inside. Four layers was back to feeling barely adequate.

When I returned to the living room minutes later, my arms were full of heavy, dusty, leather-bound books, with the emergency box holding Jupiter on top of the stack. And that was only the first batch, with the *B*, *F*, *L*, and *S* encyclopedias—for *broken bone*, *first aid* and *fracture*, *leg*, and *sprain*. Once I piled them on the coffee table, I went back to root through the other box. In it, I found a home medical guide—which looked really old based on the hairstyles of the people on the cover—and a Girl Scout handbook. *Sweet.* There must be some information inside that could guide us.

Zoe was already flipping through the *B* encyclopedia. "I looked up 'broken bone' but there isn't an entry," she said. "I don't know if these books are going to help."

"Try another one. How about *F*, for 'first aid' and 'fracture'?"

Zoe started turning the pages. "Wait, how do you spell 'fracture'?"

I spelled it out for her, hoping I got it right. When you misspell something while Googling, it helpfully suggests the correct spelling for your results. Turning pages was painfully slow, in comparison to scrolling. It was strange to think that this used to be how people got all their information, before computers and smartphones and search engines. Research projects must have taken forever back then.

I opened the home medical guide, whose pages were thick and yellowed. The illustrations were black and white, and all the medical stuff pictured appeared outdated. The sample thermometer was glass—not digital. The bandages were in a tin box. I bet they weren't even the waterproof kind. I turned back to the table of contents, then ahead to the section on first aid. "Sprains and Broken Bones" was the second header. I leaned closer, running my fingertip underneath the words as I read them.

It said that you really needed a doctor and an X-ray machine to determine if a bone was sprained or fractured, although I was pretty certain it was the latter—even if the cracking sound I'd heard when Oscar fell was from the monkey bars breaking and not his leg. Symptoms of a break were: a snapping noise during an injury (check?); bruising, puffiness and swelling, and tenderness (check); pain and difficulty moving the injured area or when the area is touched or bears weight. "Oscar," I said, "I'm going to touch your leg. Very gently. Let me know if it hurts, all right?"

He nodded. He'd become much quieter now that he was on the couch. I didn't know whether that was a good or worrisome sign. I reached out my hand, then gently pressed above his ankle. He howled like I'd punched him. I jerked my hand back. A check for that symptom too.

So, I was going to officially consider his leg broken. My stomach clenched. I turned back to the medical guide, hoping it would tell me what to do now. Its steps for treatment were:

- Get medical care immediately.
- Don't let the injured person eat or drink until you do, in case surgery is required.
- Remove clothing from the injured area.
- Apply ice.
- Keep the limb in the position you found it.
- Make a simple splint, using a board or rolled-up newsprint and elastic tape or an ACE bandage.

My heart sank while I read the list. The instructions were simple, but most I couldn't follow. There was no way to immediately seek medical care, unless we left the house and started walking—but Oscar couldn't do that with a broken leg. Anyway, it said to keep the limb the way I'd found it, but I'd found his foot gruesomely twisted, and I couldn't believe that leaving it that way would have helped him at all.

Whatever ice was unmelted in the freezer-tomb was

inaccessible to us, unless Zoe or I suddenly developed superhero strength and managed to lift the fridge back upright, which would only make it a danger again.

It was too cold to remove his clothing, and assuming it might be a while—a long while—until Oscar could see a doctor… Not eating or drinking seemed like a terrible idea. Hunger wouldn't help him. In fact, we hadn't eaten lunch, so I should already be foraging for dinner. *Dinner*. That meant it had been almost twenty-four hours. I still couldn't believe no one had come to find us yet. I didn't want to think about what that meant.

The only instruction I could follow was to make a simple splint—if I could find the right materials. I scanned the room. No boards shorter than the length of Oscar's lower leg, and the few broken bits of wood strewn across the floor looked like they might be splintery. Then my eyes stopped on a flood of glossy magazines spilling out of an overturned wicker basket. A rolled-up magazine could work the same way as a newspaper, right?

I snatched one of the magazines and wiped off the dust, then rolled it up like a sturdy tube. Measured against Oscar's lower leg, it was the perfect size. I felt a rush of satisfaction for being so resourceful—before I remembered that if I *really* was good at babysitting, he wouldn't have been climbing on an unsafe swing set in the first place, and nobody would need a homemade splint. Nor would Zoe have that deep cut.

I rubbed at my chest, coughing to clear it. "Do you guys have any ACE bandages?"

"Huh?" Zoe looked up from the encyclopedia. "What are those?"

I sighed, even though I probably didn't know what one was when I was ten. "It's a stretchy fabric you can wrap an injury in, to make a sling, or to cover a cast..." What other stretchy things we could use to fashion the splint?

When Zoe shook her head, I figured it out. She was wearing a soft, wide, *stretchy* elastic headband. I reached my fingers up to loosen the polka-dot hair tie that had been keeping my curls contained in a bun. I'd double-tied my hair yesterday morning, so there were actually two I could use.

"Give me your headband?" Dutifully, she pulled it off her hair, which still stayed pressed against her head, like a phantom headband was keeping it in place. That was probably the work of grease—we were all in need of showers. I arranged the headband around the upper part of Oscar's leg and the magazine splint, tugging it tight. Then I secured the bottom with my linked hair ties.

"We just made a splint," I said, a proud smile curling at my lips. "But I don't know how well it'll stay on—so don't move, Oscar."

He only made a sad little groan in response, and my smile vanished. Even the small successes I had were reminders of how overwhelming this all was, how utterly incapable I was of being in charge. Or to keep us safe.

kitchen floor, I scribbled *In Case of Emergency* on the front. Inside, every useful fact or tip we'd read would live. So far, I'd written two pages on identifying poisonous berries, which I'd read about in a slim, faded pamphlet on Washington flora and fauna that was tucked inside the *F* encyclopedia. Of course, the first instruction had been, "When in doubt, don't eat wild berries." Well, ideally, we wouldn't have to. At least I was certain about what a blackberry bush looked like, and I knew where clusters grew along the road. Neha and I used to walk from my house to the inlet, filling baskets with ripe ones, when they were in season.

I paused while reading the home medical guide, pressing my finger to the crease between pages while I reached for a pen. "Found instructions for a tourniquet," I said.

"What's a 'turn a kit'?" Zoe looked up at me from the Girl Scout manual. She sniffled and wiped at her nose. I hoped she wasn't getting sick.

"It's how you deal with a bad cut. You wrap a bandage super tight to stop the flow of blood."

Zoe reached for her arm, glancing down to check the still-white bandage. "Should I have had one, when I sliced my arm?" Her tone was fretful.

I shook my head. "Your cut wasn't bleeding badly enough to need one." It turned my stomach to think about gushing blood that would require an actual tourniquet. Whenever TV shows or movies showed injuries like that, I'd have to cover my eyes,

10

WE SPENT WHAT WAS left of the afternoon in the living room. Oscar rested on the couch, cuddling Jupiter and intermittently moaning when he would forget to keep still and try to move his leg. I'd ventured into the downstairs bathroom and pried open the remains of the medicine cabinet—my bravery was rewarded with children's Tylenol chewables. There were only five left rattling in the bottle. I checked the instructions, and for a kid Oscar's age that was only two full doses. Hopefully, that would be enough—and, hopefully, by the time he chewed all five, someone would've made it home and whisked him to a doctor.

While he drifted in and out of sleep, Zoe and I made use of the dwindling daylight. I divvied up between us the encyclopedias and manuals to scour for survival information. We'd spent the first twenty-four hours woefully underprepared. Whatever happened next, I was going to be ready for it. I'd found my backpack in the jumble of debris in the front hall and my almost-blank notebook inside was unscathed. Using a marker from the and ears, if they were using lots of gross sound effects. "Anyway, do you have anything for me to write down?"

"Yeah, I found a chapter on identifying animals by their tracks." She held up the book for me to see. It was dim in the living room, and I had to squint. Soon we'd need to use the flashlight and my phone to see, and then books would have to wait until morning.

"That's great information." I quickly sketched the most worrisome tracks: cougars and bears. Then, instead of copying the rest, I took a photo of the illustration of prints and tracks. In the notebook, I simply added, *See photo of tracks to identify which animals are around.* I guess my phone did still have some use besides being a flashlight.

"I know how to identify poison ivy," Oscar chimed in, his voice woozy. "It has three leaves. So does poison oak. Write that down—leaves of three, let them be. Especially don't use them to wipe your butt."

I had to laugh. "Um, okay. How do you know that?"

"One of my games," he said. "In the fourth level you're on your own in the woods, hunting bad guys. If you run into poison ivy, you get all itchy and lose points from scratching."

"That's not a real tip—that's for a video game." Zoe sniffed.

I wrote it down anyway. "Maybe so, but it can't hurt to make note of it. Thanks, Oscar." It was reassuring that he was stable enough to listen and chime in.

"There are bears in that game too. If you see them, you're supposed to make noise and back away slowly."

"Doesn't your game have hunters? Can't you just shoot the bears?" Zoe asked.

Oscar looked horrified. "It's not that kind of game!" She shrugged. I added his advice to the notebook, even though it had been years since I'd seen a bear around my house. I'm not even sure how many were still living in the forest preserve. In terms of the threats we were facing, bears were thankfully low on the list.

When I turned back to the book, I had to lean close and squint to see the words clearly. I slipped out my phone to check the time: almost seven. Before I tucked it back in my vest pocket, I tested the Wi-Fi and bars. I pressed to resend texts to my mom, my dad, Andrea, and Neha. *Hope springs eternal, like Mom always says.* But all my phone did was flash me the warning bubble that my messages would not be sent, suggesting I check my settings. I sighed. The battery was at 17 percent. It was way beyond time to use the emergency radio to crank it back to fully charged. I'd been putting it off because I hadn't wanted to remind Zoe and Oscar about the radio's existence. I didn't want them to ask to listen to the broadcasts. If I were being honest—I was afraid to listen. In a way it was easier to not hear the news, to keep pretending that on the other side of the inlet, things were back to normal.

I wonder if our moms, and my dad, are pretending that everything is okay here on Pelling. Even though I desperately wanted them to come home, if they couldn't, I almost wished that the grown-ups had forgotten about us, stranded here by the preserve. It was worse to think that they were somewhere out there, unable to reach us, worried, possibly hurt, and scared. Just like we were. I wouldn't wish these feelings on anyone.

"It's time we ate something," I said. When I rose from the couch cushion on the floor, my head spun. I squeezed my eyes shut for a moment, to make things stop swirling. I hated that light-headed feeling. Before I got the inhaler, that's how I would feel after running in gym or at soccer practice.

"Are you okay?" I opened my eyes to see Zoe watching me, her brows knitted with concern.

"I'm fine. Just a head rush. Probably because I'm hungry." I cleared my throat, then a second time. "Any requests for tonight's meal?"

"Yeah, something hot. Like mac and cheese…or noodle soup," Zoe said.

"I always have soup when I'm sick," Oscar mumbled.

I rubbed at my temples. "There isn't a way to heat up any food, unfortunately. I meant more like… Do you want granola bars or crackers and nuts?" I didn't even know if we had those. I squatted next to the food bag. There wasn't much left in it. We'd been hungry that morning.

"Whatever," Zoe said, curling down onto the cushion and hugging her arms against her chest.

I debated trying to do something with the orange powder packet in the mac-and-cheese box—maybe mix it with the water to make a paste for the crackers? But a sad imitation of mac and cheese would probably only make our bellies more aware of all the delicious things they were missing. It's funny because I always thought if I were home alone and could eat whatever I wanted, I'd never tire of stuff like chips and chocolate. But after a full day of grazing on whatever junk had survived the shaking in the pantry, what I craved was a big bowl of my mom's brown rice veggie stir fry with peanut sauce. Something fresh and crisp, warm and filling. I didn't even want the leftover chocolate eggs. Avoiding them was the least I could do to be kind to my teeth, now that I was living without a toothbrush. I ran my tongue over them again. So gross.

The house was quiet except for our chewing. And my wheezing. I swallowed the peanut butter cracker-wich I'd made and reached for the home medical guide and the *A* encyclopedia, which I'd also grabbed from the porch. I flipped to the guide's index. *Asthma, pp. 68–70.* I turned to the page and, in the waning light, started to read.

It was mostly information I'd already read or been told by the doctor: how asthma is a chronic lung condition in which the airways thin and narrow because of inflammation. Often mucus blocks the airways, too, which is gross to think about. Sometimes asthma is minor, sometimes it interferes with certain activities—like my soccer playing, I guess—and sometimes it can cause life-threatening attacks.

A lump of the cracker-wich stuck in my throat. I swallowed harder, and it wouldn't budge. Maybe I was just getting nervous. Asthma could be serious, but the doctor said that I had only moderate problems, which my inhaler could control. Without my inhaler, I wondered, could moderate become severe? And how fast? I began copying down the information in our notebook.

"If wheezing and coughing don't go away with the use of an inhaler, seek medical care. If lips or face take on a blue tinge, go to the hospital immediately." Great—there was that helpful "immediately" again. It was too dark to accurately check my color, and I didn't want to sneak into the bathroom to peek at my fun-house reflection in the cracked mirror. I doubted I was turning blue, anyway. I just had a little wheeze. And a cough. And a chest that felt like I'd put on last year's swimsuit and now it was way too tight and the fabric and straps were trying to force me into the shape of a girl I'd outgrown. I unzipped Andrea's coat past my collarbones to give myself the feeling of free space at my neck.

"What are you reading?" Zoe asked, leaning over to see the guide. I snapped it shut. I didn't want her to know that something was wrong with me too. I wanted her to think I was healthy and strong, fully able to handle the situation we were in.

Because if she wasn't confident in me—how could I be confident in myself?

"The section on…nutrition," I said. "Um, what the best foods are for energy. So I can prioritize what we have left."

"Chocolate?"

"Sure, in small doses. Hey, speaking of which," I said, putting down the books. "Did you want dessert?"

By the time we were all done picking at the food, it was pitch dark in the living room. Outside, I heard the hoot of an owl—a clear sign it was more or less time for bed. Unfortunately, Zoe and Oscar didn't agree with me.

"Tonight, I'm waiting up in case my mom comes home," Zoe said. She was perched on the arm of the couch, hovering above Oscar like a gargoyle. It made me slightly nervous—what if another aftershock happened and she fell on his leg? Zoe tilted her chin upward, defiant, daring me to tell her that, no, she'd be heading into the blanket fort to sleep. We all would, once she and I dragged the sectional cushion back underneath the blankets and rearranged Oscar on it.

"We don't know when that'll be," I said, my voice soft. I still hoped that any moment, we'd hear a car zipping up the drive, a frantic jingling of keys at the front door. But the longer it went, the more that seemed like a dream that wasn't going to come true.

"Don't try to trick me with fake texts again either." I shined the flashlight toward Zoe's face. She looked more wounded than angry. Her lips were also quivering—and teeth chattering. The temperature had dropped even lower in the house throughout the day. All our conversations were now punctuated with little puffs of breath.

"I promise I won't. But even if you don't want to sleep, will you at least help me get Oscar settled in the blanket fort? He shouldn't be up there on the couch, exposed to the cold. He needs to rest where it's warmest."

Zoe slowly nodded, scrambling down from her perch. I stood next to her, and we gently lifted Oscar off the cushion. He winced and yowled as we moved, even though I tried to keep his leg steady.

"I'm so sorry, Oscar," I whispered.

He mumbled something in response, perhaps *"I want my mom."*

When he was settled, I paced the living room, looking for extra blankets. Or throw pillows, or even area rugs—any nice, warm, soft, fabric things to pile into the fort to keep us toasty. Even with Andrea's coat still on, I couldn't stop hunching in an attempt to stay warm. It was worse near the kitchen…because the window was still open! I carefully pushed it shut. The stinky stove smell hadn't gotten any worse. We'd open the window again in the morning for fresh air. Not that there wasn't plenty of that in the living room already, thanks to the broken windows.

I crawled under the blanket flaps to find Oscar tucked neatly into the other blankets, with Zoe curled up next to him underneath a small multicolor rug. She was holding his hand. Her other arm circled protectively around Jupiter's box, which was beginning to smell like pee. My heart panged. Zoe had every right to be mad at me for lying. Otherwise, she was doing such a good job of holding it together.

"Mom was reading this book to us," she said, raising herself up on one elbow to reach for her tablet. "A chapter every night. Before bed." She held it toward me. "I think it would help him fall asleep."

"Great idea." I swiped to wake up the screen and opened the books app. They were on chapter twenty-two of a mystery set in colonial times. According to the table of contents, only four chapters remained. If it was a chapter a night, I hoped I wouldn't be finishing the story with them.

I leaned against the couch and began to read. My voice was hoarse and husky, and I stumbled over the words for the first few paragraphs. I didn't need a flashlight to see the text, thanks to the glowing screen. But the chapter was long, and the sentences were dense and detailed. I felt myself sucking in air at the end of each. My wheeze grew louder, like it was competing for attention with the story.

When I finally hit a section break, I pretended the chapter was over. Oscar was asleep already, anyway. Shining the tablet toward him, I could see his eyes were closed, his hands clenched on top of the blanket covering his softly rising and falling chest. Even asleep, his expression showed he was in pain—his brows were knitted, and his mouth had frozen at the start of a frown. *Poor Oscar.* It hurt to know that I couldn't give him the help he so badly needed.

Zoe made a snuffling noise next to him. She'd fallen asleep too. I lay back on my narrow section of the cushion, clicking off the tablet. Darkness enveloped me. It was less scary than the night before. Nighttime was a relief, actually—for now, while the kids were asleep, I had a break from the responsibility to watch over them.

And finally, a chance to recharge. I grabbed the emergency radio and hooked up my phone. I spun the knob around, and the battery icon lit up on screen. *Thank goodness this actually works.* But it took a full minute of cranking for the charge to go up just 1 percent. After ten minutes, with three breaks because my arm was getting so tired, the battery was only up to 25 percent. I decided that was enough for the night. I craved sleep.

But my brain was full of bad feelings in the way a leaky bucket holds water. If I plugged one spot—stopped one worry— another would give way and start leaking. A new concern would make itself known. Zoe and Oscar being asleep didn't give me time to rest. It only gave me time to focus hard on how badly I'd already failed them.

I shouldn't have lied about contact from their mom.

I shouldn't have let them crawl around on a floor full of sharp debris.

I shouldn't have let Oscar climb up on that swing set.

I shouldn't have let us eat so much of the food already.

My mom was right when she said that stuff like forgetting my inhaler showed I wasn't responsible enough for babysitting. It had barely been twenty-four hours, and already we had two serious injuries. How much longer would I be able to keep us safe?

I'm just a kid too.

Hot tears rolled down my cold cheeks. I tried to cry silently, which only made me cough. I pulled Andrea's coat up to cover my mouth, but the coughing fit continued. I scrambled out of the blanket fort, to get a drink of water from the sink to soothe my throat. My chest was awfully tight again, like when Neha and I, before my asthma, would try to hold our breath underwater at the community center pool. That tense, bursting feeling.

I pulled down the coat and took in a deep inhale. The air entering my lungs forced its way back out in another, more insistent cough. Fresh tears pricked at the corners of my eyes, and my hands flew up to cover my mouth. Steps from the kitchen, I stopped to sniff the air. The rotten-eggs scent was back, and this time it was stronger. The hissing sound was louder too.

It had to be a gas leak. Something had happened to the pipes during the shaking—or when the fridge fell. I fumbled to pull the fabric of my windbreaker up and over my mouth and nose to filter out the smell.

Was the gas why my breathing had gotten so much wheezier?

Had it already been poisoning us?

What were you supposed to do during a gas leak, anyway? I squeezed my eyes shut. Mrs. Pinales hadn't covered that in the babysitting course. But I'd seen a commercial on TV once about calling the gas company if you suspect a leak. My dad had muted the set for a second and turned to me. "This is good for you to know, Hannah. If you smell gas, and Mom and I aren't here, open a window. Don't turn on any lights or flip any switches and definitely don't strike a match, although you shouldn't be doing that anyway when we aren't home."

"But Neha and I love candles," I'd said. Our favorite shop was a boutique on Main Street that sold gorgeous swirly ones with scents like "Night Sky" and "Golden Birthday." Somehow the words seemed to match the smell perfectly, even though the night sky doesn't have a smell and neither does a birthday, other than sugar and frosting, maybe.

My dad had sighed. "Anyway, if you smell gas, grab your phone and run outside to call for help. That's really important, okay? That you get out fast. *Right away.*"

I'd nodded and filed the info away, even though it seemed at the time like I'd never have to use it. In the same category as the Fibonacci sequence, which is cool, but does knowing that two integers add up to the next number in the sequence actually do anything useful? Other than score you extra credit on math tests.

In the Matlocks' dark house, I didn't have to worry about turning on a light or anything, because the power was still out. And I hadn't found any candles or matches to use, although thinking about it, that would've been a decent way for us to see after dark without using up precious batteries. Many windows were already open, because they'd shattered, although I'd closed the big one in the kitchen—maybe that's why the smell had come back. The gas was getting trapped inside the room.

I shook with another cough. I felt light-headed. Each exhale came out in a wheeze.

The news broadcast had said there were fires all around Seattle. What specifically had caused them? Could it have been gas leaks?

My imagination filled with houses turned to fireballs, like I'd seen in TV shows and disaster movies. Explosions and bursts of flames, licking up the walls. The hissing seemed to grow louder around me. All it would take would be one staticky spark…

We need to get out. Right now.

11

WAKE UP, ZOE. OSCAR, get up." I don't know why I was speaking in a half whisper—we were alone in the house, after all, and there was no reason to be quiet, aside from not wanting to startle the kids. But maybe this was a time when startling was appropriate. We needed to move fast—if that was even possible with Oscar's injury.

"Guys! We have to go." My voice was still hushed but firm.

Zoe sat up, rubbing her eyes. I was amazed she'd fallen asleep so deeply, so fast. "Go where? To be with our mom?" Her voice rose with hope. I couldn't see her mouth but I could hear the smile. *Oh, I wish.*

Oscar, next to her, stirred and let out an anguished moan when he shifted his leg. I winced. Each time I was reminded of how much pain he must be in, something squeezed deep inside my chest, in sympathy.

What were we going to do about Oscar? Where were we going to go, outside, in the middle of the night? The best place would be my house, but we couldn't possibly travel there in the dark. There wasn't even any ambient light from the city to help us see; the moon and stars were shrouded by clouds. I shivered. We would be cold, damp, and exposed in the backyard. Were we just going to sit in a circle on the grass until morning? We'd freeze.

Something rattled at the other end of the living room. "The scritch-scratch!" Zoe shrieked, even though she'd been the one to tell the made-up story in the first place.

"That's not the scritch-scratch. It's the wind, blowing through the porch." *The porch.* The yard, away from the house and anything that could explode, would be safest. But because it would be too dangerous to sit out there in the dark, and we wouldn't be able to keep Oscar comfortable, the porch was second best. There, we'd at least have plenty of fresh air. And a quick path to safety if a fire did start. Unless the whole house exploded, in which case… *Stop it*, I ordered my brain.

"We're transferring the blanket fort to the porch," I said, grabbing random pillows. I whipped the tent-roof blanket from the couch, uncovering Zoe and Oscar still inside.

"Why? In the middle of the night?" Zoe grasped toward the blanket as I pulled it away.

"I'm staying right here," Oscar groaned. Which was fitting, considering he was immobilized.

I took a deep breath that still felt shallow. "Something's wrong with the stove. I think it's leaking gas. We'll be safer on the porch. It's only for tonight," I said. *Tomorrow night, you'll be home*, I promised myself. *One way or another.* But my own reassurance sounded empty.

Zoe nodded solemnly and started to gather the smaller cushions. I was proud of her for taking me seriously and for not panicking. Maybe I should've trusted her earlier with the news.

She and I moved everything—including Jupiter in his box—to the farthest corner of the screened porch, draping two blankets onto the old wicker settee like a tent. Wind rattled the screens. Thankfully, I couldn't smell anything like rotten eggs out there. When we burst back inside to get Oscar and the big cushion, the scent met us halfway to the couch.

"Yuck, it smells like Oscar farted."

Half a laugh escaped my grimace. "That's the gas, Zoe. They put a stinky scent in it so people know when it's leaking out."

"If they add the scent, why do they make it so gross?"

"To make sure you want to get away from the source."

First we moved Oscar, temporarily, back to the cushion-less couch. Zoe waited with him, holding his hand, while I ran the sectional cushion out to the porch and arranged it under the draped blankets. I tucked Jupiter's box between it and the wall. He chittered at me, annoyed—whether from being woken up or the cold air, I'm not sure. The cold, proba-bly—I think guinea pigs might be somewhat nocturnal? At least I'd heard him scuttling around when I was sleepless at night. Then I dashed back to the living room. Running to the couch, my big toe collided with something solid—maybe an overturned end table.

"Ow!" I waved my arms in the air and wobbled to keep my balance, narrowly avoiding a face-plant.

"Are you okay?" Zoe shouted.

"Yeah," I said, stopping to press on my toe. It smarted, but I could wiggle it fine inside my shoe. As urgent as it was to get outside, I had to slow down, be more careful. The last thing we needed was another injury.

Zoe and I arranged our arms underneath Oscar. When we lifted him up, somehow he seemed even heavier than earlier in the day. "How many marshmallows did you eat, Oscar?" I wheezed as we made a very deliberate, slow two-step across the living room floor. Occasionally my sneaker would crunch or crackle on the carpet. I hoped the noises weren't from anything too dear, but I'm pretty sure I stepped on the tablet.

Oscar mouthed the numbers as he counted. "Nine."

"I still don't think that explains how heavy you feel."

"Maybe our arms are just tired," Zoe piped up. "Mine hurts."

My head snapped in her direction, although I couldn't see her bandage. "Are you bleeding again?"

She was quiet for a second. "I don't think so."

"Good. Remind me to check that once we're settled."

The last few feet to the relocated blanket fort felt endless. My biceps were screaming. I wasn't sure I could keep holding Oscar up, especially because he wouldn't stay still in our arms.

"Hold on, Oscar," I said through clenched teeth. "We're almost there." Seconds later, we lowered him onto the sectional cushion, and then with a final push, we slid it fully underneath the blankets.

Zoe dropped next to him onto the cushion. "Show me your cut," I said, pulling out my phone and flipping the flashlight app on. She raised her arm and pushed away her sleeve, and I looped my fingers around her wrist, shining the light on the bandage. It still looked clean, and no fresh red had seeped through.

Back in the living room, it had been warm enough that we could spread out a bit inside the blanket fort. With all our clothes and coats on and with a blanket (or rug) tucked around us, it hadn't been comfortable but tolerable. On the porch, it was at least ten degrees cooler. The coats and blankets weren't cutting it—I could hear the kids' teeth chattering, and my shivers were involuntary.

"Let's all try to fit on the big cushion," I suggested. "And cuddle together, to stay warm." I moved closest to the exterior wall, where it was coldest. Zoe took the middle, and Oscar was on the other side—so his leg was away from both of us and any accidental nighttime kicking. The blankets and rug we piled on top of ourselves. Their weight was cozy and reassuring, but I could still feel the chilled air seeping in from the wall next to me.

At least the blanket fort now smelled like cedarwood and unwashed hair—instead of gas.

Zoe rolled to face me. *And unbrushed teeth.* I couldn't fault her. I'm sure my breath smelled abominable too.

I stared up at the ceiling. As my eyes adjusted, I could make out the fan that hung down directly above us. Its blades glinted in the moonlight. My stomach twisted. There was danger every-where. What if another aftershock hit and the fan fell down? I turned my head away. *Please let us be safe here tonight*, I pleaded with the universe.

I curled my fingers around the edge of the blanket. Maybe by the time we woke up, my mom would be sitting on the chair across from our nest. Watching over us. She'd have picked up Top Pot doughnuts on her way back, even. I knew it was ridic-ulous to hope for—both her being there and the doughnuts—but I let myself imagine that particular miracle anyway. If I kept picturing our parents safely returning home—stepping out of the car with wide, relieved smiles on their faces, arms open for a hug, not a scratch on them—I didn't think about the real possibilities of where they were. Under rubble, or in hospital beds. The photo my dad had taken of the ocean's lapping waves flashed into my head. That same water might have taken him away from me, forever.

No.

I couldn't let myself go there.

Another tear slid down my cheek, so I rolled toward the wall, to face away from Zoe. I didn't want my crying to wake her. I stifled a cough with my elbow. Then I coughed again. Nothing seemed to clear my lungs. It felt like they had been coated in peanut butter, something sticky and thick. Even though the air on the porch was crisp and thin, I couldn't get enough of it out of my lungs to get more inside me.

Oscar needed a doctor; Zoe needed a doctor. Maybe now I did too.

Something scratched at the window screen above me. *Thank goodness they're both asleep*—or surely that would've caused another scritch-scratch panic. Probably only a branch, but who knew what might be out there. Last night a bird had sneaked inside the living room, and the porch was even more exposed to the elements. What else could join us in the blanket fort? I pulled the hood of Andrea's coat away from my ears to listen for the howling I thought I'd heard the night before, but the only sound was the wind rustling trees and rattling the window frames, and Oscar's fitful, whimpering sleep.

During the babysitting course, when Mrs. Pinales had told us to get help in an emergency, she'd warned, "Don't try to be a hero in these situations."

Neha had frowned. I understood why. She was used to being a hero on the soccer field and elsewhere. When we were young, we played a game outside called "Animal Heroes," in which we pretended we'd found all kinds of injured or abandoned baby animals (really our stuffed ones) in dangerous situations and rescued them. The make-believe game I had always wanted to play was "Library," in which we'd mostly pretended to check out books to each other and collect overdue fines. Some people just seem designed to step up, take charge, and be heroic. Neha was one of them.

The world outside the porch had gotten eerily still and quiet. We were so totally alone, without even stars in the sky above us. *I would really appreciate a hero swooping in right about now.*

It's not that I didn't want to be heroic. I just knew I'm not the type. So far, I'd been doing more harm than good. The earth-quake hadn't caused Zoe's cut or Oscar's fall from the swing set—I had. I'd already failed to keep them safe.

The truth was, me being left in charge was more dangerous to them than an earthquake.

12

T HE THRUM OF RAIN hitting the roof of the porch woke me
the next morning. Zoe and Oscar were still conked out
underneath the blanket pile. I slowly peeled the covers off myself
to head for the bathroom. If I hadn't felt like I was in danger of
bursting, I don't know that anything could've convinced me to
leave the meager warmth of our fort. It would be my forever
home. When I first put my feet on the floor, it surprised me that
I didn't feel the rough-hewn beams with my toes—but I was
still wearing my sneakers. It was too cold to take off my shoes,
and anyway it seemed wise to keep them on in case we had to
race away in the middle of the night. I shuddered, partly from
the damp chill and partly from the thought of a fresh disaster
forcing us to flee from Blanket Fort 2.0.

The screened porch smelled like cedar, salt air, and fresh rain,
my favorite blend of scents. To me, that's home. But the inside
of the house still reeked of gas. I covered my nose with my sleeve
as I slalomed through the living room and kitchen to the hall.
My DIY gas mask caused me to take in even less air—like the

difference between drinking from a straw with a pin-size hole versus drinking from a straw that had been pinched shut. By the time I reached the bathroom, my chest ached and I was wheezing. Maybe the air I managed to get inside my lungs, tinged with the gas fumes, could make my asthma even worse. I shuddered from a cough.

I didn't want to stop in the kitchen to wash my hands, so I tried the faucet on the cracked bathroom sink. After a split second, a rusty brown stream spewed out. Gross flecks of something stuck to the sides of the sink's bowl. I twisted the faucet off, wondering if the color had something to do with the sink's crack. Or if all the water was like that now, which would mean it was no longer safe to drink.

Suddenly my throat felt extremely dry. I swallowed hard. Was there bottled water in the pantry somewhere? I hadn't checked because, so far, we hadn't needed it. Now we definitely would.

I zipped up Andrea's coat and prepared my sleeve-muffler to cover my face for the trip back to the porch. My feet didn't want to move. I scanned the hallway, searching for remaining signs of the cozy, welcoming house the Matlocks' had been only a few dozen hours before. A painting of an elderly woman—maybe their grandmother?—was still firmly affixed to the wall. Her eyes gazed sympathetically at me, and her half smile was reassuring. She was posed sitting in a chair, and I had this urge to climb into the painting, onto her blanket-clad lap. The woman in the portrait looked like someone who would offer a soft hug and a butterscotch candy warm from her pocket. Someone who would pat my upper back and say, soothingly, *Don't worry, darling, it'll all work out*. An adult.

I didn't want to go back to the porch, where it was so cold, damp, and exposed. But I had to. My eyes stung with tears, either from the fumes or the emotions threatening to break from my control. I coughed and sucked in more air, which only made me cough harder. My ribs now ached even when I wasn't in the middle of a fit. My gaze fluttered down from the painting to the shattered pottery and unidentified stains on the runner, the balusters from the staircase still littering the floor. I could hear a loud dripping coming from above—rainwater? There could be a hole in the roof somewhere. Or a pipe could've burst.

The noises I heard weren't the normal settling sounds a house makes. It groaned like a wounded animal. Which actually made sense—a house is like a living thing, full of internal organs that keep it alive—plumbing and heating and insulation and electricity. All that essential stuff had been injured by the earthquake. The Matlocks' house was in as much pain as we all were. But was it just sick—or was the house dying?

We could no longer depend on it for shelter; inside was no safer than outside, even on the porch. In fact, that was probably more dangerous than being out in the open, where things (such as the ceiling fan) couldn't collapse on us. Beth Kajawa had said to shelter in place, but this wasn't a shelter any longer. *It's time to head for my house.* My dad would have made sure that everything was totally up to code and earthquake-proof. Plus, I lived closer to Mr. Aranita's house and the bridge—and the rest of civilization, across the inlet. We couldn't wait at the Matlocks' forever. Not with broken bones, and cuts, and asthma. Not with a gas leak and no heat and scarce food.

But with Oscar's leg, traveling anywhere by foot would be tricky. The medical guide had said it was important to keep the injured area stable. We also couldn't head out in the middle of a downpour. Until that stopped, at least, we were stuck.

Fixing my sleeve over my mouth and nose, I jogged back to the kids. While passing the couch, I glanced through the living room window that opens into the porch. Out there, the blanket fort actually looked like a tent, pitched in between the wicker furniture. *It really is like we're camping indoors.* And then I knew what we could do, where we might be safer than inside.

On the porch, I squatted to crawl underneath the blankets, which, when I pushed them aside, I discovered were soggy from the rain drizzling through the screens. My movement, or the light from outside the fort, caused Zoe to stir. She rolled onto her back, blinking her big brown eyes up at me.

"My mom?"

I shook my head sadly. "Not yet."

She sighed. "I knew it. If she were home, she'd be cuddled up in here with us." Zoe turned her head to face Oscar, so I wouldn't see the tears welling in her eyes, but her quivering bottom lip gave her away. I reached out a hand to squeeze her shoulder, through the layers of shirt, sweatshirt, and parka. She smiled at me and wiped her eye. No more tears rolled out. I wanted to tell her it was okay to cry, but if I sneaked those words past the lump in my throat, I'd probably start to cry too. It was easier to keep my feelings as numb as my fingers felt.

"So, the gas smell got stronger. I don't think it's a great idea for us to stay inside the house today. Or even here on the porch—it's too close." I had to pause for a breath. I was feeling light-headed again. I kind of hoped Zoe didn't understand that I was worried about the house, and us, blowing up.

"Where is there to go?" Zoe tugged the blanket up closer to her chin. It's funny how the porch, which had first seemed so weird and unwelcoming during our midnight move, now was a place of comfort, which we were reluctant to leave. I decided to break the news about our relocation plans one step at a time. I'd tell her about moving to my house later.

"Do you guys have a tent?"

"Yeah!" Zoe's eyes brightened. "Mom bought us one last summer. We went camping at Ohanapecosh, at Mount Rainier."

"That's great." I'd gone hiking there with my parents once. "Because we're going camping now. For real this time—outside."

Zoe and I found the tent in the jumble of the front-hall closet, buried beneath a badminton set. Neatly folded up in its original box, still with the instructions, to my relief. Tents don't seem like particularly complicated things, but the time that Neha and I tried to pitch ours during our Girl Scout camping trip, we got all twisted up in the poles and netting, and without our troop leader's patient help, I think we would have been sleeping under the stars.

I lingered in that memory for a moment. Even though it had been difficult to get that tent set up, trying had been fun. Doing almost anything with Neha was fun—even the time she accidentally threw away her retainer at the yogurt shop and, because she'd already lost three of them, her mom made us sort through four bags of the slimy, yogurt-soaked trash to find it. We were wearing gloves, of course. It was disgusting, but we kept finding funnier and grosser stuff as we sifted, giggling nonstop. When Neha finally found her retainer, covered with goo and sprinkles, she was so excited that she jumped up and spilled half the contents of that trash bag on her sweatshirt. I laughed so hard I cried. That's the beauty of best friendship. Even the moments when you're elbow-deep in froyo trash, you find a way to have fun together.

I wondered if Neha and Marley were together somewhere right now, the bonds of their friendship knotting even tighter in the midst of the rubble.

And despite the familiar pang of jealousy that they might be together while I was alone—it made me happy, and relieved, to think that wherever she was, Neha had someone to help her through this awfulness. All the time I'd spent worrying that Neha's friendship with Marley would eclipse ours suddenly seemed kind of unnecessary. There's enough room in Neha's big heart for tons of friends. I could share her, even if she was my best. All I wanted was for her to be okay.

"Hannah?" Zoe shifted from one foot to the other. "We should get back to Oscar. I don't like leaving him alone out there. Especially with the food."

I snorted. "You think he's going to eat all that's left?" Which wasn't much.

She shook her head, her eyes wide. "No. But what if something else does?"

That snapped me back to attention. "Grab those raincoats"—I pointed to two still hanging on pegs and one crumpled on the closet floor—"and head back."

Tents are surprisingly heavy. While lugging everything back to the porch, I stopped to check the situation with the kitchen sink. Sure enough, that was spewing brown gunk too. A gallon jug of distilled water had survived the collapse of a pantry shelf, so I dragged that out to the porch along with the tent and the slickers. Zoe, I noticed, had been itching at her bandage while we were scavenging in the closet. Without clean water, we couldn't wash her wound very well. I didn't want to have to change the dressing often, so from then on, I'd have to do the heaviest carrying so the strain wouldn't reopen her cut.

Wheezing slightly, I dumped the tent and raincoats to the floor of the porch. A puddle had formed, slowly seeping closer to the blanket fort from the screen door. I hoped Oscar wasn't soaked inside. My chest squeezed as I dove under the blanket to check on him. He was on his back, eyes closed, one hand stretched out to half-heartedly pet Jupiter in his box. Nothing had bothered him, or our sad stockpile of snacks.

"Doing all right?" I asked.

He shook his head. His chin quivered. "My leg really hurts today."

My chest squeezed tighter. "Time for more Tylenol, then." *What am I going to do once it's gone?* I'd only been giving him one chewable at a time, to stretch it out.

We waited until the rain had slowed from torrents to a drizzle, and then Zoe and I zipped up our raincoats to lug the tent outside. "Oscar, it's your job to make sure Jupiter is doing okay."

"I can help with the tent," he said, sniffling. "I don't want to stay on the porch by myself again."

I dropped to my knees next to him. "You have to stay here and keep your leg stable, Oscar. This'll take just a few minutes. We're only going to be in the yard, near the firepit. Zoe will shout out progress reports for you, okay? And if you need anything, holler."

Like he wanted to make sure he was included in this arrangement, Jupiter let out a few loud chirps. "Same goes for you, Jupiter."

I hated walking away from the house with those two still inside. Every step, I worried that something awful would happen, even though we were only feet apart. What if the ceiling fan did come loose? Oscar couldn't dive out of the way. Or what if the gas leak made the house burst into... *No.* That worry, even if totally valid, was still unthinkable. At least until we were in the tent.

Zoe, next to me, kept turning back to look at the house. "One of the upstairs windows is broken," she said, pointing.

I turned. She was right—the white curtains from whichever room the window belonged to fluttered out of the frame, like a sign of surrender. Fitting, as we were abandoning the house. It was so strange that we had no idea what it was like upstairs, how much damage had been done. Or in the front yard and beyond—I hadn't so much as opened the front door to peek out; the windows in the kitchen and living room faced the backyard. For all I knew, the house was now perched on the edge of a chasm. Or there was a sand volcano the height of the second floor in the front yard. I squinted as I studied the back of the house. Was it my imagination, or was the roof sagging? I'd never noticed that the eaves were uneven before... All the better that we were moving out.

"This is a good spot," I said, motioning to a patch of grass slightly to the right of the firepit and far from the weird sand mounds, which had stopped geyser-ing at least. Nothing around could fall on us, because the trees all ringed the edges of the open yard. The closest structure was the fenced-in vegetable garden, and nothing in there stood taller than my chest, anyway.

We cleared away the strewn branches and then I pulled out the tent instructions—a single piece of paper, but a huge one with about a dozen folds. The diagrams were the maddeningly vague kind, like on IKEA furniture instructions. I have a desk from there in my room, and it took my dad *hours* to put together, along with two dollars in quarters for the profanity jar Mom has in the kitchen…and Dad's a trained architect. Making building instructions is his job.

I took a deep breath, or what now passed as deep. The instruction sheet was damp from the rain and beginning to disintegrate in my hands. I let out a sigh. *We can do this.* But the diagrams made about as much sense to me as hieroglyphs. I tried to remember how my dad started a building project—organizing his materials. "Okay, Zoe, first we need to lay the tent out on the grass."

We spread it out and then yanked all the poles out of the box. I started to stick one in the tent's loops, but Zoe stopped me. "No—the short ones go on the *other* side." She handed me a different rod.

I wiped the rain off my face. "Thanks. Actually—do *you* know how to put this thing up?"

She shrugged. "Maybe." She studied the instruction sheet, biting her lip in concentration. "I used to play with these engineering toys. I like to build stuff." While she was talking, she'd already hooked in two more poles. Apparently, Zoe was some kind of engineering genius.

"I'm going to follow your lead," I said. "Tell me how to help." I was really impressed by her skills, but watching her navigate the instructions so easily didn't exactly make me feel better about my capabilities as the person in charge.

Thanks to Zoe, the tent was up in about fifteen minutes. "My dad would be super impressed, and he builds for a living." My stomach pinched as soon as I said it. If he hadn't been building the Seaspray Resort, he'd have been in Seattle when the quake happened. Maybe he'd even have been at home on Pelling, and then he'd be here, with us. Safe. I blinked my eyes, willing myself not to cry.

We grabbed the crumpled tent box and the sodden instructions and ran back to the porch. Relief flooded me as soon as I saw Oscar, leaning back on his elbows to watch as we burst through the door.

"Everything cool in here?" I asked, scanning the space. Jupiter was still huddled in his pungent box. The ceiling fan hadn't crashed onto anyone. The rain puddle was encroaching on the blanket fort but hadn't hit quite yet. There wasn't smoke or flames from the kitchen. The muscles in my back and shoulders relaxed a tiny bit.

"Yeah. Except we're hungry," Oscar said. "And thirsty." My shoulders tensed again immediately. I'd forgotten to give the kids breakfast.

"We'll eat in the tent. First, we're going to move the fort out there." I gathered the blankets into a wad in my arms and tucked the pillows on top, underneath my chin. "Hang tight while I take this outside. Zoe, can you pull together the books, notebook, flashlight, and radio?"

I couldn't see her nod with the pillows piled up so high beneath my chin, but I heard her start stacking the books. I ran back into the yard, but after a few paces I had to stop. My chest was getting really tight again, and the grass was super slippery. I didn't want to trip on debris and sprain something—I was the only one left with the use of all their limbs.

In the tent, I dumped the pillows and blankets in a corner. Once we got Oscar inside, I'd bring out the big cushions too. Although the tent was in the middle of the yard, it already felt so much cozier inside its warm orange walls, even with the rain pelting all sides. It wasn't any colder than the house.

By the time we'd moved Oscar, Jupiter, the cushions, and all our essentials—flashlight, survival books, notebook, gallon of water, food bag, bandages, and the radio—into the tent, the rain had cleared up. I unzipped the windows so we could see into the yard. Even though it was cold, the fresh evergreen air was nice. Maybe I was imagining it, but I could breathe easier. I stared longingly in the direction of my house, even though you can't see it through all the trees. So near, and yet so far.

I flopped onto a couch cushion, staring up at the orange dome.

"What are we going to do now?" Zoe asked.

Good question. I wanted a rest, more than anything. Before I could suggest a nap, Oscar piped up, "I'm starving, and I need more Tylenol."

No rest for the weary. My mom sometimes says that. Thinking of her made my stomach drop, but I ignored the sensation and rose to my knees. Mom wouldn't want me to cry about her. She'd want me to take care of Oscar and Zoe, to be responsible—the best I could, anyway. "Let's see what we have to eat in here."

"Could we listen to the radio again?" Zoe was already fiddling with its dial. "Maybe it'll give us an update so we know when our mom will be back."

I stared at the little red radio. Just looking at it made my pulse race, my chest muscles clench tighter. I couldn't unhear whatever news the broadcasts shared, and while I knew Beth Kajawa and whoever else was reporting didn't want to frighten anyone, didn't want to share news that acted like a punch straight to your heart—that's what their broadcasts were. Everyone listening probably felt exactly like we did: scared, helpless, and desperate for reassurance that their loved ones were okay. If Beth said the f-word again—*fatalities*—I'm not sure I could bear to hear it.

But it was also possible that the radio would tell us something we *needed* to hear. Like instructions on how to get help from a doctor. Or when the power was coming back on. Or whether the brown water was safe to drink. Every time I checked on Oscar's leg, it looked worse—puffier and more deeply bruised. There were only three chewables left to dull his pain.

It would be irresponsible not to stay informed. "Okay, we can listen while we eat," I said. "I'll power it up."

Zoe passed me the radio and I flipped out the crank, then started whirling it in circles. I kept twisting and twisting; the longer I took to charge it, the longer I could delay facing the news.

"Don't you think it's done already?" Zoe eventually asked, wiping graham cracker crumbs from her mouth. "You only cranked it a little last time."

"Um, yeah. Probably." I stopped and tucked the crank back in its spot. I slowly pulled out the antenna. Then I flipped the switch.

"The rain this afternoon brings an increased risk of landslides. Emergency Management advises listening carefully for the sounds of moving debris, such as trees cracking. Avoid sheltering in low-lying areas. If you find yourself in the path of a landslide, move away from the flow of debris as quickly as possible. If escape is not possible," she paused to clear her throat. Since the last broadcast, Beth Kajawa's voice had grown raspy with exhaustion. I wondered

where she was reporting from, and how long she'd been on the air. What about her friends and family? Did she know if they were okay? I wished I could thank her, for trying to sound so calm and reassuring—and mostly succeeding. *"Curl in a ball and protect your head with your arms. Another risk facing residents of low-lying areas is liquefaction. Soil and groundwater can mix in an earthquake event as strong as this. When that happens, it causes the ground to become very soft and function almost like quicksand. Buildings may sink into it, causing tilting or even a collapse. If you notice signs of liquefaction, such as the formation of 'sand volcanoes' on the ground—use caution."*

Wait. Sand volcanoes? We had those. Now our ground could turn into quicksand? I honestly thought that didn't exist outside of chapter books and old cartoons. Kind of like the threat of slipping on a banana peel. "Don't go anywhere near the sand mounds, Zoe," I said.

"We now have an updated list of bridge closures, but remember this is only a partial list. Other bridges, especially in suburban and rural areas, may also be closed or unstable. Use extreme caution if attempting to cross. I'll say it again, folks: shelter in place." She sighed and paused for what sounded like a sip of water. *"Closures are: Ship Canal Bridge, Montlake Bridge, Murrow Memorial Bridge, Fremont Bridge, Elliott Bay Bridge, Ballard Bridge. In terms of ferry service: It's not operating, and I'm going to venture a guess that it will be a long time before it's running again. King County Metro*

Transit and Link Light Rail are not operating. Basically—a car is your only option at this point, but road conditions and closures make travel inadvisable. Unless you have an emergency need, the Office of Emergency Management still asks everyone to shelter in place. I know you've heard me say that phrase dozens of times by now, friends. But, please, listen. The first responders who are out there already have their hands full. You will be helping yourselves and everyone in the metro area if you just stay put."

Elliott Bay Bridge. Which connected Pelling Island to the rest of the world, at least by car. And if ferries weren't running—how could anyone get back to our island? Maybe if they had a boat. Otherwise, we were totally cut off.

Beth Kajawa cleared her throat, like she dreaded whichever update was next. *"Now, an update on the coastal region. The tsunami's floodwaters reached as far as two and a half miles inland."* Beth Kawaja paused. When she spoke again, her voice had taken on a tremble. *"I'm afraid to say, we've had no contact with Emergency Management west of the inundation zone. At this point, helicopters from Fort Lewis are undertaking flyovers to look for signs of…survivors."* Her voice cracked. *"Some of you listening, I know, are thinking of friends and family who were there. I—I am too. All I can say right now is, try to keep hope alive—"*

I lunged for the radio and flipped the dial off. I couldn't breathe. I froze on my hands and knees, gasping. Now it was like air was trying to get in and out of my lungs through one of those tiny coffee-stirring straws they have at gas station coffee bars, the ones not even meant for sucking up any liquid. With each gasp, my throat and chest felt tighter. I honestly thought I might suffocate. It was a full-blown asthma attack, worse than any I remembered having before.

I struggled to think of the instructions the doctor had given me, other than "use your rescue inhaler." *Keep calm. Lean forward. Take long, deep breaths. Loosen tight clothing.*

I sat cross-legged, leaning with my elbows on my thighs. I tried that yoga breathing, repeating the word *calm* over and over and over in my head. I reached up with one hand to unbutton the top of Andrea's coat and unzip my windbreaker and then my vest inside. I stretched out the neck of my long sleeve.

Calm. Calm. Calm.

I stared out the tent's clear plastic window, at the trees waving in the breeze. At the wide-open sky above them. I imagined my throat and lungs being as expansive as it. I avoided looking in the direction of Zoe and Oscar, because I could feel their eyes fixed on me. I'm sure I was really freaking them out.

It took a few minutes of focusing on the breathing exercises, but the coffee stirrer turned back into a normal straw. My hands stopped tingling. The nausea I'd begun to feel subsided.

"Are you...okay?" Zoe's voice was a notch above a whisper.

I nodded. I couldn't talk yet. A few more full breaths, and then I would try.

"Yeah." My voice was hoarse, strained.

"What happened?" Zoe was messing with her bandage again, rubbing at the skin around it.

"I had an asthma attack. But I think it's over. I'm fine now." Another lie.

With those words, I'd rebroken my promise to Zoe, but I had no other choice than to tell that lie—*I'm fine, it's okay*—to her, and myself.

13

WHEN I WAS IN fourth grade, one of our vocabulary words was *utopia*. Mrs. Simpson told us that the definition is an imaginary place where life is perfect: Everyone there gets along, and it's safe and beautiful and happy. "Like a paradise," she'd said, before asking us to please use it in a sentence.

I chewed on the eraser end of my pencil. Her definition kind of sounded like a description of Pelling Island—especially our mini neighborhood across the inlet. Mr. Aranita, the Matlocks, and my family all got along just fine and our peninsula was completely safe. I could run outside and pluck wild berries from a bush for my breakfast. There's never a lot of noise, other than chirping birds. We lived peacefully with the animals, even the coyotes and bears. The island might not be particularly sunny, except for in August, but overcast skies are beautiful too—especially the way the gray and white clouds sometimes swirl together like milk into tea. And every morning on my way to school, I had a chance of catching a glimpse of Mount Rainier and the Cascades, their snowcapped peaks reaching up toward the heavens.

So for my sentence, I wrote: *I am lucky to live in a utopia.*

Mrs. Simpson called on me to share my sentence with the rest of the class, which was slightly embarrassing. When I read it aloud, her brows furrowed and she paused for a moment before asking, "Could you tell us more about your sentence, Hannah?"

"Sure," I'd said. Then I explained everything I'd been thinking, about how I love living in a place where the air is always fresh and smells like ocean and pine, where sometimes while I'm sitting in the breakfast nook reading, I can see deer nibbling in the yard. Where on a lazy Sunday morning my dad and I will go for a bike ride through the forest preserve and stop near the bridge to skip stones into the calm, clear, silvery water. "Nothing really bad ever happens in my neighborhood, or on Pelling. Everyone's pretty happy here. So…it's a utopia. Right?"

Mrs. Simpson smiled. "Usually we use 'utopia' to mean a made-up place. But you've made a compelling point, and I have to say I agree."

I never forgot that moment in class. Afterward, whenever I came across *utopia* in print, I'd picture the view from the front door of my house. The word *utopia* would also pop into my head sometimes when I was outside in the yard, or biking along the road. *How lucky am I to live here, in this utopia.* I really believed that was true.

But as I stared out the tent window, still waiting for my breathing to return to normal, I realized that as lovely and idyllic as Pelling might be—utopias *are* fictional. No place is perfect, or perfectly safe. The earthquake had proven that. "Pellingites" were as vulnerable to disasters and trouble as people anywhere else. Maybe more so, because we were cut off from everything and everyone. Our community was fragile. That truth stung. I'd been betrayed by the island I loved so much.

But my house—maybe it was still safe. Protected from the earthquake by my dad's planning and handiwork. Warm and dry inside, with clear water and no gas smell and—most important of all—my rescue inhaler resting on top of my nightstand. If I could get it, I wouldn't have to fear another asthma attack.

I knew exactly where the first aid kit was too, and that my mom kept it stocked full of bandages and wipes and packets of children's pain relievers. We also had that emergency tub, waiting in the closet next to the kitchen.

Beth Kajawa had begged us to shelter in place, unless it was a real emergency. Although weren't we having a real emergency at the Matlocks', with our cuts and broken bones and worsening asthma? We'd resorted to living in a *tent*. It was only three-quarters of a mile between their front door and mine. *It's time to pack up and head home.*

"Hannah? Is there more water? I'm thirsty," Zoe asked.

"And I have to pee," Oscar whined.

None of us had needed a bathroom break since we had moved into the tent. Should we still use the toilet inside—and now that the water was messed up, would it flush properly? I definitely didn't want to add raw sewage to the list of problems—and smells—inside the house.

My hand fluttered to my throat as I thought about dashing back in, even for a few minutes. I was convinced the gas smell helped trigger my asthma attack. I couldn't avoid the cold, or the strong emotions, or the exertion that my doctor had said could cause a flare-up, but I could avoid those fumes.

"Hannah? I have to go *bad*." Oscar was shifting on the cushion like he was doing a lying-down version of the gotta-pee shuffle dance. "It's an emergency." Using his forearms, he lifted his bottom off the blanket—but that's as far as he could get up on his own, without shifting weight into his legs. He gasped, wincing, and lowered down.

"Hang on, we'll help you." I motioned to Zoe to take one side, and I'd get the other, after I unzipped the tent door.

When Oscar was back in our aching arms—mine felt like spaghetti from lugging him around—Zoe started to maneuver us toward the porch. "Wait! We should stay out of the bathroom for now," I said. "At least when we only have to go number one."

She looked over at me, horrified. "Then where are we supposed to do our business?"

I motioned toward the edge of the yard, hemmed in by waist-high bramble bushes and some trees. "We're camping, remember? We'll go in the woods."

Oscar giggled. "Cool," he said, his voice still weak.

"You're gross, Oscar," Zoe teased. "You're probably happy that I won't bug you about washing your hands."

I had to smile, because they were acting like themselves again. I clung to any moment of normalcy like a raft in the ocean.

We deposited Oscar next to a tree that he could lean on, turning our backs for privacy but sticking close in case he started to lose his balance. I tried not to listen to the sound of him relieving himself onto the leaves and twigs. When he was done, we slowly started back for the tent. I made a silent plea to my arms, to please give me just enough strength to get Oscar inside. Then I'd give them a rest.

Clouds still covered the sun, but the quality of its light told me that we were firmly into the afternoon. I reached through all my layers to my vest pocket to pull out my phone. That might have been the longest I'd ever gone without reaching for it. 2:00 p.m., leaving us a few hours before dusk—so it was now or never, if we were going to trek to my house. *But how?* I had to figure out how to transport Oscar—and all our essentials. Everything in the tent and maybe some more supplies too.

As we carried Oscar back, I silently brainstormed all we would need to gather before leaving: A jug of water. Any remaining food. Our survival information—at least what was transcribed in the notebook, because the books would be cumbersome to take along. Except maybe the home medical guide. That was too essential to leave behind. A safe mode of transportation for Oscar and Jupiter—a wagon or wheelbarrow? Wagon would be safer; wheelbarrows topple over pretty easily. Speaking of Jupiter, we should clean the poop out of his box before we left. Oh, and we needed the flashlight and the radio/charger. Plus blankets. And a thousand things I was either forgetting or simply not aware we needed. This would be less like a trip next door and more like leaving for the Oregon Trail.

Once Oscar was safely deposited on top of the cushion, it was time for a checkup. The magazine-scrunchie splint appeared to be holding up surprisingly well. I snapped a photo with my phone, thinking I could show it to Neha...later. Sometime. *Hopefully.* I clicked the screen off, then reached over to carefully roll up the fabric covering Oscar's injury. Expecting it would look better than the last time I'd seen it.

I choked back a gasp once his pant leg was up. The rainbow of bruising had deepened, and the whole area had swollen. I pressed lightly on his puffy, mottled skin. Before I could ask if he felt my touch, and if it hurt, he sucked in his breath sharply and let out a yelp of pain. I clenched my teeth and worked to keep my face neutral as I rolled his pant leg back down.

"How does it look?" Zoe sounded more nervous than curious.

"It looks...okay," I said. *If only we had some ice.* I felt a bubble of rage toward the refrigerator, for having the nerve to fall facedown on the kitchen floor. Had it fallen onto any of its other sides, we could've gotten inside. It was cold enough in the kitchen that it was entirely possible that the trapped ice was still perfectly usable. Another reason to get to my house ASAP.

I sat back on my heels, then reached for the notebook with all our instructions. "Okay, guys, here's the plan." I swallowed hard, hoping they'd go along with it. I was in charge—but without their cooperation, we couldn't go anywhere. "We're moving to my house."

"I don't want to leave!" Oscar cried. He reached for Jupiter in the box next to him, scooping the guinea pig up and pressing him next to his chest. Jupiter squeaked in protest too. "Neither does Jupiter."

Zoe looked thoughtful. "Why? Shouldn't we stay here, because this is where all our parents think we are? They'll be really worried if they get back and we're not waiting. And that radio lady said to shelter in place."

"True, but this isn't a safe place for us anymore. I mean, the tent is safe...*ish*. But we don't even have a bathroom at this point. The water's not working inside, and there's a gas leak. That is so, so dangerous." I peered out of the tent's unzipped door, in the direction of my house. "My dad's an architect. He knows how to reinforce things, and all about the building codes, so I'm positive our house held up well. Also, we have an emergency tub with water, food, extra batteries, and flashlights. And who knows—maybe my phone will work over there."

That wasn't an unreasonable idea. The Matlocks' house was the farthest from downtown Pelling, where the nearest cell tower was. When I'm biking in the forest preserve, my phone gets spotty service. Maybe the closer we got to the bridge and the rest of civilization, the better the chance we could communicate with the outside world. By now, they could've restored some of the network, or figured out another way to return communication to people.

It's funny how I thought of "they" as these all-knowing, super-capable experts who could problem-solve immediately. Like they weren't normal people who might also have become trapped in their homes, or injured, or worse. Like "they" didn't need passable roads or electricity or working phones to begin fixing what the earthquake had destroyed. I shuddered. The people with the skills to help might be as helpless as I was.

Zoe let out a small sigh. "I guess you're right. We can't live in a tent and pee in the woods forever, and I'm really sick of being cold and soggy."

"Zoe!" Oscar's tone was wounded. He looked at his sister like she was a traitor. "I don't want to go."

She patiently crouched at his level. "Hey, I know. But we need to, Oscar."

I knew how to convince him. "It's like in your video games— it's time to go to the next level. That's always a new place. Don't you want to level up?"

His chin quivered, but he didn't cry. "Fine." Honestly, I couldn't believe how tough he was being. He had a broken leg, after all. If I were in his situation, I would probably cry nonstop. Pride for him blossomed in my heart. *This must be how parents feel, when their kid does something good that surprises them.*

How would my parents feel if they had been watching me all this time?

I didn't know. I had made so many mistakes.

But I was also doing my best. That's what Dad always says: *All you have to do is try your best.* I really was. I hoped that would make them proud.

Zoe and I snapped into action, first by dashing over to Andrea's fenced-in garden to harvest some veggies—so we didn't have to live on the scraps of crackers and marshmallows that were left. Or maybe *pillage* was the right word—although Andrea had planted the veggies with the goal of her kids eating them someday, right?

But the plant beds only had sprouts to offer. Not even literal sprouts, like what my mom always puts in her turkey-and-avocado pitas. Sprouts like seedlings, which we couldn't eat (1) because the vegetables hadn't grown yet, and (2) because I would have felt guilty about killing the teenage plants, especially when they'd already survived an earthquake.

"So much for living off the land," I said to Zoe.

"I still don't understand why you wanted to get dirty veggies from the yard when there's probably food we missed in the house," she said.

"Because we could avoid digging through the debris piled up in the kitchen if we got our sustenance from the garden." She looked skeptical. "Fine, you're right. We'll go inside."

The truth was, going back into the house scared me. I didn't want to have to hold my breath, especially now that my breathing had calmed down. I could get enough air into my lungs, and my fingers weren't tingling, although I still had a wheeze. But even if we'd been able to collect food from the garden, there were other things inside we needed in order to leave, like food pellets for Jupiter (if we could find them), and more water. And then something to carry everything in. *Wait, we still need a way to transport Oscar so his leg stays stable.* How had I forgotten that? I massaged my temples, giving myself a moment to think the plans through again, so I wouldn't forget anything important. "Zoe, do you guys have a wagon?"

She nodded. "It's in the carport."

"Let's get that first."

We dashed to the carport. The pavement where the car normally would be parked had a long, deep crack in it. The lawnmower and various garden tools—a hoe, a shovel, and a couple of rakes—had all toppled over. A pyramid of firewood had collapsed, spreading logs and kindling across the covered area. A couple of terra-cotta flowerpots had shattered, but the metal ones looked fine, although full of rainwater. One of the rakes had fallen onto the wagon, which had rolled to the middle of the parking space, like it had taken the opportunity to sneakily steal the car's spot.

"Excellent," I said, dumping the wagon on its side and giving it a couple of shakes to get all the gunk out. Then I grabbed the handle and motioned for Zoe to follow me back to the porch.

I parked the wagon next to the door. "Okay, here's the plan. If you see food—grab whatever hasn't spoiled or opened or possibly been contaminated. We need Jupiter's food pellets. We need more bandages and pain relievers, if we can find them. And we need bottled water—or juice; anything we can drink.

"We're going to run in, gather what we can, then dash back out to the wagon. Don't breathe too much air in the kitchen. And let's be really careful moving across the floor—stuff might have shifted or fallen. We don't want to trip and get hurt."

Zoe nodded. "It's like that game show, the one where you have to get through the grocery store super fast and stay within your budget."

"Exactly like that, except our 'budget' is what we can safely carry." I craned my neck to look over at the orange tent in the middle of the yard. I cupped my hands around my mouth. "Oscar—are you and Jupiter all right in there?"

Weakly, I heard: "Yeah. If you find fruit ropes, can you bring me some?"

"We will totally do that," I bellowed back. Then I pulled my shirt over my mouth and nose again and motioned for Zoe to do the same.

"Ready? Let's go."

Reentering the house, it didn't feel like the same space at all. It had a creepy, abandoned vibe—like somehow in the few hours we'd spent outside in the tent, cobwebs had formed and dust had coated all the surfaces. Actually, all the surfaces *were* covered in a layer of grimy silt, but it was from the earthquake's damage, not neglect. Even with my ears pounding, I heard strange noises— hisses and groans and drips. I hunched forward, in a protective posture, as I stepped carefully through the living room mess and into the kitchen. Zoe followed right behind me, so close that if I paused for even a half second, we'd collide. Even with my shirt over my nose and my breath held, I could smell the gas. My heartbeat picked up its tempo.

In the kitchen, we went straight for the cupboards and countertops. There wasn't much left in them, thanks to our previous foraging. What remained was mostly unusable—like pasta you'd need to cook to eat. I grabbed a few smushed granola bars tucked in the back of the cupboard. And I found the can of refried beans that Andrea had joked we could eat if we got "desperate." It was dented but hadn't burst. *Well, we're desperate now.* Best of all, it had a pop-top lid. The odds of me being able to find a can opener in the kitchen nightmare were slim to none.

Next to a split-open bag of basmati rice on the countertop

was an intact box of matches. I swiped them. They might come in handy later—and it seemed like extremely bad judgment to leave any fire starters in a kitchen that smelled like gas. After they were zipped in my pocket, I felt like a walking bomb.

I'd only sneaked a few breaths while I'd been filling up my arms, and my chest was achy. My eyes were watering too, possibly from the fumes. I motioned to Zoe, who had turned her shirt into a makeshift basket, holding a thing of rice cakes and a fresh box of bandages—the small ones, unfortunately, but still good to have. I motioned for her to follow me back outside, grabbing my backpack on the way.

At the wagon, we took stock of the food. Not great options—but enough to get us to my house. We wouldn't need any more than that, though, right? Unlike the Matlocks', where we'd started out with little food even before the earthquake ruined most of it, my kitchen was fully stocked. Mom had gone to the grocery store the day before the quake. Once we got there, we'd be fine. And full.

"Now all we need is water and more pellets for Jupiter," I said. "Oh, and fruit ropes, for Oscar."

Zoe frowned. "I didn't see any more water. All we had was that jug—which we drank."

"There must be something inside for us to drink. To stay hydrated." I paused. "I'm going back in to check. Why don't you see how Oscar's holding up?"

Zoe nodded, taking off across the yard. As she ran, she hugged her injured arm close to her side, like it hurt to be jostled.

I took a deepish breath, then another. *Water. Pellets. Fruit ropes.* Last trip in, and then I'd be going *home*.

To my delight, I stumbled on the fruit ropes as soon as I stepped back into the kitchen—the crushed box had slid underneath the edge of the kitchen island and I almost tripped over it. *Sweet.* I tucked them under my arm. I just needed water—or juice boxes; whatever was drinkable—and pellets. The shavings for Jupiter's cage had been in a cabinet below the window. Maybe the pellets were in there too. I bent down and tried to open the door, but it was stuck shut.

Come on, I begged. I slapped my palm against the wood to jar it loose. I crammed my fingernails into the crack between the edge of the door and the rest of the cabinet, pulling to pry it open.

I sucked in another breath, my nose scrunching at the smell. I had to let it go—even if Jupiter's pellets were inside, I couldn't spend any more time trying to get them.

Fluids. I ran back to the cupboards, sweeping debris out of the way. No bottles of water; no boxes of almond milk. I shined my phone's flashlight in, hoping for the glimmer of a silver pack of juice pouches, at least. Nothing. My heart sank. I'd even take a bottle of prune juice and consider that a victory.

I turned to the sink. Maybe the water coming out of the faucet had gone back to normal. Gingerly, I turned the knob, holding my breath in hopes that the water would run out crystal clear—or at least clear-ish—but after a few seconds of a weird clanging, sucking noise, rusty brown came sputtering out again. The faucet shuddered from the effort. I turned it off. The shuddering continued.

It wasn't only the faucet. Everything was shuddering—an aftershock.

I dropped to my knees and hunched protectively, folding my arms over my head. *Why didn't I look up "earthquakes" in the encyclopedia and find out exactly what you're supposed to do when it starts shaking and you're already in a half-destroyed room full of potential missiles: heavy bags of lentils and little glass jars of spices that managed not to roll to their deaths on the floor? Not to mention swinging light fixtures and cabinet doors.* I whimpered, tightening every muscle in my body, like if somehow I turned myself rock solid, the ground would go back to being that way too.

Should I make a run for it back outside? *Outside.* What was going on out there? Were Zoe and Oscar okay? What if the tent had collapsed on them? Or what if a crack formed right underneath and then it fell inside…or the ground turned to that quicksand stuff below them. I gasped in a breath, pressing one hand to the floor. *What if* this *is the tremor that turns a gas leak into an explosion?*

I wobbled up to standing, then took off through the living room. The shaking wasn't as strong as the first aftershock. If the fridge hadn't already face-planted onto the kitchen floor, I don't think the current level of quaking could've toppled it. But still, I had to get out of the house. For all I knew, the tremor was just a warm-up.

I burst out of the screened porch, the door slamming behind me. The clatter seemed to echo in the silent outdoors. Zoe's head popped out of the opening in the cozy orange dome. Relief flooded me. They were okay.

The fish pond wasn't, though. The water in it sloshed back and forth like a wave pool at the water park. A mini tidal wave had formed. It rushed past the rocky boundary of the pond and deluged the grass. A much smaller scale of what had happened to the coast. To my dad. Had he been beyond the wave's reach? *Please don't let the wave have taken him.* I thought I might throw up.

"Hannah! It's shaking," Zoe called.

"I know!" But it was already ending. The pendulum wave in the fish pond slowed like a metronome coming to a stop.

In the newfound stillness, I fully felt how out of breath I was. I hunched with my hands on my thighs, begging my chest to relax and my lungs to fill. After they did, I put the fruit ropes in the wagon and slowly wheeled it toward the tent.

"Another aftershock," I called to Zoe, my voice portraying a calm I definitely hadn't felt while inside the trembling house. "It's over now. How's Oscar?"

Zoe shrugged. "The same, I guess."

I ducked inside the tent, which felt at least a couple of wonderful degrees warmer than outside. Body heat, I suppose. However, it was also starting to smell strongly of stinky bodies and wet socks. I sat down next to Oscar, who was lying on the cushion, his head propped up by a wad of blanket. He gazed up at me with bleary, pain-filled eyes. I thought my heart would snap into pieces.

"I got you the fruit ropes," I said gently, holding up the box. I reached in, pulled one out, and started to undo the cellophane wrapper for him. Whenever I was sick and my mom brought me Popsicles and Italian ice, she always undid the wrappers for me. Like she wanted every ounce of energy I had to go toward healing. It made me feel so safe to know that someone was there, making sure that I had all the care I could possibly need. Poor Oscar, who was hurt and also aware he wasn't getting any of the treatment he deserved. *He must be so scared.* I handed him the rope.

He stretched his arm out limply to take it. "I'm really thirsty, Hannah. But we're out of water."

"Completely?" I was hoping that at least a cup would be left, to wash down the remaining pain-reliever chewables.

He nodded.

My heart sank. I had nothing to offer him. Other than what was left in the scuzzy fish pond. This was another instance when Neha would probably be a much better, and more prepared, babysitter than me. She always has a water bottle. She says she just likes to stay hydrated, which is a good idea considering all that running on the soccer field. But I liked to tease her that the shiny silver water bottle she totes to class, on Main Street shopping trips, on the ferry, to my house, even to bed at night is her security blanket. Once she forgot it in her locker after school ended, and she actually convinced her dad to drive her back to get it.

Neha would have that water bottle on her if she were babysitting. And she probably would've had the foresight to start rationing the water, just in case, as soon as she realized that an earthquake had happened. I'd let us go through a jug in a single morning. I sighed.

There we were, stranded on an island suburb of Seattle, the city known for its constant rain—in fact, my clothes were still damp from this morning's downpour—and yet we had no water. That was irony. Water, water everywhere, and not a drop to drink.

Wait—this morning's downpour. I pictured the metal flowerpots spilling over with fresh rainwater that I'd navigated the wagon past. *We do have water.*

Except you can't drink rainwater collected from dirty metal pots. That's a surefire way to end up with some kind of horrible infection or disease like cholera. Whatever they got on the actual Oregon Trail. You'd have to purify it in order to drink it.

Another Neha memory popped into my head: standing in front of the stove with her mom, laughing as she dropped Neha's post-yogurt-shop-trash retainer into a pot of boiling water. *"Bye, yogurt germs."* Neha had looked skeptical. *"I promise this will kill them all,"* her mom had reassured.

We could drink that rainwater, if we boiled it first.

"Don't worry, we'll have plenty to drink," I said. "We just need to get that going." I pointed to the firepit.

flames—kind of like a grill? We could set the flowerpot on of that once the fire got going, which was a big help—I wouldn have to figure out how to string up the pot over an open flame.

The hardest part would be getting the fire started, and even that didn't seem terribly hard. I had matches, after all.

"These are good instructions," I said to Zoe. "Really clear." She'd penciled in tiny illustrations of each step , which made me smile:

1. Gather tinder, kindling, firewood, and a starter, such as matches.

2. Make a "bed" of tinder.

3. Arrange the kindling in a tent shape above the tinder.

4. Build a bigger tent of firewood over that.

5. Light the tinder from several sides, using the starter.

That was it. She'd even included the instructions for putting out a campfire:

14

ONE OF ZOE'S CONTRIBUTIONS to our emergency survival notebook, neatly copied from the Girl Scout Manual, was step-by-step instructions for building a fire. Of course, step one was preceded by a warning message, which she'd written in shout-y block letters: FIRES SHOULD ONLY BE BUILT AND STARTED UNDER THE SUPERVISION OF AN ADULT, SUCH AS A PARENT OR TROOP LEADER. DO NOT ATTEMPT TO START A FIRE ON YOUR OWN. WHEN BUILDING A CAMPFIRE, MAKE SURE TO DO SO IN A SAFE, DESIGNATE PLACE, SUCH AS A CAMPSITE FIREPIT. KEEP A BUCKET OF WATER (EXTINGUISHER HANDY FOR EMERGENCIES. AT ALL TIMES!!!

Well, until we started boiling it, we'd have a bucket rainwater handy. Or rather, a flowerpot. The other parts of warning message, regrettably, I had to ignore.

The Matlocks' firepit wasn't actually a pit. A small squ the yard had pebbly gravel instead of grass, bordered by stones. In the middle of the square sat a dark steel d the firepit. The top opened so you could put in logs, ar was even a flat grate over half the area that rested a

Start by sprinkling, not dumping, water on top. Stir
the embers around to make sure no sneaky coals
are left smoldering.

Zoe and I had returned to the carport and loaded the empty
wagon—we'd transferred all the food and other supplies into the
tent temporarily—with dry logs, sticks, and wads of newspaper.
Now we hunched in front of the firepit, Zoe handing me pieces
of tinder, which I tucked inside the belly of the pit. When I had
a nice little pyramid of tinder, I called for the kindling. That was
a lot harder to stack. The drawing in her instructions showed
that the sticks should rest in an upside-down cone shape. But
whenever I tried to rest them against one another, they'd topple
like dominoes. It took three tries until I got all the sticks stacked
and steady. Then I still had to pile on the big pieces of firewood,
without collapsing everything.

"Can you go get the—wait, never mind." I was going to ask Zoe
to fetch the flowerpot full of water, but then I remembered her
injury. I glanced at her arm. "How's your cut doing, by the way?"
She'd been itching at it earlier, and she still let her arm hang in her
lap, like she didn't want to overuse it. Or like it hurt to move.

She shrugged, pushing back her sleeve to check on the
bandage. It had picked up smears of dirt, but no bloodstains
were visible.

"Does it still hurt?" I asked. The skin around the bandage

looked kind of red. But maybe that was part of the healing process? I wished we'd had some antibiotic ointment to slather on it. Or that we still had water to spare—and soap—to keep it clean.

"Yeah," she answered. "But not like Oscar's leg."

No parts of us hurt like that, I supposed, feeling sympathetic pricks of pain in my own legs, from crouching.

"Wait here, and I'll get the water," I said. "Don't touch the matches!"

Zoe nodded, tapping the lid of the box.

It took me a few minutes to get over to the carport. I stopped, standing underneath its roof, and for the first time, stared at the driveway and out toward the road. Nothing stirred, not even the branches of the pine trees. What was left of them anyway. The yard was dead calm. I strained my ears, hoping to hear a sound from beyond the yard. If not a car coming along the road, then a siren from across the inlet, or an airplane overhead, making its descent into Sea-Tac.

I heard nothing. The quiet that I usually loved about our slice of the island had curdled into something worrisome.

I walked back at a quarter of my usual pokey pace, because I was terrified about spilling any water and also the full flowerpot was heavier than I expected. About halfway to the pit, my nose wrinkled. I sniffed. I smelled something like…smoke. I squinted. A parka-clad figure huddled on the log, her back to me. A curl of smoke rose above her toward the clouds.

"Zoe!" I lurched forward into a run, until water from the flowerpot sloshed onto the thick, insulated gardening gloves I'd put on. I'd figured it would be a good idea to have something like oven mitts to handle the metal pot with, once it had been heated up.

She turned in my direction. I made a very angry but slow march toward her and the crackling fire.

"What did I tell you about touching the matches?"

"Not to?" she replied. Reaching her, I gently set the water down next to the logs. The flames already licked up through the firepit's grates. It was a really good fire, actually. Not bad for our first try, especially considering how damp everything was. In addition to being a prodigy builder, Zoe must be some kind of fire-starting savant.

"You have to listen to me," I said. "I know you think you can do stuff on your own, but sometimes it's not safe. You're already hurt"—I pointed to her arm—"and I don't want anything else to happen to you." I stopped, feeling the prickle of déjà vu. Why did those words sound so familiar? Oh, right. I sounded exactly like my mom, whenever she chided me for forgetting my inhaler, or baking cookies when she wasn't home, or anything else that I was absolutely capable of doing but for some reason she refused to let me try.

You'd think that would make me take it all back, out of sympathy for Zoe. Except the person I felt sympathy for was my mom. It was *hard* being in charge of someone who thought she could handle a task that was, in fact, incredibly dangerous for her to do on her own. It was hard to feel the weight of responsibility on your shoulders, twenty-four hours of the day.

I wasn't actually angry with Zoe, I realized. She was a go-getter and smart and capable. I respected that she was eager to grow up and try things. I was only angry that there had been an opportunity for her to get hurt, and I'd failed to prevent it.

I wished I could tell my mom all that. Even more, I wished I'd understood these feelings when we had been in the car and I'd ducked her hug.

"You did a great job of starting the fire, though," I said. "You know, I'm really happy you're here to help me deal with all this." Zoe's face flushed as she hugged her coat tighter, poking at the firewood with a stick. She had a tiny smile. For a few minutes, we sat in silence, our cheeks warming as we watched the flames grow.

When they settled down a bit, I rested the flowerpot— carefully using its handle, thank goodness, so I didn't have to hold the sides right above the flames—on top of the grate. Then I closed the mesh-like dome over it.

"Should we bring Oscar out to see the fire?" Zoe asked.

"We could for a couple of minutes. I don't think that would hurt."

We settled him on the log next to Zoe. Woozy, he rested his head on her shoulder. Jupiter was safe in his box, tucked on the ground in between Zoe's feet. Jupiter! I'd forgotten about the problem of what to feed him.

"You guys don't know what guinea pigs eat other than pellets, do you?"

"We feed him carrots sometimes," Zoe said.

"We can't reach the ones in the fridge, and the garden hasn't grown any yet," I said. "Unfortunately, I couldn't get to his food. The cabinet is stuck shut."

"Just Google—oh," Oscar said.

"Yeah, I know," I said, ruefully. How weird that I wasn't even reaching for my phone anymore when I had a question.

Zoe rubbed her arm. "Look it up? In one of the encyclopedias…"

"You're right." In entries for animals, they usually tell what they eat. "I'll go get the *G* book. Don't touch anything while I'm gone." I gave Zoe a look like my mom always gives me when she knows I don't want to listen to her advice and probably won't.

It was good to step away from the firepit for a minute. The smoke wasn't helping my lungs. While crossing the yard, I went back to yoga breathing. In for four counts, out for eight. Or was it the other way around? Either way, I focused on filling both my belly and my chest with clean air. I visualized my lungs expanding like a balloon, even though they felt uninflated even at the top of a breath.

The screened porch still had a huge puddle of rainwater, but it hadn't spread to the box of books. I dug around until I found the *G* volume, which I tucked under my arm.

Turning to leave the porch, I realized how low the sun had sunk. The sky and clouds had a dusky haze. How had it gotten so late? Before we could leave for my house, we had to wait for the water to boil, then cool, pour it into the gallon jug, then pack up all our things and safely position Oscar in the wagon. Should I lock the house before we left? I didn't even know if there were keys somewhere inside. But who could possibly break in while we were gone? Anyway, the house already looked ransacked.

I would also need to leave a note for Andrea. Maybe tacked to the front door, where she'd see it right when she got back.

If she got back?

I pulled out my phone to check the time. Almost six. Realistically—at the rate we'd been moving, we wouldn't be ready before the sun set, and we absolutely couldn't travel to my house in the dark. We would need daylight to show us debris in our way, and other damage—downed wires or holes in the earth. Quicksand, like Beth Kajawa had mentioned. I shivered.

The safest thing would probably be to spend the night in the tent and go in the morning.

I slumped on the log next to the kids, resting the encyclopedia volume on my legs. "It's too late to leave for my house today."

Even though he'd fought leaving, Oscar's expression remained the same—not neutral, but pained.

"We're going to have to sleep in the tent."

"I don't mind," Zoe said, reaching to stoke the fire with her stick. She winced as she stretched her arm straight.

"Let me see your wound," I said, motioning for her to scoot toward me. She pushed up her sleeves. The skin around the bandage definitely looked redder, but maybe that was because Zoe had been itching at it all day. I worked my fingernail under the adhesive on one corner to lift it up for a peek, and I cringed.

The cut looked so much worse than yesterday. It was fiery and raised, and the swelling spread centimeters beyond the wound itself. Worse, there was a lot of yellowish…stuff.

"Oh, Zoe," I whispered. "That must be very painful." I carefully pressed the bandage back down.

She nodded, blinking back tears.

"It's okay to be upset when you're in pain," I said gently. "Why didn't you tell me it hurt so badly?"

She shrugged, apparently still unable to respond without crying.

I sighed. "Go inside the tent and rest for a few minutes. I'll finish the water and then make dinner."

We helped Oscar and Jupiter inside, and I came back out alone with the empty water jug and the big can of beans. I put on my gardening gloves and then very, very carefully transferred the bubbling pot off the grate and down to the gravel. It occurred to me that I could've gone back into the kitchen to get a real cooking pot to boil the water in, and maybe that would've been a lot easier and safer to handle. Oh well. I'd remember it for next time. There being a next time didn't seem totally unlikely.

Once it cooled, I carefully poured the contents of the pot into the water jug. It wasn't the clearest-looking water in the world, but it appeared a lot more drinkable than the gunky stuff coming out of the faucets.

I popped the top off the bean can and set it on the grating. The sun was low, and the glow of the firelight was kind of mesmerizing. It was actually a nice place to sit and rest—except for the smoke. That had thickened, and the breeze seemed to be playing a game of tag with me, so the trails of smoke followed me no matter which log I rested on. I rubbed at my eyes and coughed. My chest was tightening again. *The beans are probably warm enough. I could put the fire out.*

I trudged to the carport to get the other, smaller flowerpot of rainwater. The way the backyard curved, the carport was close to the woods. As I hefted up the pot, the breeze shifted and rustled all the surviving leaves and needles on the trees. I heard something else, a plaintive sound from deep in the forest. A coyote's howl.

Even though I was exhausted and hungry and my chest ached, and I was carrying a heavy pot of rainwater, I ran back like *I* was on fire. I dumped the water on the dying flames. I know the instructions said I should sprinkle it once the fire had shrunk to glowing embers, but I didn't want to wait in the yard for whatever was howling to find me standing there alone. It was time to hunker down in the tent for the night, that was for sure.

∧

Three spoons and one can of lumpy refried beans. Without rice or cheese, the beans weren't as tasty as I usually found them. Also, they had cooked inconsistently, with spots of the can holding much warmer bean goo than others. I swallowed the cold, dry spoonful I'd gotten and passed it to Zoe.

"When your mom was giving me instructions, she said we could eat these but only if we got 'really desperate.'" I paused. "Isn't it funny that we actually are?"

Oscar only moaned in response. He was reclining against a couch pillow that propped him up just enough to safely eat. We only had one pain-reliever chewable left, and I'd been saving it for an emergency. Like, what if one of us suddenly got a very high fever?

But looking at Oscar, weak and miserable, it seemed cruel not to give it to him right then. I kept picturing him the afternoon before the quake—jumping around on the couch, smiling and laughing. All his happy energy had curdled into fear and pain. It was heartbreaking to witness.

Zoe had gotten quieter too. She stirred her spoon in the bean can, clanging it against the sides. "I don't think it's very funny."

My shoulders curved inward like I was deflating. I shouldn't have tried to make a lighthearted joke. At least, not about something their mom had said—or our pathetic food situation. I just couldn't get over how Andrea's throwaway statement had actually come true. There were moments when I paused and thought, *Is this real life? Have we really been alone for over forty-eight hours? Are we actually living in a tent in the backyard?* If Neha were there, she'd understand. She would've laughed and riffed about us having to make literal stone soup next. Sometimes the only way to deal with the bizarreness of life is to find the humor in it—both Neha and I understood that.

I felt a pang like homesickness. *I miss her so much.* And I missed my actual home, and my parents, and the boring everyday details of life that don't seem wondrous until you no longer experience them: a sip of fresh clean water from the faucet, the buzz of a text message from a friend, the soft glow of the reading lamp you flick on at nightfall.

"We should feed Jups," Zoe reminded me.

"Right!" I said, grabbing the *G* encyclopedia. I flipped until I found the entry for guinea pigs. "Let me see…" I scanned the page. "Did you know they have tails? They're just not visible on the outside. Oh, hey! This is great. It says they don't actually require water to drink."

"No way. Jupiter sips from his water bottle all the time," Oscar said.

"That's because he eats pellets—dried food. If they're fed fresh vegetation, they don't need to drink. And look here," I pointed to the entry. "Guinea pigs eat grass." I grinned. "We still have a yard full of that. And in the morning, it will be nice and dewy too."

"I'm getting him some now. He must be starving," Zoe said, bolting for the tent door.

"Wait—" I didn't want her in the yard by herself—not after hearing howls from the woods—but she was only reaching her good arm out, tugging up handfuls of fresh, clean grass, which she plopped on the bottom of Jupiter's box. He squeaked happily and did a little hop before he started nibbling the blades.

"I'm sorry you were so hungry, Jups." I picked up a bit of the grass and rolled it between my fingers. Still damp from the rain, it would be good enough to keep Jupiter hydrated. I pulled his water bottle—mostly full—out of the box and set it next to the water jug. We'd only taken sips of the boiled rainwater during dinner, partly to ration it and partly because it had a strange metallic taste. Not surprising, considering the source.

Our next indicator of true desperation would be drinking from a guinea pig's water bottle.

I really, really hoped it wouldn't come to that.

By the time the bean can was empty, it was fully dark outside the tent—inside, we had our flashlight, whose beam was weakening. It seemed foolish to keep it on, especially when we had no idea how much juice the batteries had left. The only thing that made sense to do was go to bed.

I unzipped the tent and darted out to deposit the bean can over by the firepit. The edges were jagged, and I didn't want anyone to accidentally slice themselves. When I crawled back inside, I remembered that my phone needed to be recharged—the battery had dipped precariously low again. If it got too cold at night, it might die altogether, and what if a text finally came through? I couldn't miss it.

"Where's the emergency radio?" I asked, tossing around the blankets to find it. The more I overturned them and didn't see it, the more panic started to set in.

"Over here." Zoe motioned to the space between her and Oscar.

I exhaled, feeling the flutter in my chest release. "Thank goodness. I need to charge before we turn in."

"We're going to sleep already?" Zoe wrinkled her nose. "We just ate dinner. Our bedtime is nine."

"What else are we going to do in a totally dark tent? And aren't you exhausted?" I was bone-tired, as my grandma would say.

"No, I'm not sleepy." Zoe was getting more and more contrary. Maybe she was still mad about the lies I'd told. Or maybe it was simply because her arm hurt.

"Well, do you want to charge my phone with the radio?

Maybe that'll make you tired." I offered a smile. Also, cranking the charger took a surprising amount of effort. I didn't want to get wheezier.

She shrugged. "Sure." I handed over my phone, which she hooked into the charger part of the emergency radio. She started turning the crank, vigorously, with her uninjured arm, gripping the radio in her other hand.

"I don't think you have to spin it so fast to get it to work, and we actually do have all night." But she didn't slow down. It made me nervous how hard she was whipping the crank. "Come on, Zoe, be gentle with it. It's not a toy." I sounded just like my mom.

She didn't listen. She gripped the crank and turned it even faster, giggling. I thought of Neha in the babysitting course, asking Mrs. Pinales how to handle a kid who wouldn't listen or behave. What was I supposed to do—give her some space to settle down on her own? I watched Zoe warily. She was literally winding herself up.

The snap sounded like something heavy stepping on a brittle twig: crisp and sharp. At first, I thought it had come from outside, and I started to bring my index finger to my lips, to signal to the kids to be quiet so I could listen. But then I saw Zoe's mouth form a perfect O of surprise, which melted into a grimace after she realized that the radio no longer tethered her hands together. We both looked to the hand she held up in slow motion. The crank had been severed from the radio. The tip of the plastic was jagged, where it had broken free. It's like Zoe was brandishing a tiny sword in defiance of me.

We'd never have enough sunlight to use the radio's solar-powered option. That tiny piece of red plastic was our lifeline. Without it, the radio was worthless. Without it, we had no way to charge my phone.

No way to listen to Beth Kajawa reporting the news from the rest of the city, or bulletins that would tell us things essential to our own safety—and survival.

No way of knowing if our loved ones might be looking for us.

If they might be safe.

If they might be alive.

"Why didn't you listen to me?" My voice was a low hiss, unrecognizable to me. I began shaking, like the ground had. The feelings bubbling up in me were seismic. Every worry I'd pushed down, every drop of anger and fear and sadness and shocking disbelief. They tumbled out of me now, more powerful than I could control. "I told you to be gentle! Do you know how important that radio is? We're completely cut off without it!"

Zoe's bottom lip quivered. She looked devastated. I *knew* it was an accident, I *knew* she felt terrible now, and I *knew* I'd made plenty of mistakes of my own since the earthquake—ones with terrible consequences. Things even more precious than the radio had broken.

But I erupted anyway. "What's going to happen when my phone dies? When the flashlight batteries run out?" My gasping breaths filled the silence between my shouts. "We'll be stuck in the *dark*! Literally and figuratively! It's all *your* fault!"

"Stop yelling," Oscar cried, as he tried to turn away from me and pull the blanket over his head—but, after grimacing and yowling when he attempted to shift onto his side, he kept his supine position, covering his ears and eyes with a pillow. "Stop fighting!" Jupiter chattered as though in agreement.

I paused to catch my breath. It had felt so good to yell, to get mad. I hadn't realized how furious I was. I was a bubbling-over pot and the lid had lifted. Once the steam of bad feelings was released, I settled down immediately, and as soon as I did, I understood it wasn't Zoe I was mad at, even if she'd broken the radio. I was mad at the world. At the earth, specifically the sneaky Juan de Fuca plate, for putting us in this position, for ruining my utopia, and for hurting people I loved.

But now it was Zoe's turn to get angry. "It was an accident!" she shrieked.

Her arm was injured. She probably had a harder time cranking because of that. We were all exhausted and loopy. "I know—" I started.

"No, you *don't* know. You don't even know how to pitch a tent or build a fire. Because you're a kid, just like us. And I *don't* have to listen to you—because you're not our mother." She spoke so furiously that spittle was flying out of her raw, angry mouth. Tears streamed from her eyes. "You're a *liar*." Behind her, Oscar began to cry.

"Zoe. I'm sorry. I shouldn't have yelled at you like that." I paused. "I know it was an accident."

"Just shut up!"

"You're not supposed to say that!" Oscar wailed.

"Who cares? Mom's not here now! And we don't know if she's ever coming back. She could be dead!" Zoe, hysterical, snatched Jupiter and crawled to the far end of the tent. In between us, Oscar sobbed. I wheezed, head in my hands. I felt like I'd been punched.

She'd said it. She'd said the thing we'd all thought but were too afraid to say out loud. *Ever coming back. Could be dead.* Her words lingered in the thick air inside the tent. The orange walls pulsed with their energy, their pain, their fear.

I was both angry and relieved that she'd said it out loud. "Zoe…"

"Don't talk to me. Don't come near me. That's your side of the tent. This is mine."

I sank to my knees next to Oscar. "Are you okay?"

He nodded weakly.

"Do you need more Tylenol?" I was desperate to make something better inside the tent. Even if it meant using up the last precious chewable.

"I just want to sleep." The pillow was back over his eyes and ears.

"Okay," I said.

There was a blanket that neither had claimed next to him, balled up against the tent door. I rolled myself up in it. There was no pillow for my head, or cushions for my aching body, and the ground was surprisingly rough and spiky underneath the tent fabric. Something sharp pressed into my shoulder blades as I lay down. Even with the blanket double-wrapped around me, it was ice cold next to the ground. I shivered. What we should be doing is sleeping huddled together, to conserve body heat, but fighting really didn't allow for that.

Soon, I could hear snoring from the other parts of the tent. Two different patterns of light snores, telling me both kids had fallen asleep. I was vaguely impressed. As exhausted as I was, I didn't know if I ever would rest again. You needed a certain amount of security to fall asleep, confidence that the world will be waiting for you when you woke up. I'd lost that.

I kept stifling my coughs. Even if I couldn't sleep, it was important the kids did. If there was any hope of us making up and moving on tomorrow, it hinged on them not being exhausted and cranky. But the damp, chilly air was making my lungs worse. I rolled over, and my phone pressed sharply into my hip. It took some unraveling, but I managed to free my arm from the blanket roll to pull it out.

Ten percent battery. It wasn't going to last much longer. It would be smart to save every ounce of battery I had, in case we needed the flashlight app. But there were things I needed to say, even if the people I wanted to say them to might never have a chance to read them. To Neha:

I'm really sorry for everything I said. I didn't mean it. I want to be your friend now and forever. I don't know how many times over the past two days I've thought about you, something funny you'd say or something I wanted to share with you, or a way you'd step in and get things done like you're always so good at doing. I miss you. I realize now that no matter how many other friends we have, no matter if our activities and stuff change and we're not Always Being Partners, you're still going to be my best friend.

Because that other F in BFF means forever.

Wherever you are right now, I'm hoping you're okay.

I need you to be, all right?

I wiped away a tear and rubbed my sniffling nose. The next two were going to be even harder to type out, and not because I was in low-battery mode so the screen had started dimming if I paused in my typing for more than a half second. They were going to be the kind of messages that break what's left of your heart.

I get it now, Mom. How hard it is to be responsible for someone else and to want to keep them safe. And how to stay strong for others when you are dealing with your own stuff. I'm so sorry I was cranky in the car. I just want to go back in time and dive in

for your hug. And as long as I'm going back in time, I'd grab my inhaler off the nightstand before I left my bedroom too.

Please come home soon. I need you. And I love you.

The collar of my shirt was soaked with tears by the time I set my phone down after pressing send on that text. I knew it wasn't going anywhere, but I had to keep trying.

The last message I started and stopped. Started and stopped. Started again, and then through the tears I remembered what Beth Kajawa had said on the radio, how she was also worried about friends and family in the tsunami zone. She'd told us all to keep hope alive. So I changed my message.

I am keeping hope alive. For you.

Dad, just try your best.

Because that was what he always asked me to do.

I pressed send and curled into myself, tucking my head into the top of the blanket roll. I squeezed my eyes shut and imagined the texts zipping through wires, or space, or however text messages ping from one phone to another. I imagined Neha, my mom, and my dad all smiling as their phones lit up and they saw my messages. That was the only way I could stop the tears.

15

THERE WAS A NOISE outside the tent.

Even though I'd thought sleep would never come to me, I had eventually fallen into it deeply. I was in a weird position, so when I woke my left arm was numb and prickly, and that side of my face was freezing cold from being pressed against the tent floor. It felt like there was straw in my mouth from it being so dry. Every other part of me was damp and chilled. I wiggled my way to a seated position, because my blanket roll-up had held tight so far. Maybe I'd simply been too cold to toss and turn in my sleep.

I strained to listen. Something was moving through the brush, into the backyard. *Is someone here to help us?* I didn't have my bearings, so I wasn't sure which way I was facing in the tent. I squinted into the pitch darkness. If the zippered door was in front of me, then the house was in that direction too. The noise—swishes of grass and the occasional snap of a twig—wasn't from there. Whatever—or whoever—it was, it had come from the forest preserve.

A ranger? Hope swelled in my chest. Maybe one had been in there during the quake. Cataloging trees or something, or holed up in one of the research sheds. Maybe it had taken this long for the ranger to find a way out of the forest…but a ranger would notice the reflective fabric of our orange tent in the moonlight and then would call out to us. Right?

More twigs snapped. Whatever was lumbering toward the tent was heavy. It breathed hard—I could relate—but I'd never heard a human snuffle like that. It was a distinctly animal noise. Same as the sounds of its movement.

Coyotes didn't lumber and neither did deer. They tiptoed. None of the small creatures of the forest could make that snuffling sound—and I didn't think I was exaggerating how loud it was, just because it was dark and any middle-of-the-night backyard noises were unfamiliar and freaky.

I heard a light scraping and then the nylon fabric rippled as something, massive and furry, brushed up against the tent. My eyes had adjusted enough to the darkness so I could see an outline as it pressed its body against our little dome.

It was, unmistakably, the shape of a full-grown bear.

Our tent was full of snacks. Not to mention us. Although to the creature outside, I suppose we could be considered snacks too.

I held my breath, because I didn't want it to hear me wheeze and know that the creatures inside the tent were neither the strongest nor the most capable of fighting back or dashing away.

Weak gazelle, I thought. We couldn't even run, thanks to Oscar's leg and my asthma.

The bear hadn't brushed up against our tent again. Maybe it had only been passing through, and now it was gone on its way. With the porch door hanging open, it would be easy for the bear to get inside the house. Once in the kitchen, it would have a smorgasbord of food options—bears didn't mind finding a meal by digging through trash.

A chill ran down my spine as I pictured it hanging around the kitchen and thought about how it could have surprised us, if we'd dashed back in for supplies.

I jolted when I heard a clang from the direction of the firepit. The clang repeated, along with a light growl. *The beans of desperation!* I'd left the can out there, and even though we'd eaten the contents greedily, stubborn bean remnants stuck to the sides and especially near the sharp part around the top. The bear must've smelled the beans. That's what led him, hungry, over to us.

Why, why, why did I leave food out in the open? I knew not to do that. We had special garbage cans outside with lids that prevented bears from rooting through them. Even though my dad loves birds, we don't keep feeders in our yard—because the deer and the bears will eat all the food. And when I'd gone camping with the Girl Scouts, we'd been careful to secure our food overnight to not attract any animals. Although I'd thought they were only worried about raccoons and rodents.

The bear wouldn't find much to satisfy its hunger in that bean can. Then would it come back to sniff around us? What would we do if it tried to get inside the tent? The fabric was great at keeping out bugs and rain, but a bear's claws would slice through like our shelter was made of tissue paper.

I needed to get the bear away.

Wait... Oscar had been talking about this, when we were filling in our emergency survival notebook. I slowly inched in the direction of his cushion, where Oscar still lay fast asleep. The notebook was next to his head. I picked it up and the flashlight too. I flipped through the pages until I reached the one I was looking for. Zoe had sketched a bear standing on its hind legs next to my wobbly handwriting.

If you see a bear don't run. Make
noise, and back away slowly.

I vaguely remembered someone, maybe my mom, telling me that bears can always outrun people, so during an attack running is rarely an effective escape strategy. In terms of backing away slowly, we weren't face-to-face with a bear, so we didn't have to do that...yet. But I could make noise. If that scared it enough, maybe it would run back into the woods on its own and leave our tent alone. A totally nonconfrontational escape. That would be ideal.

My fingers were trembling so hard that I struggled to work my phone out of my pocket. I swiped to unlock the screen and pressed open the music app. I dragged the volume icon to the max point, and then I pressed play. Pop music blared, jolting everyone else in the tent awake.

"What are you doing?" Zoe yelled from the other side of the tent. "That's so loud! It's the middle of the night." Even groggy, she sounded mad at me.

I let out a nervous laugh. "Good thing there's nobody around to hear."

"But *we're* sleeping," Oscar groaned.

"I couldn't." I had to shout over the volume. "Music always helps!"

"Blasting dance music? Helps you sleep?" Zoe shouted back.

If I told them what was outside the tent, what I was trying to frighten away, they'd be too scared to ever go back to bed. They'd panic, and doesn't that attract predators like bears? Can't they smell the fear or something?

I looked down at the phone in my hand. The battery had dropped to 8 percent. I had to conserve every—amp? Volt? Watt? I don't know what unit of energy a cell phone battery is measured in. Regardless, I had few left, and they were precious. Now that the kids were awake, though, together we could make enough noise to scare Mr. Bear away.

It's funny how adding "Mr." makes even something like a hungry, prowling bear seem less terrifying.

I turned off the phone. "If it's too loud for you, we'll do this a capella." I cleared my throat and started to shout-sing the lyrics. My voice was hoarse and the lingering tightness in my chest made it kind of hard to belt out the words without feeling light-headed. When Zoe and Oscar didn't immediately chime in, I paused. "Come on, you guys! One time through, then we can go back to sleep." I grabbed a thick encyclopedia volume and beat it like a drum in time with my singing.

Oscar and Zoe joined in, their voices weak and wary. I strained to hear if there were any lingering noises outside the tent. I watched the sides to see if the fabric would be brushed up against another time. Or clawed at. I didn't hear any clanging of the bean can.

After we finished the last line, the only sound was my wheezing and Oscar whimpering. "I want the Tylenol now."

"Okay," I said, reaching through my layers into my other vest pocket, where I'd been safekeeping the vial. I handed him the last chewable. "Drink some water to wash it down." I helped him take a hearty sip from the jug. I couldn't see the water line in the dark but it felt less than half full.

"That water tastes so awful." He sputtered.

"I know—I'm sorry."

It remained quiet and still outside the tent. My heart rate slowed. We'd scared it away.

Zoe flopped back down in her corner, after tucking Jupiter safely inside the box. Oscar was already conked out in the middle. I lay back in my blanket roll, but I couldn't sleep. I wouldn't sleep. I'd let my guard down, and then a bear had come. If I hadn't woken up—would it have tried to get inside the tent? I pictured its claws—each as long and thick as one of my fingers—ripping through the tent walls. I could almost smell its meaty breath, see the saliva dripping from its part-time carnivore teeth. Would it have eaten us? What little food was in my stomach churned at the possibility.

Someone had to be vigilant at all hours, and I was the only available someone. Everyone I trusted was gone. And, like Zoe had said, they might never be coming back.

What was going to happen to us?

I didn't have the energy to wipe my tears. They felt good as they trickled down my face—clean against my dirty, cold-chapped cheeks. The harder I cried, the more shallow and ragged my breaths became. I tucked my head to my chest and scrunched down into my blanket.

We're not safe in the house. We're not safe on the porch. We're not safe in the tent. And we're not safe with me in charge.

We couldn't keep going like this. As soon as daylight arrived—ready or not, we had to leave. Thanks to Dad, we'd find safety at my house; I was sure of it. If we survived the newly remade wilderness to get there.

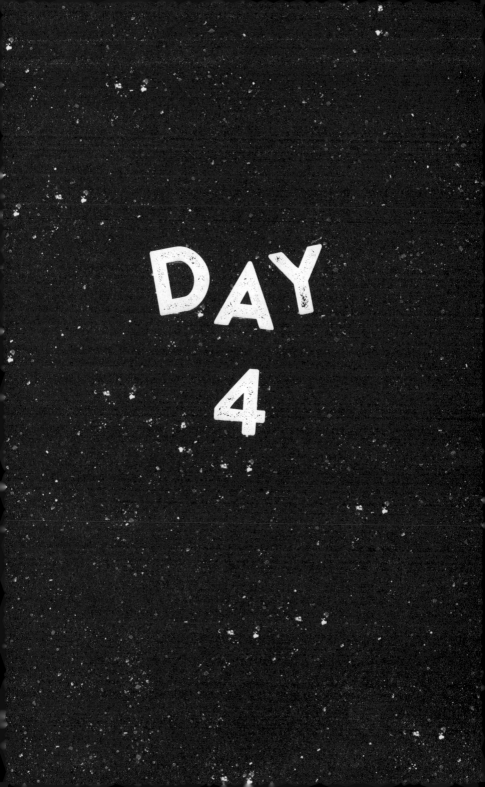

windbreaker and long sleeve, I could feel his fingers digging into my skin, desperate to stop me.

"Whoa, sorry!" He hadn't reacted so strongly any other time I'd looked at his injury. "Is the pain a lot worse today?" Between sobs, he nodded.

Enough of the fabric had been freed from underneath the splint so I could pull it back without actually touching him. When I did, I gasped. The bruising was an even deeper shade of purple. It spread up his shin and down toward his foot. The skin on the rest of his lower leg—the parts that weren't purplish—was pale, strangely tight, and shiny looking. Almost like the glistening plastic legs that Barbie dolls have. Something was very wrong.

"Can you still move your toes?"

He grimaced. "It's hard to wiggle them. Everything feels like pins and needles."

"And it wasn't like that yesterday?" He shook his head no. "I'll look this up in the medical book."

I scrounged around on the tent floor, searching for the faded blue cover of the home medical guide. When I finally found it, I flipped to the page where I'd folded the edge to mark the entry for sprains and fractures. I skimmed the text, looking for anything about shiny skin or tingling. My finger stopped on a sidebar about "Acute Compartment Syndrome":

16

"HANNAH. HANNAH." EACH CRY of my name was [...] ated by a moan. The light in the tent was dim. I [...] only getting started outside. It couldn't be later than 6:4[...]

I rubbed my eyes and sat up, surprised I'd ever fall[...] asleep, and a little disappointed in myself too. So much [...] vigilance.

"What is it, Oscar?"

"More Tylenol."

My heart sank. "We don't have any left." I unrolled [...] although somehow in the night I'd squirmed my way [...] the blanket so that my bottom half was uncovered and [...] was all twisted. When I finally tried to stand, my kne[...] made crackling noises. Every part of me ached. Probabl[...] the damp chill or how much running around I'd done [...] before, or both.

I crawled over to him. "Let me see how your leg is [...] When I adjusted the splint to roll up his pant leg, he scr[...] and grabbed my arm. Even through the layers of park[...]

This painful syndrome happens when swelling and pressure, after an injury, build up in a "compartment"— such as an arm or a leg. This may happen very suddenly after an injury, and it presents a surgical emergency. If pressure is not decreased, it can cause nerves and muscles in the affected area to die. This can begin to happen within just four to eight hours.

Watch for these warning signs of acute compartment syndrome:

- Severe pain, which may become worse with touch to or movement of the affected area
- Discomfort that is not ameliorated by pain relievers
- Loss of feeling in the area
- Skin that appears pale, shiny, and tight
- "Pins and needles" sensation, tingling, or numbness

Seek immediate medical attention. Temporary first aid may include loosening any bandages or wraps covering the area, and raising the affected limb to heart level.

I swallowed hard. Check, check, check, check, and check. We needed to get Oscar to a hospital or find a doctor. *Fast.*

First, though, I could at least loosen the hair ties that fastened his splint. "This might ease the pain. Hold my hand," I said, offering my left for him to squeeze. Oscar took it; his palms were ice-cold and clammy. I ran my thumb soothingly over the back of his hand, the way my mom always does when she holds my mine during something scary or sad or uncomfortable, like getting a filling at the dentist. I carefully slid the bottom elastic off his foot. Oscar gripped my hand so tightly it felt like he could snap my bones.

"Is that any better?" He shook his head, reconsidered, and then nodded. I really hoped the homemade splint hadn't somehow made the compartment syndrome worse, or had caused it.

Somehow Zoe slept through all this. "Zoe?" I called. We needed to pack up our essentials, get Oscar into the wagon—with his leg somehow elevated, if we could figure that out—and leave. Once we were at my house, I'd figure out what to do next. Maybe, if we were lucky, my phone would pick up service over there.

Zoe didn't stir. "Zoe!" I called again, my tone sharper. This wasn't the time for sleeping in, no matter how cozy her pile of blankets might feel.

She mumbled something at me but still didn't sit up. Grumbling, I crawled to her side of the tent. Her face was really flushed—weird, considering how cold it was inside and out. My exhales were cottony white puffs. Combined with my wheezing, it was like I was imitating a freight train struggling to push itself up a mountainside.

"I don't feel good," Zoe said, finally opening her red-rimmed eyes and squinting at me.

"What's wrong?" I reached out my hand and pressed it to her forehead, like my mom always does whenever I say those four words. Zoe's skin radiated heat. I didn't know if she was actually burning up with a fever—which is what it felt like—or if I couldn't judge temperature well because of the coldness of my hand-as-measuring-device. I pressed it to my own forehead, which felt almost as cool as my fingertips. No matter what, Zoe was too warm for someone who'd spent the night in fortyish-degree tent.

Did she have the flu? My eyes fell on the water jug and narrowed to a squint. The water was tinged greenish yellow. She could have gotten sick from it, even though we'd boiled it… Although Oscar and I had been drinking it, too, and neither of us felt feverish. *Or is she sick from her cut?*

"Hey, show me your arm." She limply raised it for me. When I pushed up her sleeves, my stomach twisted. The skin underneath was bright red, with a few fiery streaks. I scraped at the edges of her bandage and lifted a corner. Then I gagged. The wound hadn't scabbed over at all. It was an angry red, puffy and oozing something green. There was no question. It had gotten infected. Badly.

My chest became tight like a vise. I coughed to release the pressure, then again. Carefully, I pressed the bandage back down.

"Does it look gross?" Zoe asked.

I nodded. "You need antibiotics." There were some in my house. My dad had a bad cold last month, and he thought it might be a sinus infection. The doctor at the urgent-care clinic prescribed him a course of antibiotics but said to wait another day before starting them to see if he got better on his own first. And then he did, so he never used the medicine. Dad was going to return the pills to the pharmacy when we refilled my inhaler. But for now, the vial of antibiotics was still in the medicine cabinet. "Good news: there are some at my house." I know you're not supposed to share medications *ever*, but this was an emergency. What if Zoe didn't take any and wound up getting gangrene or something? What if they had to amputate her arm?

"Then let's head over there."

I smiled at her. "My thoughts exactly." She offered a half smile back. I guess we'd at least reached a truce. Or maybe she felt too awful to still be angry with me. "We have plenty of children's Tylenol at my house too."

Zoe looked sheepish, as she reached into her coat pocket with her good hand. She pulled out a red-and-white vial. "I found this in the bathroom. I kept it…for an emergency. There's only one pill left inside. It's not the children's kind, so Oscar couldn't take it," she added quickly.

And she'd kept that from me? I felt a prickle of anger that she hadn't handed it over right away. I opened my mouth, ready to snap at her to never do that again.

Then I thought of the sing-along last night; I hadn't told her or Oscar about the bear. The first morning, I had also gone into the bathroom to listen to the radio on my own. I wasn't trying to be sneaky by withholding information; I was trying to be smart. To protect them. Even if I didn't agree with what she'd done, maybe Zoe had felt the same. Maybe she had wanted a chance to be the hero.

"Exactly how old are you?" I asked.

"Ten," Zoe said. "And three months."

I thought for a moment. "You should take the medicine." I would need her help today—to get Oscar into the wagon and to carry things once we were on our way. She couldn't help us if she had a fever and if her arm was pulsing with pain. Once we got to my house, we'd have access to other medicines. Then, until the antibiotics kicked in, she could go back to taking children's Tylenol.

Zoe was tall for her age, not much smaller than me, and I had already graduated to the regular kind. But to be sure, I compared the two pill bottles. My mom always double-checked the dosage instructions before giving me any medicine. The label said the children's had 160 milligrams in each chewable, and you could take two every four hours. The adult pill was 325 milligrams, so that was about the same as one children's dose anyway.

I held out the pill while Zoe reached for the water jug, wrinkling her nose when she saw the color inside. She popped the tablet into her mouth and took a swig. I could tell she had to force down the swallow.

"Great. Now let's hitch up the wagon and go."

We lingered at the top of the driveway. Oscar lay in the red wagon, nestled atop a layer of blankets. We'd positioned couch pillows in a stack below his foot, to keep the injured leg elevated. I'll never forget how hard he cried as we lifted him in and carefully, gently arranged his leg. He convulsed with sobs, howling every time his leg moved the slightest bit. The ride to my house would be bumpy under normal conditions—Forestview Drive was old and potholey. After the quake, who knew what shape it would be in. I shuddered. It was going to hurt Oscar so much to drag him in the wagon, but that was the only way to get him help.

In his lap was Jupiter's box, which Oscar clung to with both hands. Zoe tucked our *In Case of Emergency* notebook next to him. We were all wearing the raincoats over our parkas, making us look as puffed up as Violet Beauregarde after she ate Willy Wonka's gum. The current precipitation was a light drizzle—just spitting, as my dad would say, but you never know when the sky will suddenly open up on Pelling Island.

The earth too, apparently.

I tore out a page from the notebook and scribbled a note to Andrea or anyone who might eventually come looking for us:

> We went to the Steele house next door. Will try to get help from there. O and Z are injured and need a doctor! We have Jupiter too.

I added the date and stuck it to the front door with a bandage. I felt bad using one from our small supply, but I wanted to make sure the note didn't blow away in the breeze and that was my only adhesive.

Some stuff we had to leave in the tent: the heavy encyclopedia books, the broken radio, and the larger couch cushions. We packed up the scraps of leftover food, the remaining first aid supplies, the dimming flashlight, and the mostly full water bottle from Jupiter's cage. The jug of water we'd finished off after Zoe took her pill. When I realized that none of us had needed a trip to the bathroom bushes since waking up, it seemed pretty likely that we were dehydrated.

While Zoe had been pulling things together inside the tent and Oscar was resting—meaning, he was lying down with his eyes closed, occasionally letting out a sharp exhalation of pain somewhere between a shriek and a cry—I'd sneaked over to the firepit. The bean can I found hiding behind one of the logs. Nothing was left inside, not a single speck of dried refried bean paste, but in the soft mud around the firepit, I saw the evidence I'd been looking for: paw prints. A triangular-shape pad, ringed at the top by five ovals like toe prints. With sharp notches above them, from large claws. It perfectly matched both the bear print sketched in our emergency survival notebook, for identification purposes, and also the photo that I'd taken of the prints book page.

Yup. Mr. Bear had been there.

Before we headed down the driveway, I turned to finally face the front of the house. Half the windows were shattered. Broken eaves over the door dangled. I might be imagining it, but one spot of the roof looked like it was sinking. A few sand volcanoes dotted the front yard too, and one of the big trees tilted danger-ously toward the house. If another aftershock happened—that tree could come crashing down. Maybe taking the house with it. It looked dilapidated, utterly unlike the cheery home I'd walked up to days before, after waving goodbye to Mr. Fisk and the bus. That afternoon felt like a lifetime ago.

"Let's get going," I said. "Keep pace with us, Zoe." She was on her shiny purple scooter, which we'd found, unscathed, among the rubble of the carport as we passed through. I thought it would be easier for her to scoot instead of walk alongside the wagon and me.

The condition of the driveway made me think of Neha. We loved experimenting with face masks at sleepovers, some that we mixed up using a "beauty cookbook" that Neha's mom had on the kitchen shelf: oatmeal, avocado, honey, yogurt, etc., but my favorites were always the single-use packets of mud mask from the drugstore that we bought with saved-up allowance. I liked the sensation of the creamy mud tightening on your face as it dries, and how if you make any facial expressions once the mask is set, a funny pattern of lines and cracks forms in the goo. Neha and I would have a challenge similar to a staring contest while wearing them—trying to make each other laugh, and then seeing whose mask held up the best with the least cracks.

Anyway, the driveway reminded me of those hardened masks. It had been a neat, even, unbroken black asphalt surface when I came over. Now, it was riddled with fissures and uneven spots where the pavement dipped or rose in a strange new topography. I dragged the wagon as gently as possible, and avoided going over all the fallen branches and other debris, but it could only bump along, as Oscar whimpered.

I turned back to say, "Tell me if you need to rest, Oscar." I felt like *I* would be the one needing the rest. The overloaded wagon was heavy and so was my loaded backpack. We'd barely eaten breakfast, and my stomach felt hollow and angsty. No matter how much I tried to clear my lungs with coughs, my breath came out in half-hearted wheezes. Things were a bit spinny, like how you feel after going on a carousel or trying to hold your breath underwater. I don't know if that was from lack of air or food or both.

We just have to make it to my house. It'll be okay once we're there. We'll have my inhaler. Antibiotics. Tylenol. Bandages and ointment and those little alcohol wipes. And fresh water and food.

Fresh water sounded amazing. I turned to stare at Jupiter's water bottle, tucked next to Oscar in the wagon. No, that wasn't a line I was ready to cross, drinking from a guinea pig's bottle.

You can't see the road from the Matlocks' yard, because the foliage is so thick. The trees that dot the driveway become sparse at the end, so the sky suddenly opens up and then you can clearly see the road and the forest preserve sign. As I tugged the wagon to the end, Zoe stopped rolling next to me. The mailbox had fallen down, lying in our path and marking a line between the Matlocks' and the road. Between us and the world. It was time to cross it. It was time to see what was on the other side.

17

OUR STREET—FORESTVIEW DRIVE—WAS WHERE I learned to pedal a two-wheeler, where I attempted a few almost completely unsuccessful lemonade stands. (It's hard to sell lemonade, even for a quarter, when there are no passersby. One time I was saved when a group of people on a bike tour stopped and took pity on me.) I knew each of its gentle curves, alongside of which thin white fencing separated the shoulder from the grass and evergreens. I'm pretty sure that even blindfolded, I would be able to walk the length of Forestview without trouble.

After the quake, I didn't recognize it.

The asphalt had broken up like pan of peppermint bark after it's cooled—a once smooth, unbroken (minus a few potholes) surface splintered into uneven chunks and crumbles. In some places there was just a small fissure between the pieces; in others, a big crevasse had formed. Below the layer of blacktop, sandy soil like a graham-cracker crust was visible. The speed limit signpost across from the end of the Matlocks' driveway had slumped so far toward a rising chunk of road that the sign almost kissed the pavement. The normally neat, clearly defined shoulder was a jumble of rocks, dirt, and grass. Fallen trees were splayed across the road, their big branches tickling into the cracks.

It was eerily quiet all around us. Even the breeze was missing. In the stillness we stood, gaping at the path we had to take, the obstacles we were going to have to cross. The sky above was the color of Earl Grey tea. The clouds hung heavy with impending rain. For a moment, I thought about turning around, heading straight back to the tent. I tried to rationalize staying put: *What if one of our parents makes it back to the Matlocks' house and somehow misses us on the way? And our note has blown away, so they don't know where we are...* Well, then they would keep looking for us. That wasn't going to happen, anyway. Forestview Drive is the only road into the preserve and past our houses. We would be on it till we got to my house. Then, once we were inside, one of us could keep watch on the road through the picture window in the living room. We could also stick up a few emergency cones, which my dad has stacked in the garage, and put a sign in the street. Then nobody would miss us.

We cannot stay here. No matter how scary it was to leave. I reminded myself of all we needed: More supplies. A place where my phone might work, while it still had a charge. A way to get help from a doctor.

And then there was Mr. Bear, who might come back again in the night. Or in the daytime, if he (or she, I really didn't know) was as desperate as we'd become for food. Maybe the bear was in a similar predicament. Its house in the forest could have been destroyed too. Sympathy didn't make me less scared of it, though.

I looked at the cracked road, then over at Zoe. "I don't think you can scoot through this, Zoe. Maybe it's best to leave that here." I pointed to her scooter. She nodded and lowered it to the grass. "I'll walk in front of the wagon to pull—you can watch the back, make sure nothing falls off."

We moved slowly. Every time we crossed onto a new chunk of asphalt, I tensed, hoping that this one would be as stable as the last, and that the wagon wouldn't get stuck in a crack. Up close, some of the gaps were even larger than I'd expected. These slots in the earth were deep and wide enough that someone Oscar's size could get stuck in them. Not to mention Jupiter. If we suddenly tilted and his box went flying… He'd be lost forever.

I found a rhythm as we walked, a few quick steps followed by a tug to get the wagon onto the next piece of road, then a moment to pause while I calculated our next move and caught my breath. My chest ached so badly. I wanted to lie down for just a minute, try to stop wheezing.

Keep going. You're almost halfway there. Your inhaler is going to fix this. It's waiting for you at home.

I pictured my kitchen. The phone on the countertop, next to

the coffee canisters. I imagined lifting the handset off the base and pressing the button, hearing a miraculous dial tone. They could've restored the landlines by now, right? Then I pictured opening the cupboards, pulling out toaster pastries and peanut butter and fresh, clean bottles of water. Soon we'd be sitting in the living room, with plenty to eat, watching out the window for the arrival of the help we'd been able to call.

If I kept picturing the scene, embellishing the details with each step, it felt easier to keep going.

Next, I imagined my parents pulling up in the car, not even bothering to turn off the engine before they jumped out on either side, racing for the door, ecstatic smiles of relief stretching their tired faces…

"Stop," I called, flinging my arm back in case Zoe hadn't heard me or was zoning out or just being obstinate again. She skidded to a halt next to me. We were exactly half the distance between our two driveways. Ahead, a downed utility pole, or what was left of it, stretched across the road. Standing up, those things never look especially tall or heavy, but this pole was big, and it completely blocked our path. Strands of black power lines, like long thick hair, spread out across the road.

Never, ever go near a downed power cable, my dad always said. Except we had no choice. "We're gonna have to figure out a way around that," I said, grimacing. The downed pole was cutting us off from the rest of the neighborhood, the island, and the world. *Leaving the Matlocks' is definitely the right choice.* No one who wasn't already looking for us was going to venture past it to where we'd been waiting.

The power lines had all landed onto the asphalt—on the grassy shoulder was only the cracked, splintery pole. One low-hanging cable dipped above, but it was high enough that we could slip underneath. We would simply need to move quickly in case it came swinging down.

The ground was too crumbly and uneven for me to pull the wagon on the shoulder. "Do you think you can help me lift the wagon?" I asked Zoe.

She nodded and, without instructions, moved to the back end, positioning her fingers below the metal edge. Oscar watched us with wide, pain-glazed eyes.

"I can get out. I'll try to walk." His weak voice cracked with an ache.

"Absolutely not. You can help us by holding Jupiter very steady. Maybe close the top of his box, for this part." *So he doesn't catapult into a crack*, I thought but didn't dare say out loud.

When the box was secured in his hands, I bent down and positioned mine at the front of the wagon, pressing my fingertips into the rusted metal lip for a good grip. It made them feel even colder. "Ready? One, two, three."

Zoe and I lifted up. The wagon was unbelievably heavy. We could only raise it a foot or so off the ground. My arms ached from the strain. Zoe gasped, then pursed her lips with determination. "Step really carefully," I warned her. "I'll lead."

Please, please, please, please don't let us drop the wagon and Oscar.

We moved painfully slowly until, after four or five steps, Zoe suddenly cried out. The wagon wavered. The flashlight, resting by Oscar's feet, tumbled out and rolled along the asphalt as we watched helplessly. Seconds later, we heard the thud as it hit the bottom of a crack in the road. Zoe groaned.

"The flashlight doesn't matter, just keep the wagon steady!" I yelled.

"My arm!" she wailed back.

"Lower the wagon for a break!" I counted to three out loud to coordinate the movement. As soon as the wheels touched the road, Zoe sank back onto her heels, cradling her injured arm against her chest.

Oscar stared up at me from the wagon, still afraid to move. He clutched Jupiter's box so tightly, his fingertips and knuckles appeared bloodless. "It's okay," I said, my voice a croak. "We'll get to the other side."

After a few minutes of rest, we heaved the wagon up and began to creep forward. Parallel with the end of the pole, the ground shifted below my foot, crumbling and making me slide along with it. I screamed, wobbling and struggling to catch myself, because I couldn't let go of the wagon to flap my arms for balance. "Careful!" After a few tense seconds, I found my footing.

Zoe gritted her teeth and stepped around my mini landslide while I paused, gasping and waiting for the adrenaline to stop flooding my system.

I longed to set the wagon down, even for a second, but it wasn't safe on such uneven ground, near frayed power lines. I was also afraid that if we took another break, we'd never have the strength to pick it back up again.

"Your breathing sounds really weird," Zoe said. "Are you okay?"

"I'm just...winded," I said. As much to convince myself as her that I wasn't sounding—and feeling—much worse than the days before.

Finally, we made it off the shoulder and back onto the road, the utility pole behind us. It was the only one between our houses. Now we were in the home stretch, literally. Zoe and I eased the wagon to the pavement. Releasing the weight felt sublime. My muscles were like noodles. Zoe cradled her injured forearm.

"You're really tough," I said.

She nodded in thanks. "So are you."

It had been a long time since I felt like that could be true.

The road was still damaged on the other side of the pole, but without any huge gaps between us and my drive. Based on how hard I was wheezing, I knew I should take it slow the rest of the way. Bumps were hard on Oscar, but I couldn't wait for my house to come into view. To see it standing safe and secure, a refuge in this bizarre, challenging new landscape. I tugged the wagon onward, walking twice as fast as before. Up ahead was our mailbox, robin's-egg blue, still perched at the edge of the driveway. *Almost there.* I sped up even more.

Until my sneaker caught on the uneven pavement. I crumpled down, dropping the wagon handle with a clatter. Pain shot through my right leg. "Ow!" I pressed my hand to my thigh. Even though I was wearing thick leggings, the fabric had shredded up the side I'd landed on, my reddening skin peeking through. The palms of my hands stung. I held them out and studied the scrapes covering them, budding with blood.

It's funny how now that blood didn't bother me in the slightest. I'd dealt with so much worse. I scrambled back to standing.

"Are you okay?" Zoe asked. "Do you need to rest?"

"I'm fine," I reassured. "Just keep moving." I tugged the wagon forward, only a touch slower. Zoe kept pace behind me. When we finally reached my blue mailbox, I had an urge to wrap my arms around it in a hug.

"We did it." I raised my hand for a high five from Zoe. Only when her palm met mine did I remember the scrapes, and I winced. *But we made it home. Everything's going to be okay.* A huge smile spread across my face.

I turned to gaze up the driveway. My smile froze in a grimace.

All of me froze. Zoe, panting, came up next to me. "What..." she started to say, and then she had no other words.

18

FIRST, THERE WERE NO cars in the driveway. It had been a ridiculous, unrealistic hope that we'd arrive and one of my parents would be waiting there, but I'd harbored it anyway.

The scene was worse than an empty driveway, though. Our house has a modern, boxy design, with lines of wood siding that run perfectly parallel to the front yard. The roof is mostly flat—that's why my dad was able to easily turn it into a green roof, with grasses and succulents growing up top. Now those siding lines were running at steep angles, and the roof plants had tilted or toppled. Half the house appeared to be slowly sinking down into the earth, like it was stuck in quicksand. *Like Beth Kajawa warned us about.* The ground was almost up to the first-floor windows on one side, and the sides of the house were bowed. One time my dad made an architectural model of a building to show a client, and when he was lifting the board it was glued to out of the back seat of the car, a gust of wind knocked it to the ground. The side of the model house that landed on the pavement was slightly smushed. Now our house had that same crumpled look.

The big tree outside the living room window—my favorite tree—had fallen over, its roots ripping up the front yard and sticking in the air like muddy tentacles. The trunk of the tree pressed against the gutters, completely blocking the steps and the front door. Its overgrown branches covered the house and roof like a veil. I could only see hints of the bright yellow door peeking through the leaves. The front yard looked like it had been sprinkled with glitter, as the shards of broken glass reflected the daylight and raindrops.

There was no way we could go inside. Not through the front door, and definitely not into a house that was sinking slowly into the ground. It had to be that thing Beth Kajawa had mentioned—liquefaction, when normally solid ground turns to a liquid. So now my house was damaged, unstable, and sinking. It might collapse and crush us if we tried to go inside. It didn't matter that my inhaler was somewhere in there, as was medicine and water and food and batteries and a flashlight to replace the one we'd dropped into the earth. My house might as well have fallen down one of the holes in the road. No matter how badly I wanted to start trying to salvage my things, salvage my life—I couldn't. Not if I wanted us to stay living.

My house is gone. So is my mom. So is my dad. Maybe…forever.

Tears rolled down my cheeks. My hands were busy as I coughed, clutching at my chest. I was gasping again. The coffee-stirrer straw through which I breathed had become bent and blocked. No matter how purposefully I inhaled, it wasn't giving me air. Panicked, I turned to Zoe. "I can't breathe," I sputtered. "I'm…having…an…asthma…attack." Spots danced at the edges of my vision. I tried harder and harder to suck in air. My hands started tingling, my eyes widened with panic.

Zoe fumbled for the notebook in the wagon, flipping through a few pages before stopping to read something I'd written. "Sit, but stay upright!" I sat down on the front walkway, leaning forward slightly. "Loosen any tight clothing!"

I unfastened the neck of my raincoat and the top of Andrea's parka below it.

"Be calm!" Zoe said. She squinted at the book. "No, I'm supposed to be calm. Uh, it's going to be okay!" That's not a very convincing thing to hear from a person who is shouting through tears.

"Take long, deep breaths," Zoe said. I closed my eyes and tried Ms. Whalen's breathing exercise. Inhale for four counts, pause, exhale for eight. Repeat. Repeat again. I focused on a random patch of grass in front of me. If I closed my eyes, I'd picture what my house *should* look like. That would only make it all worse.

"Hold Jupiter," Oscar said. "He's calming." Zoe took him from the box and gently placed him in my lap. My hands found his warm body and stroked his fur. He purred and nestled into me. He was indeed very comforting.

Slowly, I started to feel less like I was suffocating. The tension in my stomach and chest relaxed, slightly. "I think it's getting better," I croaked. I continued staring at the grass. I didn't want to have to face the world around me. I didn't want to see my collapsing house. I didn't know what to do, and I didn't have the will to figure it out. I closed my eyes, giving in to the sadness.

We should just stay here, sitting in the road. Wait for whatever happens next. Mr. Bear, or another aftershock, or quicksand to swallow us up. We're powerless, anyway. Even though my eyes were closed, fresh tears slid out and down my cheeks.

"Hannah?" After a few beats, I opened my eyes.

Zoe was hunched over the wagon. In it, Oscar was lying back, perfectly still. I hadn't checked on his leg since we left the tent. I'm sure it wasn't any better. It worried me that he'd stopped moaning. Like now he was in too much pain to even vocalize it. Zoe was holding his hand, while watching me.

The guilt felt like a slap. Not for what had happened to them, which really wasn't my fault. But guilt for giving up. I blinked and turned to face my tilting house. That day when my dad's model had gotten smushed, he'd been frustrated, but he'd just walked back into his workroom to fix it. "When life happens," he'd said, "you have to take a deep breath and keep on trying." When Neha missed a goal—she turned around and focused on making the next one. What was my mom always telling me to work on? Follow-through.

I couldn't stop trying, even if I wanted to, because Zoe and Oscar were still here, and they deserved to have someone in charge of them who wouldn't give up and who would keep fighting. Maybe I deserved to keep going for myself too.

But where *to* go? There was nothing for us at the Matlocks' house—just a tent, unless Mr. Bear had already found his way inside it, and I'm not even sure we could lift the wagon a third time to get past the downed pole in order to get back there.

My house had been a beacon this whole time. I really believed getting there would rescue us, but it couldn't offer us any shelter.

We could only move forward, not back. We'd head toward the bridge and hope that it could still carry us to safety. We'd try to rescue ourselves.

19

EVEN THOUGH THE ROAD was in slightly better shape on the other side of my house, we moved at a much slower pace. We all were hungry and weak. I didn't think I could run even if I wanted to. It felt like my shoes were filled with lead. The faster I walked, the more I worried I'd have another asthma attack. I hadn't recovered from the one I'd had in front of my house. My chest still ached. I might be getting a third of the air I should be with each inhale. I was dizzy and tired.

A few hundred feet past my driveway, Zoe called for me to stop. She pointed at the blackberry bushes on the side of the road. "Food," she said.

We needed something in our bellies, badly. I'd been banking on there being food at my house, and inside, there was. We just couldn't get anywhere near it. What was in my backpack, we had to ration.

Zoe was already at the bush, plucking berries. Once she had a handful, I expected her to start gobbling them up. Instead, she carried them over to the wagon. To feed Oscar?

She grabbed the emergency survival notebook tucked next to him. He barely stirred. I honestly wasn't sure whether Oscar was simply sleepy or whether he was on the verge of passing out. I moved Jupiter's box off his lap, settling it in the back of the wagon. He wasn't even holding on to it anymore. Wedged in the back was a safer place. When I peeked inside to check on Jupiter, he barely squeaked at me. Even he was fading.

Zoe sat down on the road and opened the notebook. She studied the berries in her palm against something on the pages. "What are you looking at?" I walked over to the bush and pulled off a few for myself even though I knew that at this time of year, they weren't ready to eat. They were bright green and firm—not black or blue in the slightest.

"I'm checking to make sure these are safe to eat and not poisonous," Zoe said.

She wasn't looking at me, so she couldn't see me shake my head. "I've eaten from these bushes almost my whole life. Trust me, they're blackberries. They're just not ripe!" I said, shoving one into my mouth. It was a lot firmer and starchier than usual blackberries, tart and without a trace of sweetness. Not great, but it was food.

Zoe didn't eat any of hers until she found whatever she was looking for in the notebook. Then she popped one into her mouth. "Here, Oscar," she said, holding her grubby hand out with the rest. He kind of grunted at her but didn't move to take any.

"We need to keep going." His lack of responsiveness troubled me.

I kept thinking I heard something off in the distance as we walked. A honking or beeping. "Wait," I said, motioning for Zoe to stop. We paused before a midsize crack in the road. I strained to find the sound again, hoping it would grow louder, and that flashing lights would suddenly appear on the horizon. Or my mom's car. Or even one of the many doppelgänger Subarus.

But all I heard were seabirds and the wind in the trees. Whatever that noise had been, it was gone, and it had probably been far in the distance, only audible to us because of the direction of the wind and the unusual silence of a world without power.

We kept walking. Every few feet I had to stop to rest, either because my hands felt raw and numb from the scrapes and the cold or because I was wheezing badly again. At one point, after I'd doubled over with a cough, I caught Zoe studying my face with concern.

"Hannah, I think your mouth is stained from the berries!" she exclaimed. "Your lips are kind of blue." Except the berries had been mostly green. Lips tinted blue was one of the asthma warning signs the home medical guide had listed… I started my breathing exercises again. My hands were shaking. *I don't know how much longer I can keep it together.*

Try your best. I heard my dad say it. I rolled back my shoulders, grasped the wagon pull. Wherever he was, I wanted him to keep trying too.

We stopped feet away from Mr. Aranita's mailbox and his driveway. Unlike my house and the Matlocks', his cozy craftsman bungalow is set close to the road. From what I could tell, it had survived the earthquake surprisingly well. No trees had come crashing down, and it wasn't visibly sinking into the earth. His car was parked in the driveway. *Wait... Could Mr. Aranita actually be at home?* Maybe the noise I'd heard earlier had been coming from his house!

"Let's see if Mr. Aranita is here," I said to Zoe and Oscar, although Oscar appeared to be asleep again. I leaned down and pressed my fingers to his tiny wrist, feeling the weak flutter of his pulse. It was horrifying that I'd felt the need to check for it.

I dragged the wagon across the yard, stopping at the front steps. Zoe sat on the bottom one, resting her head on her knees. "How are you feeling?" I asked. She shrugged her shoulders without raising her head. I pressed the back of my hand to her neck. It was burning hot again. Whatever relief the Tylenol had given her, it had faded.

"I'm going to knock," I said, walking up the steps. They weren't even steep, but it felt as effortful as climbing Mount Rainier. The porch wasn't in as good shape as I'd thought from the road—the swing was hanging by only one chain, and it must have swung backward at some point and shattered the big window behind it. Glass littered the floorboards. All of Mr. Aranita's potted plants (and he had a lot—when we would drive past, he'd most often wave at us with a gardening glove, watering can in his other hand) had split open and spilled dirt and flowers all over. It was botanical carnage on the porch.

I pressed the doorbell and didn't hear a chime from inside—so his house probably didn't have power either. I rapped with the door knocker. The sound echoed through our silent neighborhood. I knocked again, harder.

"Mr. Aranita?" My voice wasn't very strong. I cleared my throat and moved to stand next to the broken window, poking my head inside through the jagged opening. "Mr. Aranita!" I heard a creak from somewhere deep inside the house. Was it possible he hadn't heard me? Or he had, but…he couldn't get to me?

Inside, the house appeared as disheveled as the Matlocks' had been. A painting had fallen off the wall and been speared by a fireplace poker. Furniture was overturned, and plaster dust covered everything, but I didn't smell gas or smoke or anything dangerous.

Even if he wasn't there to help us, Mr. Aranita might have things we needed to keep going to and across the bridge, like antibiotics, Tylenol, food, and water. I hurried back to the front door and jiggled the handle. Locked, the door wouldn't budge. The panes of glass in the second window had broken cleanly, leaving no shards at the edges. If I was careful, I could crawl through, but I couldn't bring Oscar and Zoe in with me, even if I unlocked the front door once I was in. I didn't know what risks lurked in the house. It was like every place on the island had become booby-trapped: their house, my house, even Forestview Drive.

I took off my backpack and raincoat, so I could move more easily—Andrea had much longer arms than I did, and even though I rolled up the sleeves they kept sliding down. The bottom hem hung below my knees and made walking awkward. I glanced down at Zoe and Oscar. Oscar's eyelids fluttered open, and he gazed at the house with a glazed expression. Zoe, sensing I was watching them, looked up at me. "Mr. Aranita's not home, right?"

"If he is, he's not answering." I warily glanced back at the house. Is it breaking and entering if the windows are already broken for you? Mr. Aranita, though, would surely understand why I'd gone inside and, if I was successful in finding more supplies for us, why I'd taken them. I'd replace anything we took. I could always use my babysitting money. "I'm going to double-check he's not here and also try to find water and food and medicine."

"Okay," Zoe said, slowly rising to stand.

"No—you guys should stay out here."

Her head snapped in my direction. "What? Alone?"

I chewed on my lip and nodded. "It'll be faster, easier—and probably safer—if it's just me. I don't really know what the conditions are like in there, other than bad, and it takes so long to get Oscar settled."

Zoe looked uncertain. "You'll come back out?"

"Right away. Keep an eye on them, okay?" I motioned to Oscar and Jupiter. Oscar's eyes were still open, his head now turned mournfully in the direction of home.

"Okay," Zoe said. But she sounded as uncertain as I'd felt every moment since Andrea had left the house. Before Zoe could change her mind, I turned away from her, cleared my throat, and walked back to the window. The floorboards of the porch groaned ominously from my steps. I walked faster.

I reached my arms inside the window frame, first using my sleeve to wipe away any lingering glass shards. I don't think I'd ever been inside Mr. Aranita's house before. Sometimes when his grandkids from Portland visited, I'd play with them in the yard. The house was small and all on one level, and prior to the earthquake, must have been cute. But this wasn't the time to poke around. I needed to find the kitchen and the bathroom. Everything we needed should be in those two rooms.

"Mr. Aranita?" I called again, in case he hadn't heard me. My grandmother uses hearing aids, and when she turns them off, you can be in the same room and she won't know you're there. If Mr. Aranita had hearing aids, and he hadn't been able to recharge, then he might not be able to hear things in his home. Although, if he *were* home, wouldn't he be moving around, starting to fix things? Unless he was trapped by damage somewhere in the house, injured or…worse.

I squeezed my eyes shut, trying to erase that gruesome thought.

Across the narrow hallway from the living room was the bathroom. A large, mirrored medicine cabinet lay facedown on the cracked tile floor, reminding me of the fridge in the Matlocks' kitchen. I flipped it over and a ton of toiletries spilled out: flossers and toothpaste and over-the-counter nasal spray and...antibiotic ointment! I shoved it in my pocket. I took a few squirts of the nasal spray, in case that would somehow help my nose to better take in air. There was a bottle of Tylenol too, and a fresh package of big bandages. There were a lot of prescription bottles. As I rummaged through the pile, I kept hoping that Mr. Aranita had been prescribed an inhaler. But if he had, it wasn't there.

I tried turning on the water, but nothing came out of the faucet. It made the same shuddering sounds as the Matlocks' had.

I rose back to standing, feeling slightly dizzy, and stumbled into the hallway. It looked like the kitchen might be at the end of it—there was an open doorway. I carefully stepped in that direction, avoiding a puddle of...something. A leak from the ceiling above? Even though the hallway was dim and cramped, it was so much easier to move around without Oscar's wagon and Zoe behind me. At the rate we were going, we'd be lucky to make it to our side of the bridge by nightfall. If I were walking on my own—even wheezing—I could get there faster. Something to consider.

Movement flashed past the kitchen doorway. I froze. "Mr. Aranita?" I called again, my voice wavering. I thought of all the things that could be in his kitchen, if not him: A bear. A burglar? The scritch-scratch, even—shadows were cast everywhere.

Should I keep going? I stood still, working up the nerve. And then something brushed against my leggings. I screamed and jumped, twisting back with my hands out to protect myself.

Meow.

One of Mr. Aranita's cats hissed and raced past me into the kitchen, its tail up. I leaned against the wall, closing my eyes, waiting for my pulse to settle.

After a few moments, I continued on to join the cat in the kitchen. I stopped in the doorway and sniffed. No gas smell. No cat either—I hoped I hadn't scared it outside. His are indoor cats. Mr. Aranita's fridge was still standing. I tiptoed through the mess on the floor and yanked the door open. Inside, it smelled like sour milk, but there was a bottle of apple juice and a carton of OJ. When I shook the OJ, I found it empty. I grabbed the apple juice and started chugging. Even slightly warm—I've never tasted anything so wonderful in my whole life.

His cupboards had spilled food, too, but a lot was intact. *Zoe and Oscar could be safe inside this house, even with all the damage.* They'd have plenty of things to eat. They would have shelter from the rain and from wild animals, except for the freaked-out cat(s). I thought again about heading for the bridge on my own.

Maybe that was the best thing to do, to get help as fast as possible. Sticking together, we were slow.

"Mr. Aranita?" I called one more time. Nothing.

I made my way back from the hallway, still clutching the half-drunk bottle of apple juice. I unlocked the front door and, with a bit of tugging, opened it wide. Zoe and Oscar stared up eagerly from their spot at the bottom of the steps. They had their hoods up—the spitting had grown to real rain.

"Mr. Aranita's house is in pretty good shape. I'll get you guys settled in there, and then I'm going to run to the bridge, see if I can flag help."

"You're going to leave us in there alone?" Zoe asked, her voice rising with disbelief. "And you're going to *run?*" I didn't fault her skepticism about that.

"I don't want to go in this house," Oscar cried. "I want to go home."

"We can't, Oscar," I said, frustrated. "And we need to get help fast. Which isn't possible with you in the wagon. Once I find someone who can contact a doctor, I'll come back for you right away."

Zoe shook her head. "No. You promised we'd stay together!" Her tone was more pleading than angry.

My stomach twisted, maybe from hunger or maybe from guilt. I had promised that.

I pictured Zoe and Oscar left in this unfamiliar house. What if one suddenly got much sicker? What if Jupiter got loose—and encountered a hungry cat? What if Mr. Aranita's house started sinking into the ground too, and something collapsed...or his fridge fell over? What if a fire started? Oscar couldn't move without help, and Zoe couldn't move him on her own. They'd be unable to escape. Vulnerable and completely trapped.

Even if they were slowing me down—it would be wrong to abandon them. When Andrea had called and asked me to take on the job of being their babysitter, it had seemed like a not-big deal. But it actually *was* a big deal to be in charge—whether for a couple of hours or...indefinitely, as I was now. Sure, I had made mistakes. But maybe I didn't need to be perfect. Like Dad said, I simply needed to try my best. Sometimes that alone was heroic.

Mrs. Pinales's instruction was right: babysitters shouldn't do more than was safe or they were capable of, but I was capable of more than I'd thought—we all were. We'd made it this long and far. Being a hero, right now, was necessary, and that meant sticking together even though that was the much harder thing to do.

"You're right, Zoe. I promised that." I pulled Mr. Aranita's door shut and walked toward the porch steps. "We'll stick together." As though in response to my decision, Jupiter started scratching and squeaking inside the box.

Zoe peeled back the flaps to check on him, as my eyes fluttered up to the trees. The birds were cawing and taking off for the rain-heavy clouds. Just like they had that first afternoon.

"Oh no," I whispered. Below my feet, I could feel it starting again. The shaking.

20

IT FELT LIKE TRYING to balance on a paddleboard even though my feet were planted on the ground, firmly, which the ground suddenly wasn't. The grass almost appeared to roll in waves, as we wobbled on it like fledgling surfers. I jerked my arm up to steady myself, spilling all the remaining apple juice down the front of Andrea's parka.

"Get down on your knees and cover your head!" I shrieked to Zoe. Oscar looked up from the wagon, which was swaying back and forth. I crawled on my hands and knees to him and threw my body over his head, covering mine with my scraped and blistered palms.

I looked to the right and saw another mini tidal wave sloshing in the birdbath.

I snapped my head and hands to the left, following the sound of creaking and groaning. Mr. Aranita's car was shaking back and forth, like an invisible someone was pushing it. *Please don't start rolling and run us over.*

From inside the house, I heard all kinds of crashing sounds. Rattling and shattering. It sounded like an angry person was throwing dishes against a wall. I'd passed a china cabinet on my way into the hallway through Mr. Aranita's living room. I hoped the noise wasn't his dishes being smashed one by one, but that's probably what it was. *Are the cats okay in there?*

The shaking probably only lasted for thirty seconds, maybe a minute at most. It was hard to tell when it did stop, because I felt so dizzy and unbalanced afterward. I couldn't tell if the ground was still moving or if it was only that I felt like it was in motion—the same sensation as when you get off a boat or a Tilt-A-Whirl at the fair. I couldn't have walked a straight line right then, no matter how hard I tried. Bile rose up my throat.

I waited until the sounds of destruction had mostly stopped, the crashes and thuds spaced out by a few moments instead of happening in rapid-fire succession. Eventually, I lifted myself away from protecting Oscar's head.

"You can sit up now," I said to Zoe.

She uncovered her head, looking woozy. She blinked a couple of times and then pointed at the grass. "Look!" A small crack had formed, snaking through the yard. Our eyes followed it to Mr. Aranita's walkway, where a block of cement had split in two. *That is bananas.*

I stared up at the house. One of the eaves had sunk further. The porch swing had snapped its tether. The other picture window had shattered. Big glass shards had made it all the way into the front yard.

What would have happened if we'd all been on the porch? Would the sheets of glass have come flying at us? I couldn't believe I'd even considered leaving Zoe and Oscar in his house alone, like sitting ducks.

"What do we do now?" Zoe asked, her voice wavering. "Should we go back to the tent?"

I stared at the crack in the walkway. We'd crossed splits in the road much larger and longer than that. If this aftershock had been powerful enough to make fresh cuts in the earth, the gaps we'd passed earlier must have widened. I wasn't strong enough to lift up the wagon to cross them, and neither was Zoe. It didn't matter, though. The only thing the tent could offer us was cover from the rain—not food, not water, not warmth, and definitely not safety from peckish bears.

There was nothing left for us on Forestview Drive. We had to cross the inlet. Now or never.

"We're going to the bridge," I said.

"Shouldn't we wait to make sure this is over?"

Even if there was more shaking, we'd probably be safer on the road, where there were only trees and the occasional road sign to fall on us. "No. We don't have a ton of time before dark." As I rose to standing, I heard Mr. Aranita's bottle of Tylenol rattle in my pocket. It had been more than four hours since Zoe had swallowed a dose. "Take one of these; it'll make you feel better while we're walking."

Zoe stuck out her hand for a pill. "Water?"

I turned to the wagon. I'd spilled all the juice. The only liquid left was in the guinea pig bottle.

I held it out for Zoe. She wrinkled her nose. "Jupiter's bottle? Really?"

"It's all we have." I unscrewed the cap, so at least she wouldn't have to drink from the little metal tip.

"Do you need some, Oscar?" I asked.

He shook his head no. His eyes were glassy, his face slack. The medical guide had said we had only hours before his leg would be seriously, possibly permanently damaged.

"We're getting you help," I said, my voice filling with confidence and determination I hadn't known I had. Neha's level of determination. "Right now." *Before it's too late.*

As we started walking, the scent curled under my nose, so slight at first that I thought it lingered from last night's campfire, but it grew stronger the more I sniffed.

"Do you smell that?" I asked Zoe. She was behind the wagon, her shoulders slumped, her feet dragging across the asphalt. The last section of the road between Mr. Aranita's house and the bridge never seemed long in the car, but now that it had been reduced to rubble by the earthquake and aftershocks, it was never-ending. Trees ahead of us, trees behind us, and we hadn't even gotten to the hill right before the bridge. We were still on road that was flat, or once had been.

Zoe lifted her head and sniffed at the air. "Smoke," she said.

I nodded grimly. "Something's on fire." It shouldn't have been so surprising. We lived adjacent to a forest preserve, after all, and Beth Kajawa had said that fires were burning all around the city.

Maybe the gas in the Matlocks' kitchen had ignited during the last aftershock, or maybe a downed power line had sparked a flame.

"Walk faster," I said. Wherever the smoke was coming from, I didn't want it to catch up with us.

Instead, Zoe stopped. "I can't anymore. I feel...too sick."

I dropped the wagon handle and pressed my palm—raw and cold—to her forehead. She was burning up again, even though she'd just taken more medicine.

I glanced at the wagon. If we got rid of everything but Oscar and Jupiter in it, Zoe could squeeze inside. Oscar's leg could be elevated on her instead of on top of the pillows. "Climb in," I said. "Careful of your brother. Put his foot in your lap."

"You're going to pull us both?" she asked.

"Yes," I replied. I had no idea how, but I was going to.

We left our belongings, including my backpack, in a little pile by the side of the road. Zoe climbed in the wagon, and Oscar barely whimpered as we adjusted his leg. I don't know whether he was too exhausted to react to the pain, or whether he had become numb. Both were frightening possibilities. As soon as the kids were settled, I grabbed the wagon pull and tugged. The first step took all my strength. I sucked in more air. *Keep going. Try your best.*

The hardest I'd ever ran, in gym class or on the soccer field, hadn't felt a third as challenging as pulling the wagon. My muscles burned. My palms bled. Each breath was a gasp. Overexertion would trigger my asthma; I knew that, but I couldn't stop or slow down. We had to reach the bridge before dusk. Before fire caught up to us. Before a bear wandered out of the woods. Before another terrible thing happened to one of the kids.

I heard faint noise in the distance, something like a honk. Although it was probably just geese, I pretended it was Mr. Fisk's bus. That kept me going. I pictured us cresting the last hill before the bridge and seeing him below, speeding up to save us. Even better, an ambulance. I squeezed my eyes shut. *You got this!* Neha told me. Like she always used to before games. *It's only a little farther*, I told myself, reopening my eyes. But even a little distance was a long way.

The rain began falling in big splashy drops. I'd left Andrea's raincoat on Mr. Aranita's porch. Her parka was soaked, and I could feel the dampness spreading through the rest of my layers, chilling me to my core. *At least that might stop a fire.* The squeak of the wagon's wheels was punctuated by my wheezing. Either the daylight was beginning to fade, or fog was filling the air, or I was becoming faint—things grew dim and fuzzy around me. I fixed my eyes on the road, so I could avoid stumbling on the cracks or falling into one. I could hear Zoe weeping in the front of the wagon. Jupiter's nails occasionally scratched the cardboard as he scrambled inside the box. Oscar was scarily silent. I kept pushing myself forward. My chest clenched like a fist.

The pavement began its incline. *Finally.* The last stretch before the bridge. Going down the hill is always my favorite part of the bus ride from school; it means I'm almost home. Now, I was overjoyed, because it meant I was almost away. The bridge would lead us back to civilization. To safety. To help. The road was slick with rain, the shoulder turning into a mud puddle. My sneakers slid dangerously on the asphalt. My lungs ached, and my head spun. It felt like I was suffocating again. *"Keep going, you can do it."* Neha's voice egged me on. I pictured my dad, safe, smiling, waiting somewhere for me. My mom whispering in my ear, "I'm so proud of you."

Going up the hill is where you can see Rainier when "the mountain is out." I stared in its direction, although the rain clouds hid it. Now I knew just how much power the mountains—and the tectonic plates deep below them—really held. *Sneaky Juan de Fuca.* I turned ahead to face the road. I was small, an ant in comparison.

But I was not powerless.

Even though everything ached, even though I convulsed with shivers, even though the light was starting to fade, even though in so many ways it would have been easier to give in and give up—I kept pulling us toward the top. The wagon groaned to a stop next to me at the peak. *We made it.* The bridge was just down the hill.

I blinked, not understanding what I was seeing. Water brown as chocolate milk was everywhere, covering the low-lying end of the road and surrounding grass. The inlet had flooded. The bridge rose out of the floodwaters, but it was now a bridge to nowhere, a slab of concrete that stretched a few yards out over the inlet and then ended in midair. A section had collapsed. Even if we waded through the swirling floodwaters, the bridge couldn't lead us to help, but only to a drop-off into the rising waters below.

I sank to the ground. We were trapped. *Fires and floods.* Tears streamed from my eyes. We'd made it all the way here, but there was nowhere left to go.

I closed my eyes. A humming filled my ears. I struggled to breathe.

Zoe tapped my shoulder. "Do you see that?"

"See what?" I managed, between gasping breaths. "The bridge? Yeah…it's broken. I'm so sorry."

"No, the lights." I lifted my head. Zoe was pointing toward the water. No, *across* the water. I squinted. Through the rain, I could see where the road continued on the other side, connecting our home to the rest of Pelling. The humming hadn't been in my ears. There were flashing lights, bright and orange, from a parked utility truck. Next to it, a big yellow school bus—was it Mr. Fisk's? *He had honked! The honk tolled for me!* A person in a blue slicker, setting down shiny emergency cones. Bobbing in the water in front of him, a small motorboat, also with flashing lights—maybe a police boat.

I didn't know if they'd seen us. I raised my arm to wave. I stood up, even though I knew I should sit during an asthma attack. The joy from seeing other people—grown-ups—was like a shot of adrenaline. They were the first we'd seen in days. They were the *helpers.*

I did it. I got us to them, and they're going to get us to safety.

And if I had managed to do that—maybe our families and friends had survived too. Hope filled my heart.

The bus's door suddenly flung open. A figure came tumbling out.

I think they see us.

The person who had rushed out now ran to the water's edge, toward the boat still on their side. She waved her arms, frantically. She cupped her hands around her mouth. I recognized her purple coat.

And her voice, forcing its way across the water. Both panicked and euphoric. "Hannah!"

I sank to my knees, tears of joy and disbelief, and relief, streaming down my face.

The voice belonged to my mother.

TRANSCRIPT OF "THE DISASTER DAYS"

A SPECIAL SEGMENT OF "SEATTLE AFTER CASCADIA"

Beth Kajawa: This is Beth Kajawa with KUOW News. As part of our "Seattle after Cascadia" series and ongoing coverage of the earthquake and recovery efforts, I want to share an incredible story of an unlikely hero in the immediate aftermath—Hannah Steele, a thirteen-year-old babysitter who found herself stranded with her two young charges for more than three days in an isolated neighborhood on Pelling Island. I'm reporting from Pelling Island Middle School, where Hannah and her parents are taking part in the cleanup efforts. Today they are sharing their experiences of the quake and the "disaster days" after.

Hannah's mother, Ellen Steele, a librarian at Seattle Public Library's Central Library, survived the earthquake with only bruises from falling books. However, she found herself trapped in the chaos of downtown Seattle for days afterward. With the Elliott Bay Bridge closed and ferry service not running, she had no way to get home to the island and her daughter.

Ellen Steele: To finally get back to Pelling, I begged a ride on a police boat. That was on the third day after the quake. I told them that my daughter was on the island, babysitting our neighbor's two smaller children, when the quake hit. I had no idea if my neighbor had been able to get back to them, or if any emergency personnel on the island were even aware that these kids were stranded alone. When Seattle police heard the panic in my voice and saw the tearstains on my face, they whisked me back to Pelling on the next boat out—I was so grateful.

But I ran into another hurdle once I made it to the island. When I got to my car in the ferry lot, I found it destroyed. Fred Fisk happened to be there and was able to give me a ride in the school bus, which he'd been using to distribute supplies. He remembered dropping Hannah off at her babysitting gig shortly before the quake. We raced toward the house only to find that the bridge that connects my neighborhood to the rest of Pelling had partially collapsed.

Beth Kajawa: You must have been terrified.

Ellen Steele: Oh, absolutely. There was smoke in the distance too—turns out a ranger station had caught fire during an aftershock. We honked and honked, hoping someone would come out on the other side, so I'd know the kids were okay. I even considered trying to swim across, but the inlet had flooded and the current was too strong... Eventually I got my head together, and Fred and I raced back to the emergency response staging area, where I alerted the authorities that my daughter and her charges were trapped across the inlet. We drove back to the bridge to wait for help. The rescue boat had just arrived when I saw, at the top of the hill on the other side, Hannah pull up with a wagon loaded with the two kids. And guinea pig.

Beth Kajawa: How did it feel, seeing your daughter?

Ellen Steele: Incredible relief. And pride. I'm still in awe of how Hannah took charge of the situation. From quick thinking to treating injuries to looking up print resources to simply staying calm. Even once we got the kids on the rescue boat, Hannah insisted on staying with Zoe and Oscar as they were transported to the hospital—she said they were sticking together, no matter what. My daughter really showed a lot of bravery and responsibility. I knew she had it in her—she's one strong girl.

Beth Kajawa: It would take days before Hannah's father, Peter Steele, would hear of his daughter's ordeal. He was in the middle of a struggle for survival of his own.

An architect, he had been away on the day of the quake, working on a hotel project on the Washington coast. Peter had left the tsunami inundation zone just twenty minutes before the earthquake, on a run for supplies with a coworker. That meant he was safely—miraculously—out of the zone at the time the devastating wave hit. However, he found himself stranded in the chaos inland, with no way to get home or communicate with his family to let them know he was safe.

Peter Steele: I can't tell you what it was like, when I was finally able to reach my wife and daughter on a satellite phone days after the tsunami, and to finally know they were okay. There just aren't words. I never doubted Hannah was tough, that she would try her best to get help—but I was still terrified for her.

Beth Kajawa: I can only imagine. Now, I want to mention that local artist Andrea Matlock, the mother of Zoe and Oscar, the two children Hannah was babysitting, was seriously injured while attending a gallery event when the quake hit. During the days after, she was treated at Virginia Mason Hospital. Andrea is at physical therapy today, but she's expected to make a full recovery from her injuries.

But before these happy reunions—there was the young babysitter's ordeal of being stranded in a damaged house with no power, water, heat, or a phone. Here we have Hannah herself, who's going to tell our listeners about her experience. Hannah, did you ever expect that your after-school babysitting gig would turn into several days of being in charge, in a survival situation?

Hannah Steele: It was only my second time babysitting, and the first time that Ms. Matlock went farther away than Main Street. So I was nervous going in, I guess, even when I thought it would be a normal afternoon.

Beth Kajawa: How did you know what to do during the quake?

Hannah Steele: I really didn't. At first, we were all just shocked. Without our phones, the internet, and TV, or even electricity—it was a whole new world. We did have an emergency radio for a few of the days. And, actually, your broadcasts helped me to know what was going on. Your voice was so reassuring.

Beth Kajawa: That's... [clears throat] That's really wonderful to hear. Thank you.

Hannah Steele: I also used the training I had learned in Mrs. Pinales's babysitting course. We relied on some encyclopedias we found for advice, plus a Girl Scout manual and a super-old home medical guide. That's how we figured out how to start a fire and what to do when Zoe and Oscar both got injured. I couldn't just Google for answers or call a doctor, you know?

Beth Kajawa: That must have been very strange for you!

Hannah Steele: [laughs] Yeah, it took some getting used to, for sure.

Beth Kajawa: Oscar broke his leg in a fall, and although he faced complications—compartment syndrome—it's now healing well. His older sister, Zoe, suffered a cut from debris that became infected, but thanks to antibiotic treatment, she's doing fine. That's in part because of Hannah's bravery in seeking out help on the third day after the quake. Despite her own health concerns—repeated asthma attacks—she led the children and their pet guinea pig, Jupiter, to rescuers at the site of the collapsed inlet bridge. How is your health now, Hannah?

Hannah Steele: I'm doing well. I'm much better about

remembering to bring my rescue inhaler along with me when I go places, and I'm learning to live with asthma and not let it limit me.

Beth Kajawa: That's great. Hannah, how did you keep calm during those long days when you were stranded? You encountered a gas leak in one home, several aftershocks, impassable roads, flooding and liquefaction, and even a brush with a bear?

Hannah Steele: My dad always tells me just to try my best. That's what I did. I also thought a lot about my best friend, Neha. She's right over there, with our friend Marley. Hey, Neha! [interview briefly pauses for friend to join] She's the most encouraging person I know. I imagined the pep talks she would give to keep me going whenever I started to feel like I couldn't.

Beth Kajawa: Neha, where were you during the quake?

Neha Jain: My soccer team was sheltered in Bremerton, because we'd just finished a game. I was in the middle of texting with Hannah when the quake hit. I knew she was alone with the kids, and I was so worried about her. When cell service was finally restored and I got her messages and knew she was okay, that was, like, the happiest I've ever felt.

Hannah Steele: Same.

Neha Jain: Honestly, now Hannah's the one inspiring me. She's a hero.

Beth Kajawa: I can tell you two are really great friends. So, Hannah, what is life like on Pelling Island after the quake?

Hannah Steele: Well, my house was really damaged. Soil liquefaction made it sink into the ground—I knew what that was thanks to your reporting! While my dad is working to fix it, we're temporarily living in our other next-door neighbor's house, which was faster to fix up. Mr. Aranita is away, helping with his grandkids in Portland—that's where he was during the quake.

They say that rebuilding Pelling Island will take a long time and a lot of work. It's not the utopia I thought it was—except for our community. People have really come together to help one another out and restore our island. It's been nice to be part of that.

Beth Kajawa: I agree. Even in the midst of a heart-wrenching disaster, there can be happiness in watching a community join together. Now, I have to ask—do you think you'll ever babysit again?

Hannah Steele: Actually, I've been babysitting for the Matlocks a lot already, while Andrea is still recuperating. But I don't babysit alone. I have a deputy—Zoe. She was a huge help during the disaster days. She was actually the one to start the campfire and figure out how to pitch the tent in the backyard. I couldn't have survived without her or Oscar. Or Jupiter! He was like an emotional support guinea pig.

Beth Kajawa: Your teamwork is really exemplary. Still, I hope now your time together isn't so eventful!

Hannah Steele: [laughs] Yeah, me too. When I come over to their temporary apartment, where they're staying till the house repairs are done, the kids do homework and spend plenty of time playing video games and with their tablets, like before the quake. What's different is that we definitely don't take electricity for granted...or having food and water.

But sometimes we'll build a blanket fort, like we did to stay warm after the quake, or even make microwave s'mores. We spend more afternoons outside, playing "survival." Zoe and I are still updating our notebook with instructions and tips. Anyway, being outdoors feels different now. It's like... I'm aware of how powerful the environment around us is. It's a good and bad thing.

Beth Kajawa: That's very insightful. Any last words of advice for our listeners?

Hannah Steele: My babysitting bag is also my go-bag. I pack a first aid kit, a spare inhaler, snacks and water, a flashlight with fresh batteries, my babysitting course manual, and our notebook. I always take that stuff with me.

Just in case of emergency.

AUTHOR'S NOTE

H ANNAH'S STORY OF SURVIVAL during a major earthquake in the Pacific Northwest is fiction, but it is rooted in facts. Pelling may be a made-up island community across Elliott Bay from Seattle, but the post-quake threats Hannah, Zoe, and Oscar face there—from liquefaction to lumbering bears, seiches (a back-and-forth wave in an enclosed body of water, like what Hannah witnessed in the fish pond) to sand volcanoes—are all realistic.

Major earthquakes—above a magnitude 7.0—have happened along the Cascadia Subduction Zone (CSZ) in the past; the most recent occurred on January 26, 1700, with an estimated magnitude of around 9.0. It's certain other very large "megathrust" earthquakes will happen in this area in the future, although we don't know when. Unlike other subduction zones, the CSZ usually doesn't produce smaller quakes. It could very well be decades before another major earthquake happens. That means we may have lots of time to prepare.

Natural disasters, like the earthquake described in this book, are sadly regular phenomena. Perhaps your community has been affected by a hurricane, tornado, wildfire, blizzard, landslide, drought, or flood. These events are "natural" in the sense that weather and earth changes cause them, but their size, frequency, and levels of destruction can all be impacted by things humans do. As our climate changes, scientists predict that natural disasters will become more prevalent and more damaging.

It's scary to think about a natural disaster harming our homes and families, but thinking ahead is how we can keep ourselves safe. Talk to your loved ones about preparedness. You may want to set up a plan for communication in the event of an emergency, and it's always smart to keep an emergency kit and "go bags" stocked. For more information on emergency preparedness, visit the website for your local office of emergency management or the Red Cross.

If you'd like to help others who have been affected by natural disasters, a good place to start is ready.gov/volunteer.

For additional resources about the CSZ, earthquake science, and emergency preparedness, visit the author's website at rebeccabehrens.com/resources.

ACKNOWLEDGMENTS

A magnitude of thanks to:

Annie Berger, for rooting for these characters and sharing her editorial insight to shape their story of survival, and to the wonderful team at Sourcebooks—especially Sarah Kasman, Steve Geck, Dominique Raccah, Todd Stocke, Cassie Gutman, Rebecca Sage, Nicole Hower, Heather Moore, Margaret Coffee, Heidi Weiland, Valerie Pierce, Ashlyn Keil—for all it takes to turn a manuscript on an author's computer into a book in a reader's hands.

Suzie Townsend, for being the best advocate an author could ask for, and to Cassandra Baim and Dani Segelbaum, for their skilled support, and to the whole team at New Leaf Literary for their hard work and hustle, especially Joanna Volpe and Pouya Shahbazian.

Dr. Amy Williamson, postdoctoral researcher at the University of Oregon, for graciously reviewing the earthquake and scientific details in this book and offering her feedback. Any mistakes are my own.

Kathryn Schulz, for writing "The Really Big One," the unputdownable *New Yorker* article that sparked my idea for this story.

Beth Behrens and Michelle Schusterman, for reading and cheerleading.

Jessica, David, and Daisy Matlock for answering all those random Seattleite questions, and for letting me borrow their last name.

Teachers, librarians, and booksellers for all that they do to create and champion readers and writers.

My friends and family for their love and unshakable support.

Blake, for being my emergency contact and so much more.

ABOUT THE AUTHOR

Rebecca Behrens is the author of the critically acclaimed middle-grade novels *When Audrey Met Alice*, *Summer of Lost and Found*, and *The Last Grand Adventure*. She grew up in Wisconsin, studied in Chicago, and now lives with her husband in New York City. You can visit her online and learn more about her books at rebeccabehrens.com.